SUNALAKA

Cinzia Dal Lago

SUNALAKA, LLC.

SunAlaka

Cover designed by Melissa Peizer
Book edited by Patricia Richker and Michelle Horkings-Brigham

ISBN: 978-1-7362113-0-4

SunAlaka, LLC.

P.O Box 800
Somers, MT 59932, U.S.A.
https://sunalaka.com/
info@sunalaka.com

Summary: Winning *The Last Templar* comes to Erin with no surprise. She doesn't know failure, and if she does, she never admits it. But the decision to accept the prize — a science Expedition to Inner Earth — involves betrayal. Little does she realize her impending destiny will reveal all of her self-deception and fragility.

Only when pushed to the limits of endurance does Erin become aware of her mortal existence and insolence. In a surprising turn of events, she is able to find her inner strength, apply skills expanded through knowledge, and transform her weakness into power. A mystical journey unfolds that brings danger, friendship, and many a strange encounter.

Realizing her purpose, Erin finds the courage to make the only decision that will save her life and bring her friends home.

Key words: Inner Earth, Exploration, Aliens, Hummingbird, Time Travel, Shadow Government, Friendship, Betrayal.

SPECIAL THANKS

Although this book has been for the most part a solitary journey, there are some incredible people who I would like to acknowledge and thank.

Marcus, my amazing spouse and best friend, for the time, space, encouragement, love, ideas, and support to write this book. I love you.

Patricia Richker, an incredible person, who edited and proofread my manuscript. Pat led me through this process as a mentor and friend, and her talent and huge heart helped me to understand the importance of patience.

Michelle Horkings-Brigham (author of *Cannabis the Conundrum*), is an extraordinarily talented person. She spent hours reading my book and challenging my thinking. It wasn't always easy for me to delete or change parts of the manuscript, but her suggestions answered many of my questions and strengthened the story I had wanted to tell.

My deepest appreciation and gratitude go to all the spiritual beings and sapient entities who have shown me the hidden potentials within me and, through their selfless life, taught me that there is greatness in humanity.

To all the friends and relatives who, in one way or another, shared their support, thank you.

Finally, I would like to thank God for having answered many of my prayers.

This story is dedicated to all the people who have lost their lives in the line of duty.

Dear Reader,

When I first decided to write this book, I thought I had a story to tell, but I was wrong because I didn't realize that it was the story that came in search of me.

I chose to start this adventure without knowing that it would transport me to places where I had never been, to meet people that I had never met, and live experiences I had never lived.

For me it has been a journey of discovery, the one that carries the "wow feeling" until the end.

May this book bring the same wonder to you.

TABLE OF CONTENTS

ITHAKA

As you set out for Ithaka
hope your road is a long one,
full of adventure, full of discovery.
Laistrygonians, Cyclops,
angry Poseidon — don't be afraid of them:
you'll never find things like that on your way
as long as you keep your thoughts raised high,
as long as a rare excitement
stirs your spirit and your body.
Laistrygonians, Cyclops,
wild Poseidon — you won't encounter them
unless you bring them along inside your soul,
unless your soul sets them up in front of you.

Hope your road is a long one.
May there be many summer mornings when,
with what pleasure, what joy,
you enter harbors you're seeing for the first time;
may you stop at Phoenician trading stations
to buy fine things,
mother of pearl and coral, amber and ebony,
sensual perfume of every kind —
as many sensual perfumes as you can;
and may you visit many Egyptian cities
to learn and go on learning from their scholars.

Keep Ithaka always in your mind.
Arriving there is what you're destined for.
But don't hurry the journey at all.
Better if it lasts for years,
so you're old by the time you reach the island,
wealthy with all you've gained on the way,
not expecting Ithaka to make you rich.

Ithaka gave you the marvelous journey.
Without her you wouldn't have set out.
She has nothing left to give you now.

And if you find her poor,
Ithaka won't have fooled you.
Wise as you will have become,
so full of experience,
you'll have understood by then
what these Ithakas mean.

— C.P. Cavafy

SUNALAKA

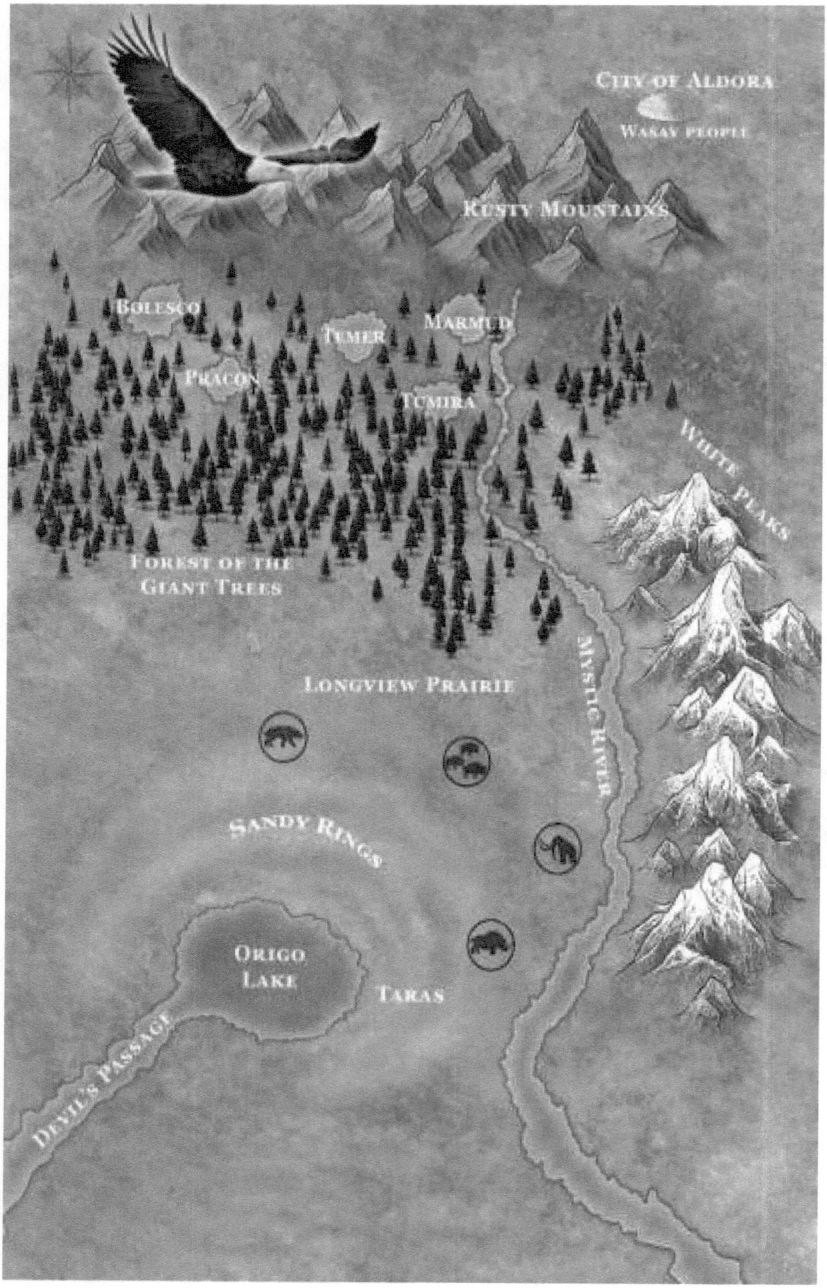
City of Aldora
Wasay people
Rusty Mountains
Bolesco
Temer
Marmud
Pracon
Tumira
White Peaks
Forest of the
Giant Trees
Longview Prairie
Mystic River
Sandy Rings
Origo
Lake
Taras
Devil's Passage

PROLOGUE

THE LAST TEMPLAR – DAY 45

Competitiveness, or the inclination to compete, is an innate, psychological trait. Although for the most part associated with the urge of survival, competitive emotions are not always about winning or getting ahead. True champions, individualistic and determined, can also be highly compassionate when it matters most in the game.

Such was the case when Jessica entered *The Last Templar* elimination challenge. She noted that her best friend and fellow competitor had little chance of accomplishing the test. Hitting a moving target using bow and arrow while standing on a slender beam was something Jessica knew she was particularly skilled at, despite the gnawing pain of her wound. Erin, on the other hand, had shown signs of distress in the past couple of days. At this stage of the game, losing one single contest was unaffordable, because it meant losing everything. Jessica sensed that victory would soon be hers to enjoy.

Unbeknownst to Terrence, it was unanimously decided by the four remaining players that he would be the next person to be voted out that night. Jessica and Erin had no concerns regarding his elimination; however, Jessica had decided to take her imminent success one step further in demonstration of her sincere friendship for Erin. It was the first time in *The Last Templar* competition, after countless challenges had tested her skills of endurance and survival, that Jessica's desire to give up the talisman was stronger than the need to possess it for herself. If achieved, the trophy would allow Erin to be immune from elimination and to move one step further in the game. Whether an act of selfless compassion or driven by some other emotion,

Jessica did not pause to consider. All she cared about was that her friend and ally remained with her in the game. And so when Jessica intentionally fell from the narrow platform, therefore missing the target, it appeared to everyone observing as an unfortunate and natural occurrence.

By deliberately losing the challenge, Jessica had won peace. Her fall allowed Erin to claim the victory for herself.

On their way back to the castle, being absorbed in the ebullient emotions that accompanied her success, Erin didn't immediately notice that her friend was limping.

Just a few days earlier, while hunting in the woods, Jessica had fallen on a pine root. A shallow wound had sliced the flesh of her left leg, but it hadn't really bothered her too much as it quickly healed over. Yet following the challenge, red welts had appeared on her calf that had only deepened over the past few hours.

Anxious about her friend's well-being, Erin suggested with genuine concern, "Should we call the medical team and ask them to examine your wound?"

Jessica's eyes revealed her distress as she laid her hand on Erin's shoulder. Her normally golden skin had turned pale. Eventually she said, "I don't know what to say. I've been feeling good all day," but the tense expression on her face showed a different reality as she closed her eyes to cope with the pain.

A few hours later, following a brief examination, the decision was made to pull Jessica from the game. "It is too risky to let you continue," stated the doctor matter-of-factly.

Erin found herself saying good-bye to the only person she felt cared about her and promised in deep sincerity, "I will win this game for both of us! One for all ..." But it was the joy of hearing "... and all for one" that gave Jessica solace in her loss.

That night, reflecting on the meaning of her promise and the many pledges that accompany such a game, Erin came to a bitter realization: She might win the final prize but the talisman wasn't a trophy she could be proud of. What she had envisioned as victory had become nothing more than a painful choice.

CHAPTER 1: THE LAST TEMPLAR

10th ANNIVERSARY OF *THE LAST TEMPLAR*
Live – FOX Studios Center – Los Angeles, California
Saturday, February 21

The night was pleasant in Los Angeles. A gentle breeze whispered the last winter magic through the bended branches of the palm trees — the perfect prelude for a refreshing, upcoming spring.

Inside the FOX Studios Center, the arena was crowded with people, mostly fans, families, and friends of the show. The stage was set. Everybody in the audience knew that the 10th season of *The Last Templar* was about to bring a new twist. The level of excitement was high by virtue of the fact that a new revelation was about to be made. As the lights of the theater dimmed, the people in the studio were instructed to take their seats.

Brian entered the theater with the Knights Templar jar containing the votes. While making his way along the hallway that led him to the main stage, he heard the audience cheering and shouting his name, "Brian … Brian … Brian." That night he would introduce the show one final time. It seemed as if the news of his departure had already spread — unsurprisingly so! He felt the overwhelming emotions surging in his heart. His eyes teared up a little bit, causing him to hesitate for a moment. Then a sparkle of joy and a sense of accomplishment spurred him forward while a smile of satisfaction illuminated his face. He had been hosting the show since day one. He remembered the first day as if it were yesterday: the abandoned medieval ruin in the Pyrenees, season one, in the year 2017. Now, after many years and ten seasons, everything was about to come to completion.

Brian took the stage and set the Knights Templar jar on the stand. He turned his glance toward the public and, absorbing one last fragment of the gratifying view, he smiled. The usual words "thank you for coming" were pronounced almost mechanically.

The stage had been set to represent the Council of Troyes. On the edges, there were tall Roman columns resembling Soloman's Temple, while The Arc of the Covenant was set in the center of the arena. The seventeen contestants composing the jury were sitting in a semicircle around the wooden chest. On the other side were the three finalists: Mark, Erin, and Satomi.

"All right, WOW! Mark, Erin, Satomi ... I have to say, from start to finish you had to earn it during this season. Through the eliminations, the blindsides, the injuries, it was a nonstop drama from start to finish. Now it comes down to this point: Have you played strategically? The final twist of the game is the Council of Troyes. The same people that you decided to expel from the castle will now decide who will be *The Last Templar*. The question is: Did you make the right choice?" Brian paused to give a good look at the three contestants who were starting to show signs of anxiety. Eventually he continued. "This year marks the 10th anniversary of *The Last Templar*. As many of you already know, tonight's winner will be given not only a check for one million dollars but also granted a spot on the upcoming Expedition to Inner Earth. The winner will be one of three civilians participating in this extraordinary journey. Everybody is talking about that, but we will discuss those details later. Now I will read the votes."

The public's attention turned back to the three finalists, who were excitedly holding hands.

Brian opened the lid of the jar and picked the first vote, Erin.

The audience was cheering again. The names of the three contestants were shouted randomly from every corner of the theater. The second vote, Mark, came immediately after.

"One vote for Erin, one vote for Mark." Brian's announcement caused Satomi to smile nervously. Why didn't her name come up yet? Brian continued with the drawing of the names, "Mark, Erin, Satomi."

The atmosphere was filled with excitement. A few more seconds and everything would be over. Satomi was becoming more and more concerned. She thought she had it "in the bag," but now the votes were telling a different story — Erin, Erin, Mark.

Brian paused for a second and looked at the three finalists before saying, "We have seven votes for Erin, six votes for Mark, and two votes for Satomi. Satomi, you are out of the game."

Mark and Erin looked at each other. They knew the winner would be one of them. Brian pulled another vote from the jar and read, "Mark. Seven votes for Mark, seven votes for Erin. We have a tie." Then with fanfare, he picked the last vote from the jar and, with a smile on his face, exclaimed, "The winner of this season of *The Last Templar* is Erin!"

The audience exploded in a roaring applause. People were running onto the stage, hugging each other. Erin managed to escape the crowd and opted to reunite with her family, who were still in the audience — perhaps just an attempt to evaporate some of her emotions. Tears of joy were washing freely down her face. The tension was over. But was it?

Sooner than expected, Brian was behind Erin with a one-million-dollar check in his hand, reminding her that she was not done yet. There was one more thing to discuss, a final question to answer. She needed to go back on the stage.

Erin's excitement took a hit. Her face, that only a few moments before had expressed joy, started to show signs of anxiety. She returned to the stage, feeling rather uncomfortable in newly acquired high heels. Her mind was scattered, and she needed to regroup her thoughts in order to focus on the present moment. Erin looked at the jury. Jessica was sitting there, calmly looking directly at her. Did Erin perceive a glimmer of satisfaction in Jessica's eyes? Or was it just her imagination?

"Come on, Erin, take your spot." Brian's words brought her back to reality. She forced a smile.

He then announced, "Erin, congratulations. You are the winner of *The Last Templar*, season ten." A brief pause followed.

"You know what this means; right?" Smiling, Brian looked at Erin, but without giving her the time to respond. "For the first time in the history of *The Last Templar*, the winner will win not only the one-million-dollar check but also a spot on the Expedition to Inner Earth. How does this make you feel?"

Despite her fascination with the situation, Erin looked around in search of comfort from the public. So high was the pressure that she felt unable to respond.

Brian continued. "But as we all know, *The Last Templar* never ceases to surprise us. Now is the moment that you, Erin, make your final decision." The pause grew even longer. Time seemed to have stopped, and Erin started to feel the tension rising. The only thing she could come up with was a feeble "I know."

"There is something I want you to see." Brian turned his back to the audience and looked directly at the big screen at the rear of the stage. They were playing a scene from the game showing Jessica, Erin's ally and best friend, being pulled from the game due to a bad infection on her leg. Jessica was crying, so intense was her agony. Erin, kneeling close to her, held her hands in an effort to provide some comfort and strength.

Sitting uncomfortably on her chair, Erin bit her lips at the sound of her own words. "I will win this game for both of us! One for all and all for one." Then her heart sank as she observed herself declaring, "I give you my word, Jessica, that if I win this game, I will give you the spot on the Expedition. I promise!" Jessica's face was contorted with pain, but she still managed to pull up a smile for her dear friend Erin. Being removed from the show when there were only five people left was really sad and unfair. Jessica knew, however, that she had gained something more important and priceless. She had found a loyal friend, Erin, or at least that was what she had thought. The short clip ended with a long, emotional hug between the two friends moments before Jessica was taken away by helicopter to the nearest hospital.

The lights went up again and all eyes were now focused on Erin in anticipation. She felt her heart beating faster and knew that a decision had to be made quickly. Would she be able and willing to honor her promise, or had she changed her mind?

Brian noted the uneasiness in Erin and didn't wait long before asking, "Here in my hand I have the certificate of participation to the Expedition, but it is still without a name. Erin, you promised your friend Jessica that if victorious, you would gift her the spot on the Expedition. Now I need to ask you again, are you still willing to do that?"

Jessica was a fresh graduate with a degree in biology. Erin knew how much this Expedition could have meant for her career. With the early loss of both parents, life had not been very kind toward Jessica. For most of their time during the game, Erin had worked hard trying to make her friend happy, but now that the show was over, their lives had been separated in many ways. It was evident that there was something different in her relationship with Jessica, but it never occurred to Erin to understand what.

Erin looked at her parents in the arena, hoping for a suggestion. She was proud of her family ties.

Brian took a deep breath. "This is *The Last Templar*, and as you know, there are very few rules in this game. You can change your mind at any time. The purpose of this game is to win as much as you can." Brian paused for effect, then continued. "Having said that, are you still willing to keep your promise to Jessica, or has your mind changed?"

Erin looked at Jessica and said, "I have been thinking about this since day 45. Obviously, at that time I didn't know I was going to be the winner. This is now a reality, and I didn't expect it to be so hard."

She looked at Brian for some sign of support. The air was filled with expectation, and the silence was almost unbearable.

Brian continued. "So what do you think now? I mean, this is your game, your victory. You must have played better than all the other contestants or you would not be sitting here having to make this decision. The title of '*The Last Templar*' and the spot onboard the Expedition are things you have earned by playing in the way that you did."

Erin thought so too.

Brian was looking at Erin with a hint of compassion.

Eventually Erin, ignoring the promise made to her friend Jessica, pronounced two fateful words, "I can't."

The audience, quiet up to that moment, started murmuring.

Erin continued. "You might call me selfish, but I see it more as honest. No one wants to give away something that might help them in the future. I am not responsible for Jessica's injury and I didn't create her defeat. I didn't make her choices, so I am not taking on the guilt either."

Brian responded, "Nobody thinks you are responsible for Jessica. But you must admit that you are responsible for your words. Do you agree?"

"I do. But I am a different person now. My mind has changed."

"So are you saying that your decision is to keep the spot on the Expedition for yourself?"

"Yes, indeed. Despite what I promised to Jessica, I won't be able to gift her my place in the Expedition." Erin's voice was loud again. It sounded as if she had reclaimed her confidence. Looking back at her friend, Erin said, "I'm sorry, Jessica, but I can't do it."

Jessica forced a smile, but her level of disappointment was apparent.

Brian asked if she wanted to say something, and Jessica, seizing the opportunity, responded immediately. "I trusted you,

Erin. I was genuine with you. I was honest with you. What you are doing now hurts. It really hurts."

Despite her friend's reaction, Erin was feeling free. The burden had been lifted from her chest. "I'm sorry, Jessica, but this is the opportunity of a lifetime. When I made that promise to you, I had no idea I was going to win. You were in such pain. This game took so much power from me, I almost handed away the keys to my mind, my body, and my soul. I am sorry that I was not able to stand up for myself sooner. This is the only thing I am truly sorry for; everything else I did was defensive. I sincerely hope you will be able to understand my position and forgive me one day."

A brief look into Erin's eyes was enough for Jessica to understand that she was already yesterday's news. Erin had been the most fun person to be around during the game, a great companion in all those days spent joking, laughing, and suffering fatigue and near starvation together. It wasn't the fact that Erin had not fulfilled her promise that upset Jessica the most. It was the realization that her friend had grown entitled, arrogant, and her empathy had become a deception.

Jessica was almost in tears when she said, "Had I not been busy trying to survive the game, I could have discovered this about you earlier, Erin. I used to look into your eyes and see sincerity and determination, but what I saw and loved in you has been replaced with egoism. I wish I had paid more attention to your real intentions because I would never have allowed myself to be trapped in your bogus game! I was honest with you, sincerely devoted, but you have made it all worthless."

"I can see there is some animosity here," Brian exclaimed, trying to neutralize any possible escalation of the situation. Then turning his gaze toward Erin, he pronounced, "Congratulations! I'm going to write your name on this certificate of participation and give it to you."

Without further ado, Brian took a pen from the pocket of his Knights Templar vest and signed the parchment before handing it to Erin. And, in closing, he stood up, took a few steps toward the audience, and for the last time in his career as a host of *The Last Templar* he proclaimed the final words, "This, ladies and gentlemen, concludes the 10th season of *The Last Templar*. From the FOX Studios Center of Los Angeles, that's all. I wish you all a good night, a kind farewell, and stay tuned for the next season of *The Last Templar*."

For the last time, Brian saluted the audience, then calmly walked backstage until no one could see him any longer.

The lights in the arena slowly dimmed until the studio went almost dark. There was still enough light for Erin to open the envelope containing the certificate of participation to the Expedition. Beside the elegant parchment was a small brochure containing a program and a round-trip plane ticket to Tromso, Norway, departing from Boston on March 4 and returning on March 9. Erin was expected to be in Norway during that time for a press conference and some basic training. The decision to keep the spot on the Expedition had been made, and her immediate future was set without her consent on the details.

This wasn't a game anymore.

CHAPTER 2: TROMSO

INNER EARTH EXPLORATION CENTER
Tromso, Norway – 217 miles inside the Arctic Circle
Saturday, March 8, ten days before departure to the South Pole

The conference room was filled with frenzied people. Erin, Charlie, and Jake, the only three civilians participating in the Expedition, timidly walked to their assigned seats: row 17, seat numbers 176, 177, and 178, located at the very end toward the main corridor. The front lines were reserved for specialized personnel, a few politicians, and crew members. Researchers and scientists who participated in the project, but who were not taking part in the Expedition, were seated on the left side of the stage, while a small team of construction engineers was located in the opposite section. Most of the back rows were assigned to family members, interns, and journalists.

The stage was elegantly set. A long table covered with a green, silk tablecloth stood in the middle of the platform, surrounded by ornate plants. There were six chairs, and in front of each was placed a microphone and nametag. A tray with some bottles of water and glasses stood in the middle of the table. Erin looked around. The conference room was getting full, a sign that the presentation was about to start. She had exchanged only a few words with Charlie and Jake. They seemed to be at ease with the situation, and she did not want to give the impression of being distressed by asking too many questions.

"Oh, good!" said a young, red-headed lady. "I see that you have found your seats," and she grabbed three booklets from the pile she was holding and distributed one to each. She continued. "Sorry, I didn't mean to be rude. I should have introduced myself. My name is Lucy. I will be the coordinator for the day.

11

If you need anything or if you have any questions or concerns, please come and see me. I will be seated in row 4, seat 45, toward the sidewall. The conference will start in about 20 minutes. You still have time for a short break, if you like. There is coffee outside, and the restrooms are located in the hall, just in front of the main door." She paused and smiled. "I hope you enjoy the presentation. It is supposed to be very interesting." But she couldn't finish the sentence because a tall man, wearing a blue suit with a green tie, pulled her aside whispering, "Lucy, we need you this way." The two of them walked away. Lucy looked back and waved. Erin could read her lips saying, "Talk to you later." Maybe she was just assisting in the unfoldment of a secret love affair, or maybe Lucy simply needed to be somewhere else, Erin mused.

She smiled and looked at her two companions who were already reviewing the booklet, making comments and sharing opinions. She decided to go out for a coffee instead.

The line at the coffee bar was quite short. "Good timing," she thought. She ordered a mocha breve tall, paid in cash, and walked toward the main entrance of the building. From the door's window she could see outside. It was a sunlit day in early spring, and the sky held a promising, soft-blue glow.

"I wonder if where I'm going, nature will always be this kind," Erin pondered while her eyes followed a flock of wild geese crossing the horizon. "Rhetorical questions usually arise in the morning while sipping coffee," she thought, before tossing the empty cup away and returning to her seat.

Twenty minutes had passed since meeting Lucy, and the conference was supposed to start any time now. Letting her mind indulge in anticipation, she fantasized about the adventure ahead.

Her dream state was suddenly interrupted by a voice on the microphone. "Ladies and Gentlemen, please take your seats. The presentation will be starting in a few minutes. Thank you."

Soon the lights in the room dimmed.

A short, Oriental-looking man walked toward the middle of the stage aiming directly for the reading desk.

"Ladies and gentlemen, welcome to the first Inner Earth Exploration Summit. For those of you who are following via livestream, thank you so much for joining us today and welcome to the show! I will give you a rundown of the schedule for the day. The first speaker will be Vice Admiral Richard A. Windsor of the U.S. Navy. Mr. Windsor has a distinguished career as an astronaut and polar explorer. He has led many expeditions to the Arctic Circle, including a personal flight over the North Pole last September. He is one of the top dogs on this project. He will talk about his early missions in space exploration and the first discovery of the Hollow Earth, with the possibility of a sun and a small ocean inside our planet. Mr. Windsor has been all over this topic for many years, speaking on national and local radio stations. I personally think his discovery is one of the most important of the century.

"The next speaker will be Captain Jeff Miller, Jr., the man at the head of the Expedition. Mr. Miller is a former United States Navy Admiral who served as director of the National Security Agency for over 20 years. During his tenure he helped to develop new technology for the exploration of outer space and Inner Earth. He will talk more about the purpose and details of this Expedition. If you have any questions, he would be the right person to ask."

The speaker adjusted the tie on his blazer and stepped away from the microphone. Erin noticed in that moment how ordinary the lecturer appeared: conventional clothing and speaking simply, but very direct in delivering his message.

She scanned the audience. "There was something convenient about being part of a group," she thought. Everybody was quiet at the same time, cheering at the same time, feeling the same emotion together. But despite that awareness, Erin felt a sort of loneliness, something that she rarely experienced when she was by herself. She took a deep breath and a quick glance at her companions for a flicker of recognition, but they both seemed very involved in what the speaker was saying.

Erin, on the other hand, felt an urgent need to leave the room. She was begging for some fresh air and sunshine. She had the impression that time was passing like cement; one minute seemed like an hour.

She retrieved the folder from her purse and her attention was immediately captivated by the majestic vessel on the front page.

Admiral Q-Oho:
- *approximately 25,000 tons*
- *530 feet long*
- *propelled by 6 diesel engines*
- *able to reach a speed of 3 knots in 7 feet of ice; maximum speed 30 knots*
- *capacity of accommodation: 40 special personnel and 15 crew members*
- *endurance, 95 days*
- *equipped with 4 large snowcats, 10 snowmobiles, and 10 four-wheelers*
- *can operate at a reduced draft of 25 feet in shallow waters*
- *aviation facilities: 2 helipads and hangar for 2 helicopters*
- *cost of construction and operation: 8.5 billion U.S. dollars*

On the successive pages were photographs of the vessel with some captions depicting the inside. Side pictures showed close-ups of all specialized personnel and staff members. Erin immediately noticed that her headshot was there too, on the very bottom of the list:

Erin Palmer – The Last Templar winner, civilian

"Last, but not least," she whispered to herself. There was a sense of arrogance in being under the spotlight. If only for a brief moment, Erin felt energized and almost invincible.

The lunch break was finally announced, and she couldn't wait to get up and rush into the line for the buffet. Already a few people were standing, but the majority of the audience were still chatting inside the conference room.

Erin opted for some steamed vegetables, smoked salmon, and vanilla pudding. She found an empty spot at a table by the window.

The man sitting opposite gave Erin a quick smile of acknowledgment.

From the window of the restaurant, the view was marvelous. There was a lake that Erin later discovered was a fjord. The water was deep blue, surrounded by heavily wooded mountains down to the water's edge with ribbons of faded green, where avalanches had cleared away the trees.

"Do you know what they say?" asked the man. "If you come here once, you will always feel the desire to return. There is something magical about this place that can hardly be described in words."

It took a second or two for Erin to realize the man was talking to her. She looked at the stranger, who took a sip of his wine, and offered no further conversation.

She decided to respond to his comment, "I agree, there is something beautiful about this place."

Erin looked at the man again and caught his eye. She had to admit he was very attractive, although he wasn't her type. But there was something of a champion in him, combined with a gentleness, that made her want to know him better.

"Will you be taking part in the Expedition or are you here just to …? Sorry, I don't think I have properly introduced myself. My name is Erin. I'm one of the three civilians who won the spot."

The man didn't let her finish. "How wonderful!" he exclaimed, offering his hand to Erin to shake with a formal introduction. "My name is Roger, and I'm pleased to know that such a lovely lady will be part of our Expedition."

Erin felt positively overwhelmed by his manners. "Our Expedition? So you are going too?" She looked at Roger waiting for him to speak.

"Yes, I'm a geologist and I have published many articles about Inner Earth. I was so happy when I was selected to be part of this mission! Being able to participate in such an Expedition is something I have been dreaming of ever since I was a kid."

"That's impressive! I've never met someone who was able to maintain an aspiration for such a long time. Usually people forget about their dreams when they grow up. I would love to know more about your articles if you don't mind telling me." She looked at Roger. He was playing with his fork without saying a word.

He checked his phone and exclaimed, "I would love to tell you more about my research, but I really need to grab some fresh air outside. The day is perfect for a short walk. You are more than welcome to join me if you like. We still have an hour before the conference reconvenes. Would you like to accompany me? This place is really beautiful!"

Erin looked down at her empty plate hoping that Roger would go on, but he didn't. She swallowed and, adjusting her posture on the chair, responded, "One cannot refuse a tour of such a marvelous place, especially on a lovely day like this!"

That day the air was filled with stillness and a brittle silence. Both Roger and Erin underestimated the cold outside, so they traded a longer walk for something indoors. The two of them wandered in silence through the center of Tromso, passing a small bank and a butcher with his cuts of meat on display. It was early Saturday afternoon and the town was serene and dormant. The only café open was the Old Goblin Tavern.

From the outside, the place looked well-maintained and charming. The painted glass of the big, medieval-style windows made it difficult to see through, but the pleasant atmosphere could be felt from the outside. On the inside the place looked very old but appealing. Two big wooden beams were supporting the upper floor, and two gigantic, steel candelabrums were hanging from them. The orange-colored walls were decorated with many sorts of pictures, paintings, objects, and tools, and each table was adorned with candles and pinecones. A few tables were occupied by folks who were clearly having a good time. Erin and Roger opted for a small table, close to the open fireplace. Erin's fingers felt numb and she realized that the tip of her nose was red. She was definitely craving something warm. Following Roger's suggestion, she ordered a hot cider and a slice of homemade rhubarb pie.

"You seem at home here," Erin said, crossing her legs under the table.

"I feel that way. When I was young, I used to spend my summers in this area. Two of the things that I will never forget are the northern lights and the rhubarb pie," said Roger.

Erin scratched her nose. "I have never seen the northern lights. Can you believe that?"

"Only a few people have been able to observe them. They are mostly seen at very high altitudes, mainly in the Arctic and Antarctic regions. Tromso is one of the best places to see the northern lights." He paused to finish his bite, then continued. "You said this is the first time you have come this far from the equator; right?"

They looked at each other. Erin nodded. She was feeling invigorated and quite confident in the situation, so she decided to ask Roger about his research.

"I thought you would never ask," Roger replied, clearing his throat. "Where do you want me to start? There is so much I could say but we only have about half an hour."

"Tell me about when you first had the desire to go to Inner Earth. How did you know there was an Inner Earth at such a young age? This is all so new to me."

"I told you that when I was a child, I spent most of my summers in this area. My grandparents used to own a farm in a village not far from here. It was normal for me to see the northern lights almost every night. I have always wondered where those lights were coming from. The best explanation I was able to come up with was that there must have been a hole in the poles and that the aurora was coming from inside the Earth. It was then that I decided to become a scientist, to be able to provide an explanation. The fact that the Earth is made of several layers has been known for many years, but it is only recently that scientists have been able to prove that our planet is actually hollow." He paused for a moment, reached for his drink, then started again. "There is an old expression that says, *'The moon is made of cheese.'* This, of course, refers to the fact that the lunar craters resemble cheese. But what if the holes were not just the surface? What if the whole moon was hollow? Would this be enough to assume that maybe many or even all the planets could be empty inside?"

Erin opened her eyes wide and a small smile played on her lips. It wasn't what Roger said but the persuasiveness of his tone of voice that captivated her the most. She scratched her head and suddenly remembered something she learned at school. "I know that all the planets in our solar system have a rotational movement. Would it be correct to assume that the centrifugal force pushes everything outward?"

Roger looked at Erin, nodding and waiting for her to go on, so she continued. "If the Earth is spinning on its axis, would it be plausible to think that the inside is hollow because of its centrifugal force?"

"Yes, this is a good observation, and it would be reasonable to assume that, especially considering that the Earth spins on its axis at a speed of over 1,000 mph, and at mid-altitudes, the speed of the Earth's rotation decreases to roughly 800 mph. On top of that, one needs to remember that the Earth also spins around the sun at a velocity of almost 1,700 mph. Despite this evidence, however, the scientific community decided to dismiss the Hollow Earth argument for many years, considering it more a conspiracy theory than something to question."

"Why do you think the theory was rejected for so long if it seems so simple and rational?" asked Erin.

"That is a very good question. I have been asking myself the same thing for many years. As a researcher, I can tell you this: Sometimes scientists are in the business of discovering; other times they are in the business of hiding. I think in this case, the main business was hiding."

"Hiding what? A possibility?" Erin asked.

"We are about to find out. I have published many articles providing evidence that the Earth's composition does not increase in density, pressure, and heat the closer we get to the core. I believe the Earth is entirely hollow or contains a substantial inner space that might accommodate ecosystems with a diversity of biological organisms. We have finally reached a level of agreement in the scientific community that has led us to conclude that we need to explore this prospect."

Erin had the thought, "There are many discoveries of ancient, underground cities. Do you think this could be used as evidence for the Hollow Earth theory?"

"I would say yes. There are several historical examples of entire civilizations living deep within the Earth. Even the most agnostic anthropologists have come to this conclusion." Roger reached for his drink. "Tell me more about you. What is your interest in participating in this Expedition? I know you won your spot, but what is your motivation? What are you hoping to find?"

This sudden and direct question left Erin speechless for a few moments. Although she had spent many nights con-templating the nature of her fate, she had never been able to come up with a good answer. The only thing that kept coming to her mind was the embarrassment in betraying Jessica's trust and friendship.

"I don't know what to say. I have just graduated from law school, and besides waitressing and babysitting I have zero working experience. I'm very happy for this opportunity but, to be honest, I don't think I'm very qualified. I feel a little uncomfortable being among all these scientists because it looks like I have nothing to contribute. I guess my greatest motivation for being here is just to be here, and I hope this experience will boost my career when I return home."

"I think you have a lot more in common with the first explorers — much more than you think." Roger's comment confused Erin.

"I do?" Erin thought Roger was kidding, but he seemed utterly serious.

"Most of the participants in the earliest explorations were people who hadn't accomplished much in life. The sailors were usually folks that had no family, no place to stay. Some of them were outcasts of society or prisoners used for free labor. Remember, in those days the living conditions, especially on a ship, were so harsh that only a few people were able to survive the journey. Others were murdered by the native populations. Think of Christopher Columbus, for example. He was a man with a vision, but most of the sailors who went with him didn't know much, hadn't done much in life. They were prisoners forced to go or, in the best-case scenario, they saw an opportunity to make a buck and took it. Without knowing, they became part of one of the most remarkable expeditions in history. No one remembers them, but a lot of the success of those crusades depended on their hard work."

"One thing I have been successful at is knowing how to survive in a hostile environment," Erin said in her defense.

"You sure do! Your skills will come in handy. You'll see."

"Are you saying the habitat we are about to explore could be dangerous?" Erin was starting to feel somewhat disturbed by the conversation.

"What I am saying is that the reality we are about to uncover could be inhospitable for human life. We only know a little about Inner Earth, and I hope we will have a better idea and more information by the end of this Exploration. Like Pythagoras once said, *'The wise man should be prepared for everything that does not lie within his control,'* and this is why we have a ship like our icebreaker, Admiral Q-Oho!" Roger finished his drink and reached for his watch inside his coat pocket. It was time to return.

Erin was silent on the way back. There was a lot to contemplate about what Roger just told her. Had she been underestimating the risk and the cost of the Exploration? Erin knew that her reasons for participating were separate from her qualifications. She had no experience, after all. But what were her motivations? She'd imagined the journalists talking about her returning home after a successful Expedition. The overall feeling was a sense of privilege and importance, but nothing else. A calm settled over Erin because she knew there was a limit to thinking. She decided instead to allow her ego to be nourished by the images taking form in her mind.

That afternoon the U.S. Navy Officer, who happened to be the ship's Captain, Jeff Miller, talked about the icebreaker named Admiral Q-Oho, although Erin preferred to call it "the big boat." The most intriguing detail of the presentation was the map of tunnels leading to underground rivers that were identified as the opening toward Inner Earth.

Erin thought there was something fascinating about that map. It was telling the tale of a journey to be — and what now appeared to be a highly dangerous one. Erin soon realized that as their adventure unfolded, it would eventually be written down, adding a new section to the depiction of what was already known. This Summit was the beginning of a slow and methodical process that would ultimately result in the success (or not) of Admiral Q-Oho's Expedition. The potential cost of the quest, however, seemed to have disappeared beneath the emphasis on the adventure.

The last slide of the presentation was a quote from the past:

"NOTICE: Men wanted for hazardous journey. Small wages, bitter cold. Long months of complete darkness. Constant danger. Safe return doubtful. Honor and recognition in case of success."

— Ernest Shackleton

It is said that the best time to start a new adventure is after having successfully completed the previous one. Maybe it was this kind of optimism that **inspired** Erin, or perhaps the inexperience of her youthful mind, but all that she remembered after reading the quote was "honor and recognition."

CHAPTER 3: USHUAIA

USHUAIA, ARGENTINA
March 17, Saint Patrick's Day, one day before departure

The enchanting town of Ushuaia, located on the southern coast of Tierra del Fuego Island, was known as the southernmost city in the world. As a major tourist town, Ushuaia was complete with casinos, nice restaurants, outdoor clothing stores and museums, although in the past it had been mainly a missionary base and a penal colony for the Argentine Navy.

Admiral Q-Oho was expected to leave the next day at noon, sailing toward the dangerous waters of Antarctica before proceeding toward Inner Earth.

Erin and her parents decided to spend the last few days together in Ushuaia, attempting to enjoy each other's company before their separation.

Erin knew that the best way to know a place was to talk with the people who live there. As much as she enjoyed spending time with her beloved mother visiting museums with marine wildlife, or shopping with her father for outdoor gear and old books, what Erin loved the most was to talk to the locals, especially the elder ones. She was aware of the fact that the older folk were the true keepers of culture and traditions.

There was one lady, in particular, who played a crucial role in Erin's adventure, like few others did. Her name was Ula, and she managed a small store of used books and ancient maps. Ula was one of those women, half-witch, perhaps, who had an answer for every question. Her shop was located in a favorite spot of Erin's mother: facing the picturesque port, not too far from a distinctive diner. While her parents were at the coffee bar enjoying the late, sunny morning and a hot Fernet, Erin decided to go shopping.

It was while searching for old maps that she met Ula for the first time.

The people of Ushuaia were in general very friendly, and it wasn't difficult to start a conversation. Most spoke good English because of the large flow of tourism in the area. Due to it being the last day before departure, Erin was feeling ecstatic. Her uplifted attitude was immediately acknowledged by Ula. "Miss, are you finding what you are looking for? I have more items in the back of the store if you tell me what you need."

Erin responded by saying that she was looking for the original maps used in the earliest expeditions. At the sound of those words, Ula smiled. "Are you one of the members of the Expedition that is leaving tomorrow?"

"Yes, I am," said Erin proudly, stretching her back to become taller, perhaps attempting to assume importance.

"I think I have something you might like," said Ula before disappearing behind the counter. She came back a few minutes later with an old book and some scrolls of parchment.

"I want to show you something," she said, inviting Erin to come closer. Ula opened the book and, pointing to a modest man in the picture, continued. "This is my great-grandfather. He was one of the leaders of the Qom tribe. Today there are only a few members left, and I am one of them. My great-grandfather participated in three of the earliest expeditions to Inner Earth."

"Wow!" exclaimed Erin. "Has he ever told you anything about that? Such as ... did he find anything?"

"Oh, yes. He told me many things! He believed that the portal to Inner Earth was known way before such was admitted by the scientific community. Some of the native people of my tribe have known about it for a long time. There are plenty of legends about Inner Earth. It is said that many people attempted to enter but only a few were lucky enough to ever come back."

Erin didn't let the woman finish. She found the last statement a bit conspiratorial. Without trying to disappoint the old lady, she started looking in her purse for her wallet, signaling that she was ready to leave the store.

Perceiving Erin's sudden rush as a sign of skepticism, Ula proposed an original invitation. "We are committed to keeping the old traditions alive. There is a ritual tonight. It is a sacred observance that people of this town perform the night before any given expedition. It is by invitation only. Would you like to participate?"

Erin was confused. She knew fairly well that it wasn't wise to accept the invite of a stranger, but something loud and clear whispered in her inner ear that this time it was safe to comply.

Ula seemed to notice the young lady's perplexity and continued. "Oh, don't worry. It is like a ceremony to bless the sailors and to wish them a safe trip. It is a very ancient, tribal tradition and just a few people know about it. One can attend only if invited by the native people. We are trying to keep the ritual as pristine as possible, and any form of publicity, including the press, cannot come. But since you have shown much interest in the history and the culture of this place, I thought it could be something you would be pleased to see. Trust me, you will never read about this in books and definitely you will never hear anything about it on television."

Ula's gracious and unexpected demonstration of trust brought fresh enthusiasm to Erin's heart. Intrigued by the unusual invitation, she replied, "Tell me more about it," and placed the wallet back in her purse.

"In the old days ..." Beginning with that one phrase, Ula evoked the magical secrecy of the rituals of Ushuaia and the ancient mysteries of venerable tribes who had long gone, leaving behind their traditions and their divine spirit. It was a journey of emotions that, almost like an enchantment, transported Erin to worlds she had never known existed.

When Erin left the store, it was already late afternoon. She did not realize she had been talking to Ula for over an hour. "Don't tell anyone. It is a sacred and secret ritual," were the parting words of the venerable, old lady.

Erin waved at her mom and dad who were still at the diner, apparently having a good time. She had not seen her parents that happy for a very long time. She briefly told them about Ula, the old maps, the tribe of Qom, and the earliest expeditions, even carefully mentioning something about the ancient ritual but conscientiously leaving out the fact that she had just been invited to participate in one of them.

In ancient times, Ushuaia was believed to be the end of the world and, as such, it was a renowned pilgrimage destination for those who wanted to make offerings to the deities of the ocean. Many local fishermen still believed in the presence of strange divinities living in the water, and on the eve of every expedition, a secret ritual was performed to bless the brave sailors. Every expedition was celebrated as a form of death, the end of life on Earth, that was believed to be the beginning of a journey of awakening for the soul. To ensure a safe course, offerings were made to the Gods, and animal spirits were evoked to provide power and strength. Traditional foods and special herbs were served; dances and popular chants performed.

At the end of the ceremony, a small quantity of whale oil was spread on each sailor's forehead to symbolize the awakening of the great inner spirit for guidance and protection. Erin was given a new name, "SunAlaka," which is an old idiom meaning "hummingbird." She was told she must invoke qualities of those creatures, such as adaptability, endurance, and courage in order to survive the journey. The last words of the shaman still echoed in Erin's mind. "Your spirit is weak and will bring death with your journey. The only thing that will save you is the ability to change, something that you now lack. You need to learn this because your life will depend on it. Remember, sometimes big is small and small is big. Expand your thinking to understand what I mean. There are no coincidences. Do you believe? May your life be long and your journey blessed."

The following day Erin left for Inner Earth.

All that her parents asked was that she come back safe. Their last hug expressed a deep connection within each other's soul and, with a simple kiss, they said good-bye.

Everyone understood it was the beginning of a journey that might not have a good end. Despite a little anxiety in the back of her mind, Erin felt somehow privileged. *"There are no coincidences,"* she reminded herself and, with a smile on her face, proudly walked past the gate where no one, except those authorized, could follow.

CHAPTER 4: ANTARCTICA

Inner Earth was a secret and dangerous place to explore. But on the ice-clogged seas of the Southern Hemisphere is where Erin's adventure began.

The passageway to Inner Earth was an underground river called "Devil's Passage," and it took about three days for Admiral Q-Oho to get there.

On the first night after departing Ushuaia, the sky was dark and starry, majestic enough to ignite the inspiration of every artist. There were no familiar sounds, except ice cracking at the passing of the vessel. It was freezing. Erin, eager to experience the night, walked outside on the deck. The confluence of the black ocean and dark sky evoked in her a sense of something strange and yet familiar. She gazed at the starry heavens. It was fascinating to think how the same stars and constellations that had witnessed the life of a myriad of people and entire civilizations passing by were now looking down in that instant. Erin felt the magnitude of that moment.

A tap on her shoulder caused her to suddenly turn away. "Afraid to miss something or simply unable to sleep?" Roger was wrapping his arms tighter around himself. His jacket was zipped all the way, partially covering his face, but his breath was visible under the sporadic lights on deck.

"A little of both," Erin replied. The air was so chilly it almost hurt her to breathe. Erin had never experienced such a low temperature. "I don't think I can resist much longer. I'm starting to have frostbite on my toes," she added, shivering.

Roger placed his arm around her shoulder and, as a good friend would do, guided her inside. "How about some hot tea?"

The break room was deserted. Despite the aluminum tables and benches sealed to the floor, Erin thought it quite romantic. Most of all, it was warm.

Occasionally Roger had the ability to amaze Erin with his remarks. And so it happened that his next question again surprised her. "Have you ever heard of 'Operation High Jump'?"

No, of course not. Why would she? Erin didn't like to admit her inexperience in so many topics, so opted to "plead the fifth" even if there was nothing to be ashamed of in her ignorance. Her face, however, could not disguise her embarrassment. Roger smiled and then continued. "A friend of mine gave me a book. It talks about an expedition called 'Operation High Jump.' Very interesting work! I was wondering if maybe you had a chance to read it yourself."

"I have never heard of that book. But now I'm curious. What is Operation 'jumping high' about?" Erin was holding her teacup with both hands in an attempt to warm them up.

"High Jump, not jumping high."

Roger seemed amused by Erin's jovial attitude. "Well, just after WWII, in 1947, the Secretary of the Navy, James Forrestal, sent a naval task force to the South Pole called 'Operation High Jump.' It was publicized as an expedition to find coal and other useful resources. But the real, undisclosed purpose was to find the alleged underground base of the Germans. It looks like the Nazis had some business in Antarctica.

"During 'Operation High Jump,' the reading of the magnetometers showed anomalies in the Earth's magnetism as if there were a 'hollow' place under the surface of the ice. But this is where the story gets even more interesting. When the data was reported back, it became classified as 'top secret.' Soon after his return, Forrestal was placed in a psychiatric hospital and prevented from seeing anyone, including his wife. After a couple of years, he was found dead. It was ruled a suicide, and the case was closed. I find that strange, don't you?"

"Strange what? That he died?" Erin's response didn't show much concern.

"No. Don't you find it strange that he ended up committing suicide after he found some magnetic distortions that could have proven that the Earth was hollow?"

"Whoa ... yes, that's weird," Erin commented with a critical gesture.

Roger didn't hesitate to go on. "Notice how this happened in 1949, at a time when the scientific community was still in denial of any possibility of an Inner Earth. But even so, why would he kill himself? Forrestal is said to have been depressed and suicidal, but there is very little evidence regarding his mental state at the time of death. There was never a police investigation and that fact set me thinking. I have read a lot of detective and investigative books. To my knowledge, when someone dies forcefully or suspiciously, the first question that one needs to ask is: Was there a motive for murder? The next question is: Did the victim have any enemies and would someone benefit from his death?"

"I didn't know you had a passion for criminal investigations." Erin was absorbed in Roger's detailed knowledge of events.

"Yes, my dad was a police detective and I have learned a lot from him. One of my dreams was to become an investigator."

"Why didn't you pursue it? Oh, yes, your quest about the northern lights and the desire to become a scientist to provide answers. I remember now." Erin looked down at her empty cup of tea and said nothing else.

"Yes, that's true. But the main reason was that my father was killed during a sting operation. I did not want to end up like him, so I decided to study geology instead. Supposedly, being a scientist is a safer job, but I don't know the truth of that statement anymore." A sad smile painted Roger's face and his eyes almost closed.

Roger's sadness was evident to Erin. "I'm sorry about your dad. You must miss him a lot." Erin moved forward on the bench trying to get closer to Roger.

"I'm fine, thank you. But the death of my father did not prevent me from studying criminology and investigative science. I don't have much practical experience, but I have enough knowledge to understand when something is wrong. And I can see that there is something awry with this picture. The story of Forrestal was sold by the media as a suicide, but the only serious government investigation of his death was kept secret from the public. The book I was reading had the same conclusion, but I'm not inclined to buy that simplistic and convenient a narrative."

"What are you saying? Do you think there was some sort of cover-up?"

"I actually do. I think that Forrestal found something back in 1947 but there was a strong interest in keeping his discovery silent. I hope our Expedition will be able to finish what he started a long time ago."

"Unless we become suicidal too." Erin thought she was being funny, but Roger didn't laugh. He raised his eyes before continuing. His tone of voice had become serious.

"I don't mean to scare you, but I hope you are wrong." He paused for a moment drumming his fingers on the table. "I'm not really supposed to share this with you, but one of the purposes of our Exploration is to collect a sample of a deadly virus that was discovered during an expedition a few years back. This will be a secondary objective, as much of our effort will be focused on Inner Earth Exploration. When the discovery of the deadly virus was first published at the beginning of the twenty-first century, not many people paid attention to it because they assumed that since Antarctica was so far away, there was no reason to be alarmed. Also, the fact that the virus was detected deep in the permafrost implicated a lower risk of infection for the rest of the planet. Are you still following?"

"Right, sooo ... why bother?"

"Well, at first there was a certain level of alarmism due to the fact that if the temperature of the planet had risen, the virus could have easily reproduced itself, posing a serious risk to any ecosystem on the planet. My point, however, is much simpler, and yet missed by many people. Per definition, a virus is a small, infectious agent that replicates only inside the living cells of another organism. Now the question we need to ask is: If the only animals who can survive in Antarctica are penguins, where does that virus come from?"

Erin took no time to respond. "Penguins!" she said proudly.

"Yes, and that would be the logical conclusion of any person with common sense," added Roger.

"You sound sarcastic. Am I missing something?"

"What if I told you that neither people nor animals have immunity from that virus?"

"What do you mean? I'm not following."

"Well, when a new virus is discovered, the first question that specialists ask is, 'Where does it come from?' That's important in order to find an antidote. Viruses move in wondrous ways but not under their own power. They need a living organism in order to replicate and survive. If the virus found in the permafrost originated from penguins, it would have drastically reduced their population because penguins do not have immunity from that pathogen. In other words, penguins don't carry the virus. So the question remains: What is the source of the deadly virus in Antarctica where only penguins can survive in all that ice? The scientific community is still unable to provide an answer."

"Wow! That's ... almost scary! So if the virus didn't come from penguins, what is your assumption?"

"I'm not sure yet. I'm among those scientists who believe that the permafrost might contain evidence of prehistoric forms of life. That could easily explain the origins of the deadly virus. But there are also people who think the Germans had underground facilities in the South Pole and that the virus could have been genetically engineered in those secret laboratories."

Roger took his last sip of tea before continuing. "Did you know that Antarctica is the only continent that hasn't been claimed by anybody, and yet all the major nations have permanent exploration centers down there? What justifies all this interest in 'nobody's land'? And why isn't anyone releasing information to the public? What are they looking for exactly? Whatever the pursuit is, it makes Forrestal's death even more suspicious. I keep asking myself what did he find that was too inconvenient to be disclosed?"

Erin met Roger's eyes for what seemed a long moment. Everything about his face communicated trust and respect. "I'm happy I have met you" were the only words that she was able to say.

Roger smiled timidly, realizing how much Erin reminded him of his wife. But he did not want to uncover the sorrowful past so he looked away, trying to avoid her eyes. It wasn't long before the door of the break room opened and two men entered carrying a pile of documents. They gave Erin and Roger a brief glance, nodding their heads in acknowledgment. Then without saying a word, they sat at a far table in the corner of the room.

The atmosphere swiftly changed.

Erin could hear the two men speaking, but she was unable to recognize their tongue. Roger was also paying attention to their movements. When he saw that Erin was about to speak, he put his finger in front of his mouth indicating silence. "Not English," he whispered, reading Erin's mind.

"Do you know them?" asked Erin keeping a soft tone of voice.

"No, but I saw them earlier this afternoon. They were talking to Miller."

"Miller, the Captain?"

"Yes, exactly." Roger revealed a slight concern in his voice and turned his head slowly in their direction. He didn't like the fact that they were sitting behind him. As a good investigator, he knew the importance of having things under control, and sometimes that meant in plain sight.

"Is your detective instinct telling you something?" Erin was feeling quite amused by the situation.

"I don't like the fact that they are speaking a foreign language," Roger stated, trying to justify his palpable anxiety. "It seems to me they might have something to hide."

Erin found the whole situation rather entertaining. "I think you're reading too much into this. They appear to be friends."

"They ARE friends," Roger replied, marking his words and lowering his voice even more.

"I think you're just imagining. There's nothing wrong in trying to keep some things private. As a matter of fact, we're perfect strangers to them." Erin felt the desire to hearten the man sitting in front of her.

But Roger didn't need to be reassured. "Rule number one: When your privacy is a big deal, there must be a reason. People are usually rational beings, and there is always a logic for the way they act."

"Okay, Sherlock Holmes, I trust you. They must be plotting something really bad."

"Erin, you should be aware of your surroundings! Assuming that everything is under control affects your vigilance. You have to keep yourself in the right mind-set because things can easily lead to a routine and therefore to complacency. Especially when you're in a survival situation, like the one we are in, always be prepared for changes around you. Remember: Awareness is a choice! You need to choose to pay attention."

Erin's eyes were wide open. It wasn't what Roger said but the confidence of his tone of voice that impressed her. "You studied geology and criminology. They seem to be two very different sciences. Were you able to find something in common between the two?"

"Good question." Roger took a deep breath. "As a geologist, I measure phenomena that can be assessed by theorizing a series of hypotheses. If the hypothesis is validated, I come to a conclusion. If it is not validated, I need to come up with a different one that can be confirmed. In criminology, like in all other intelligence analysis, I rarely have access to the observable object, the culprit, for example, and I need to gather information indirectly. Sometimes I have to use my intuition or my experience. From that observation, I need to provide a good theory that can explain the event until I reach a valid conclusion. Another important difference is that as a geologist, I study one hypothesis at a time, while as a detective I can compare multiple assumptions simultaneously. As you can see, they are two different sciences."

Erin loved talking to Roger because he didn't think conventionally like everyone else. After every conversation with Roger, Erin felt reinvigorated rather than disturbed by the lack of mental flexibility that most of the people seemed to have.

"Which kind of approach do you think we will be using when exploring Inner Earth?"

"Definitely the geologist one. We will most likely be collecting samples of dirt, rock, water, air, and any potential form of life we might find. Those samples will then be analyzed in a laboratory and compared with other samples we already have. Conclusions will be made, and maybe we will go home with something worth the cost of this project. Our camp is situated at the edge of the known area of Inner Earth, just at the end of the underground river. I believe another function of our Expedition is to expand our presence in the area and our knowledge of the territory."

"Do you think that's why those foreigners are studying a map?" Erin was looking past Roger's shoulder.

Roger felt the urge to turn and look himself but he didn't want to be noticed, so he decided to rely on Erin's words. "How do you know they are studying maps?" he asked.

"I can tell ..." but she couldn't provide a more specific explanation.

"You might be right. They could be reading a map. Maybe they are part of the task team that will explore the unknown area surrounding our base camp."

As soon as Roger finished his sentence, the door of the kitchen opened again, this time forcibly. Another person entered the room and went straight to the table where the men were sitting. Apparently unaware of Roger and Erin, he said out loud, "Sir, we have a problem!" The man was holding a phone in his hand and his tone of voice appeared anxious.

Roger's suspicions grew stronger. What was the problem? In his mind he was ready for action.

"Stay here," he instructed Erin while standing up and opening his jacket to reveal his badge.

Then he walked toward the three men and said with a polite expression on his face, "Good evening, gentlemen. I just heard someone saying that there is a problem. Is there something I should be informed of?"

The three men looked at each other, not sure what to say. It seemed that nobody wanted to take responsibility in providing a response. It took a moment or two before one of the men, who appeared to be the leader, replied. "Good evening, sir, and ... you would be?"

"My name is Roger Wood and I'm in charge of the scientific crew during this Exploration. I see you have military badges, so I must assume you are government representatives."

"Yes, sir, we are. We are part of the United States Marine Corps. We are sorry if we disrupted your conversation with your lovely lady, sir, but there is nothing you need to worry about," and he turned his head away from Roger, cutting off the conversation.

Generally speaking, Roger didn't like to be silenced, but after taking note of the situation, he decided to let it go. However, when he returned to their table, the expression on his face was one of perplexity. Erin could not hide her delight in seeing Roger left without words. She had known him for just a few days, but she had quickly learned how difficult it was for him not to have the last word in a conversation. She decided to let the situation unfold without saying anything, but inside she did feel some sympathy for him.

After a short silence, Roger made his decision. "I'm tired. If you would like to excuse me, I think I'll go to my room now."

Erin only had time to say good night before he turned his back and walked out of the break room. She watched him disappear in the dim corridor.

"What a day," she said to herself, once back in her cabin. It was the first night since *The Last Templar* had ended that she didn't have to wait long before falling asleep.

Her dreams carried her to the middle of a forest. She was in a gloomy woodland, looking for a way out, but the woods were dense with towering, frightening-looking trees, and recognizable landmarks were hidden behind heavy shrubs. It was cold and pitch-black. Erin perceived a soreness growing in her chest, like a compression that pressed deeper and deeper. She felt the urge to escape, but there was no way to determine which direction to go. The ground was crumbling under her feet, causing her to run. Even the air she was breathing seemed to be strangling her. A huge shadow loomed closer and more ominous … it assumed the shape of an enormous, terrifying owl. Erin started running without direction. She felt hopeless and almost out of breath. Her heart was pumping sporadically. Racing for her life, Erin looked back and, with horror in her eyes, saw that the owl had now become two, then three, four … Her feet were moving as fast as they could, without control, in search of a place to hide. In the deep darkness, Erin didn't see the precipice in front of her and fell into a black, bottomless abyss.

CHAPTER 5: DEVIL'S PASSAGE

A necessity, when committing to a long journey, is a good map. But what if a place to be explored is mostly unknown, unfamiliar, and no map exists to fully describe it? What if you are about to embark on an adventure that is both fascinating and mysterious but with the potential of being dangerous and grotesque? The Expedition's map of Inner Earth was as discouraging as it was helpful. Due to the unfamiliar territory, it was drawn on a small scale, enabling the already known, geographical characteristics to be included, but lacking details, as those needed to be discovered and added later.

Eventually at the end of the third day, the Admiral Q-Oho reached what was considered the end of the known world and finally approached the portal to Inner Earth called Devil's Passage.

Devil's Passage, as previous explorers had named it, referred to a long, underground tunnel with narrow walls and deadly, freezing temperatures. The tunnel itself was not easy to find, as it lay amidst a multitude of rivers, all of them disappearing in the deep ice of the South Pole. But one — located in the middle of a very hostile area named The White Southern Tundra — did not vanish into the ice but continued making its way inside the bowels of the Earth, creating an icy tunnel. The river was called Victorem. It was the only known access to Devil's Passage and subsequently to Inner Earth.

The easiest way to find Victorem River was by locating two high, pyramid-shaped, volcanic mountains — Taurus Hill and Ursus Hill — situated on either side of the river, at its confluence with the southern ocean. The two mountains were leaning toward each other forming what looked like a majestic gate, defining the entrance to Inner Earth. The river was difficult to navigate, the consequence of endless rapids and constant, strong winds. Even a 25-thousand-ton vessel was at the mercy of such inhospitable conditions, making the navigation of the river and the passing of the tunnel one of the most difficult and dangerous challenges in the Expedition.

Those least interested in this type of adventure would call the crossing a nasty and disturbing experience. Roger was one of them. His passion was exploration in a safe and predictable environment, but due to the importance of the mission he was willing to expose himself to such discomfort. He did it, however, alone from the inside of his cabin. Curious gossip makers onboard wondered if he would still be safe and sound on arrival.

The until-then jovial atmosphere on the vessel was suddenly interrupted on the third evening when the Captain announced their proximity to Taurus Hill and Ursus Hill. Everyone knew what that meant: the easy part was over and the real adventure about to begin.

"Ladies and gentlemen, this is your Captain speaking with some information. Coming up we will be catching a glimpse of Taurus Hill and Ursus Hill. On the left, in just a few minutes, will be the largest iceberg so far. Our latitude is -82.8627 and our longitude 135, with a current speed of 12 knots. A few more facts: We will be slowly decreasing our speed due to approaching a vortex in the proximity of Victorem River. If you have a weak stomach, please be prepared for some rough waters. We should be able to access Victorem River in about 45 minutes. Crew, please be prepared. Dinner will be served a little later tonight to allow Admiral Q-Oho to safely enter the waters of Victorem River. We are planning to begin crossing Devil's Passage at around 11.30 this evening. Thank you. Please relax and enjoy the next phase of this Expedition."

With Roger holed up in his cabin, Erin felt vulnerable. "Why can't he have some fun? He could be here with me enjoying this adventure instead of hiding his head under the covers!"

The reality was that Erin was scared. Besides the basic training received in Tromso, she had not spent much time in preparing for the journey, and now she had to prove that she was capable of keeping her composure in such a situation. The navigation so far had been smooth and pleasant. She took a peek outside and noted the two massive mountains reaching up into the darkened sky. They were probably less than a mile away. The wind was pushing the ocean, morphing the water into furious waves. The vessel was under pressure, but for the most part seemed to handle the struggle with hardly any shaking.

Precisely three-quarters of an hour later, another announcement from the Captain informed the passengers that the passage to Victorem River had been successfully completed and that the descent to Inner Earth had begun. The ship would cruise at half speed with a starboard declination of 10 degrees. The river itself was large, but the depth of the water decreased drastically to fewer than 500 feet. All security measures were in place and everything seemed normal. Dinner that evening consisted of a sandwich and ice cream, but only a few people showed up. The majority of travelers not involved in the ship's maneuvers opted to stay in their cabins. Always curious, Erin decided to take the opportunity to explore more of the vessel and eventually found herself back in the engine room. Nothing would normally have induced Erin to look for company or any sort of assistance, but it soon became clear to her that the journey she had begun was not meant to be lived alone.

Alan was a curious, old man with a long beard. He wore a red bandana on his head and a pocket watch inside a leather case on his hip. His responsibility was the engine room. Erin remembered Alan the first day telling stories about a giant squid who became angry and flew out of the water to attack and eat the ships of the pirates. Alan felt a tenderness for Erin but in a fatherly way. He liked to call her *Milady*. It was the only way he knew how to address a lovely and beautiful woman. He even serenaded her on that first meeting with a short song that he wrote many years before:

Can your eyes really see
the giant squid from the sea?
Black ink is her left-behind trail.
Did she have too much kale?
Only the pirates she likes to eat,
all of them but their smelly feet,
spitting shoes and people's hairs,
that's how much she really cares.
And when you think she's finally gone,
here she throws out another bone.

Erin and Alan had already developed a good friendship. From time to time she would bring him a cup of hot chocolate and some cookies, confiscated from the cafeteria, and the two of them would spend time together. Erin would tell him about her recent experience in *The Last Templar*, how she accomplished making it to the end and her strategies to win, the people she hurt, but especially her regret with Jessica. Alan would smile and listen to his young friend. "You are a fine lady," he would repeat over and over, perhaps wishing he was younger.

That night Alan was unusually busy and did not immediately notice Erin in the room. She decided to remain silent and listen to what he was saying. "The fuel is too rich on the left engine. I need to regulate it." Then while typing something on the computer, he added, "The pressure indicator is normal; everything else seems to be fine." Eventually he turned around and a big smile crossed his face when he saw Erin. "Another song for you, Milady:"

The engine is now good,
I did everything I could!
Oh, Milady, you have appeared.
Should I have shaved my very long beard?
And since you like my expertise,
why didn't you bring me some more cheese?
Milk and cookies, I do crave,

but this time you were not so brave!
Please come in and take a seat.
Happy I am whenever we meet.

Alan would always improvise a song using his spontaneous doggerel before exploding into impetuous laughter and opening his arms to hug his dear companion. One could easily tell that his affection for Erin was genuine.

The river's current was getting stronger. The vessel was at the mercy of the wind like a toy, and onboard the ship there was no staying still without being anchored to something.

"The wind is now so strong it could easily pick up a man and fling him into the ocean," warned Alan. He told Erin to hold onto something. "Don't be afraid, Milady. This won't last long. We should be entering the underground tunnel in less than two hours, but ... oh, boy! This is a heck of a ride ... oh, yeah, baby ... bring it on!"

From time to time Alan would act as if he were the captain of the boat. Other times he would pretend to be the helmsman — all in grand style but with a constant, lighthearted attitude. Alan had a genuine passion for adventure and life in general. To say it in his own words, he loved "everything that makes you late at night." Erin enjoyed spending time just watching him. Sometimes she caught herself wondering if Alan had been one of the pirates eaten by the giant squid in one of his previous lives. She also pondered if, more realistically, he had been one of those meager sailors in earlier times who only took the job to earn a penny or two. Erin knew Alan had the sincere heart of a sailor, but she never shared her thoughts with him.

Another announcement from the Captain brought Erin back to the present. "Ladies and gentlemen, this is your Captain speaking. It is almost 11.30 p.m. and we are about to enter the underground river called Devil's Passage. But before we do, please enjoy for a moment the aurora australis. I will slow the ship as much as I can so those of you who would like to film, document, or take pictures will have the time to do so. The rest of us can simply relax, smoke a cigar if you wish, and relish this wonderful gift from nature. You will be informed before we resume normal speed. But just for now, please don't worry about the journey ahead, and Godspeed!"

Alan smiled while adjusting the engine to its lowest speed. "Did he just say Godspeed? Oh, I love that guy! He is a good man. You go, Milady. I need to stay here just in case the glossy-mossy-bossy needs some more *Godspeeding* from me," and he pushed her gently out the door.

Erin chuckled, amused, and without arguing she ran up the stairs as fast as she could.

The sky was a brilliant pink in one moment and a multitude of different colors dancing and fading into each other in the next. It looked as though a conscious mind filled the sky, and even the darkness seemed to be alive, as if a substantial presence was surrounding the boat. Erin perceived that the spirit of nature was talking in the aurora lights, and something both ominous and auspicious embraced her.

She soon realized this would be her last glimpse of the sky, at least for a while. In her mind, the words of the shaman arose once again. *"Remember, sometimes big is small and small is big. Expand your thinking to understand what I mean. There are no coincidences. Do you believe? May your life be long and your journey blessed."* And with that contemplation, Erin cried.

What seemed to be an otherworldly voice started lower than a whisper, but it soon became so loud that it could not be ignored. "SunAlaka … SunAlaka … are you paying attention, SunAlaka?" These were not Erin's thoughts. It was more like something foreign coming from the outside. Erin looked up and around trying to detect the origin of the sound, but all that she saw were folks having a good time, despite the freezing temperature. Gradually a large shadow formed at the horizon in front of her, causing Erin to shiver for a moment. She then realized that the ship was approaching the dreaded Devil's Passage. Almost at the same time, the Captain announced that the vessel was about to regain speed and everyone was invited to go back inside.

Devil's Passage began as a long, dark tunnel with narrow walls and shallow water. One small mistake and the ship would have grounded. During the descent, the angle had to be 23 degrees with a starboard declination of 22 degrees. It was a difficult maneuver. Afterward, the inclination of the port would have to be increased to 25 degrees for a length of less than a quarter of a mile, before ascending again to 28 degrees. The crossing through the tunnel was supposed to take all week, with arrival expected to be at early morning on the seventh day, assuming, of course, that everything went well.

Erin went back inside and down to the engine room where a joyful Alan welcomed her with his usual laughter and conventional little refrain. *"Milady, you're back down here. Come on in and have no fear."*

It now occurred to her that approaching the tunnel to Inner Earth was of small concern. Her mind was more entranced and fascinated by the inexplicable voice she had heard a few minutes prior. When her eyes finally fell on the calm and skillful Alan, she decided to tell him everything, hoping to attain some answers. Erin talked and talked for what seemed a long time, providing a very detailed description of the ritual in Ushuaia, the name given to her by the shaman but, more importantly, the voice she had heard not long before. Alan listened patiently, without removing his eyes from the engine computer screen.

He took a deep breath before speaking. "Once upon a time, the South Pole was a green, grassy land covered with flowers and a diversity of small animals. It was also the home of tiny people called Brevis. The Brevis had seven fingers on each hand, no beard, and long, blue or green hair. These little people were divided into two kingdoms: the kingdom of *Eic,* formed by the Brevis with green hair, and the kingdom of *Wosn,* inhabited by those with blue hair.

"The Brevis were an amazing population, very intelligent and very friendly. They knew how to live harmoniously, and they existed this way for thousands of years! Until one day — I think it was a Wednesday at about 3 o'clock in the afternoon — the King of *Eic* thought it was time to demonstrate that the Brevis, despite the color of their hair, could live together in one kingdom. He decided to summon the King of *Wosn* to make a deal. But after three long days of negotiations, the two kings were unable to come to an agreement. What happened next is that instead of going back to the way they used to live, a harshness began to spread among the Brevis. What had once been a good and solid friendship became competition and the desire for supremacy.

"Soon enough, the two Brevis tribes began to fight against each other, and it was only a matter of time before the green, beautiful land was reduced to a mere pile of blood and dirt. The little animals that once inhabited the land all went extinct, killed by the evolving fury of the Brevis. The desperation grew larger and larger till one day — and I remember that very well; it was early Saturday morning — the Goddess of the South Pole, called Floridus, who created the Brevis out of her own breath, decided that she had had enough. Although devastated with sadness, she transformed every single one of the Brevis into particles of snow and ice. From that moment on, the South Pole became covered with a white mantle. The words "snow and ice" are anagrams derived from the original Brevis kingdoms *Wosn* (snow) and *Eic* (ice). Legend says that the voice of Floridus moaning in sadness can still be heard by certain sailors who dare to venture to the South Pole. It is also believed that Floridus has the ability to give courage to those who hear her voice and have a good heart."

Alan paused and looked at Erin with his watchful eye. "If you heard that voice, Milady, you must be a fine fellow. I will make a song for you." And then he said no more.

Erin sat quietly in the back of the engine room contemplating Alan's words. She noted that he seemed unusually worried. The inconsistency in oil pressure was keeping him occupied and somehow flustered. After what seemed a long time, Erin decided it was better to go back upstairs. Maybe Roger had changed his mind and with some luck, she would see him walking around. Erin gave Alan an innocent kiss and, after whispering a quick good-bye in his ear, left the engine room making sure to close the door behind her.

Once on the main level, she noted that only a handful of people were still up and around, mostly faces she had never seen before. Unfortunately, Roger was nowhere to be found. Erin had to admit how much she missed him, even though the past few days with Alan had been quite amusing.

The lack of phone communication with the external world made it seem so very far away, and a sense of estrangement was becoming more intense inside Erin.

Her usual strategy was to look for oblivion in situations where she needed to escape, but this experience was different. Erin was starting to recognize a hidden part of herself that needed to be revealed to open a path to her innermost feelings and memories. It was as though the tunnel through Devil's Passage was leading from one level of reality to the next and seemed to be anchored in different stages of awareness in her mind. Yet Erin wasn't ready to let go. She wasn't willing to look deeply at herself, so instead found pleasure in seeing the anonymous faces around her as a sort of liberation from her own limited existence. She was the winner of *The Last Templar*, after all! She knew how to endure an unfamiliar environment and dangerous situation alone and without fear.

Erin felt she was entering a new phase of her brightness, but without realizing it, she silenced (once again) the urge of her soul.

It didn't take long before a loud and violent sound, similar to an explosion, traveled through the air. The sudden change of pressure inside the vessel caused Erin to lose balance and forcefully pushed her against the wall. It took a minute or two to regain awareness of the situation. When she opened her eyes, people were yelling and running in all directions. The Captain's voice over the microphone endeavored to comfort, but the only information Erin was able to fathom was that there had been a hazardous event. Everyone was being asked to sit down and remain calm.

A young nurse intercepted Erin before she had time to hide or leave the main level. The nurse, whose name was Megan, guided Erin to a nearby chair and then commenced with a series of questions. "Are you okay? Do you feel pain anywhere? I need to check your eyes. Please, let me feel your pulse."

Erin tried to look as strong as possible, but she felt more like a bad actor playing a role. Besides a bruise on her left arm, however, she was surprisingly unharmed. In the midst of the confusion, Erin was able to comprehend that there had been a mechanical explosion. "The situation is under control," said the attendant. "There was an explosion due to the cracking of a pressurized liquid tank. The specialized crew is taking care of the situation. Fortunately, we were able to avoid major damages, so there is no need to worry. The ship will continue cruising to its destination, but the time of arrival will be slightly delayed."

Megan's comforting smile was enough to reassure Erin for a few moments, but soon the thought of Alan pierced her mind like a dart. Erin needed to find out what had happened to her friend. She rose to her feet, but her head was spinning fiercely, making it difficult to keep her balance. She was about to fall, when a gentle touch on her arm pushed her back into the chair. When she turned around, she almost burst into tears realizing that Roger was finally there. Without thinking, she threw her arms around his neck and the two of them remained bonded in an innocent embrace for a few moments.

"Are you okay?" Roger's voice was soft. His hands were holding Erin's palms in a strong clasp. Erin could see the worry in his face, and the black rings under his eyes showed a lack of sleep.

Still heavily disarrayed, Erin responded, "I feel fine, thank you. Do you know what happened?" The sound of her own voice brought her back to awareness, and assuming a solemn posture, she continued. "They say there has been an explosion. Is it true?

Why aren't they telling us anything, except to remain calm? What the hell is happening?"

But instead of answering, Roger changed the topic. "Are you thirsty? I brought you some water."

"That doesn't answer my questions!" blurted Erin in frustration. "What's wrong with you? You don't even seem human … Something bad just happened. We are in the middle of nowhere, stuck in a freaking tunnel, going to a place that nobody knows … and all that you have to say is that you brought me some water?"

Roger was speechless for a moment. "I'm as human as you are," he finally responded. "I was serious when I said this journey had the potential to become ugly," but he soon realized Erin was not in the mood to talk nor comprehend the meaning of his words. He wanted to suggest that it was natural to feel this way but being unsure about the truth of his own statement, he decided to say no more.

Erin, gathering her strength, gave him a challenging glance and walked away, annoyed. Roger understood the conversation had been his first opportunity to test the limits of disagreement and compromise with Erin. He watched her lovely figure walk away, sipping the water. In that moment it was clear to him that doing business with Erin would never be an easy task.

Several hours later, the situation inside the vessel was calm again, almost as if nothing had happened. Small groups of people were gathered together chatting, while most of the crew had already returned to their cabins.

When Erin learned that the explosion had occurred in the engine room, as much as she tried to hold back, tears began spilling down her face. Her crying wasn't hysterical. She quietly sniffled into her sleeve. Despite her sorrow, she was hoping that Alan would surprise her again with another of his songs and sonorous laughter.

She stared around those gathered, looking for clues, but everything seemed exactly the same.

Medical staff passed her by, carrying bags of equipment. Erin noticed they had no blood on their uniforms, and the assessment made her feel a little more optimistic, although a slender fear prevented her from asking any questions.

She stood there, for what seemed to be a long time, wondering if something or someone could offer any encouragement.

Finally, a man wearing blue scrubs approached her. She was pleased to note his silver hair, reassuring her of experience, but his soldier-like posture made her feel somewhat uncomfortable. Erin noticed his badge — "Dr. Scott Anderson, trauma surgeon" — the one person she had not wanted to see!

Dr. Anderson briefly introduced himself. Erin could not explain how he knew about her close friendship with Alan but did not bother to ask. She tried to be as professional as possible while listening to the doctor's words. "Alan has suffered major burns from the explosion and is being treated by specialized staff while in a coma-induced state ..."

Alan was still alive, but those were not the words she had hoped to hear. Erin stared at the doctor. He was emphasizing every sentence with unhurried and meticulous hand movements. His voice was deep and slow and, for the most part, Erin was able to comprehend what he was saying.

"Once we arrive at Taras, Alan will be transferred to our most equipped medical facility and you will be able to see him again," were the last comforting words of the doctor.

With some peace restored in her mind, Erin finally decided to get some rest. She looked for her backpack, found on the bench not far from where she was standing. She couldn't remember placing it there, but in all the chaos, it was probable that someone else did.

When she went to retrieve it, she noticed a small piece of paper protruding from the front pocket, another oddity that she did not recall. "I must have been really confused," Erin said to herself before opening the folded slip of paper.

Inside was an old map and a new song.

DEVIL'S PASSAGE

Milady, follow well this map.
I promise you this is not a trap.
What you will find
will open your mind.
Beyond the cold and the snow,
there is so much more you just don't know.
Keep your heart open and pure.
I warn you, there is no other cure.
And when life should give you a surprise,
know that you know how to be wise.
Life is a gift,
but sometimes we need to shift.
What once was true,
is no more than a clue.
If you listen well to this old boy,
I promise you a life of joy.
Always keep the heart of a child,
but always live well and always stay wild.
For heaven's sake, stop the guessing
and never forget to count your blessings.
I say good-bye, Milady, my dear,
smile, have a beer, and forever cheer!

CHAPTER 6: TARAS

Devil's Passage was worthy of any self-respecting story. At the end of the tunnel, a surreal light grew bigger and brighter — the kind that makes you want to cover and protect your eyes after days of traveling in darkness along the river — and then a stunning opening that appeared magical to Erin. The landscape was almost lunar, virtually without color.

The sky was a solid gray and the air still, but after days of rough weather and dangerous sailing, the lack of excitement was perceived more as a relief rather than a disappointment.

Toward the end of Devil's Passage, the river converged on a small lake named Origo Lake. It was deep and similar to a reservoir.

The first thing Erin noticed was the military base. It looked much like a small citadel with a tall tower in the middle, a kind of lookout. Taras was the name of the base, and after many days at sea, it was the nearest thing to remind Erin of home.

Taras was located in a desert area on the edge of Sandy Rings, a name that was given due to the circular platforms formed naturally at increasing elevations. The lower ring was called Inferior Ring, followed by a central Medium Ring and the Superior Ring on top. Crossing Sandy Rings would take an average person about two walking days. The crew didn't have to be concerned about that, at least for now, because in Taras, everybody would be spending the first few days acclimating to the new environment.

There were four exploration crews, each consisting of five people.

The mission of each group was simple: expanding government research into Inner Earth, gradually working their way out from the base camp at Taras.

Erin's team was christened "team Delta" and was composed of:

- Roger: Expedition scientist – geologist. The man who knew it all. His motto? "I don't know everything, but I have the phone number of those who do."
- Matt: Expedition guide and navigator. Marine veteran, expert in combat and survival techniques. He didn't like to talk much, but when he had something to say, it was usually important. He wasn't fond of repeating himself either.
- Rachel: Expedition scientist – biologist. She loved being the observer more than she liked to be a participant. Rachel was usually the last one to arrive but the first one to notice things.
- Steve: Expedition photographer. Nicknamed "the witness." His only purpose was to make others see what he saw, hear what he heard, feel what he felt.
- Erin: Civilian – winner of *The Last Templar*. Her job was to take notes from observations and follow team directions. She was quickly nicknamed "the investigator" for her acute mind as well as her instinctive and relentless ability to ask questions.

Of the three civilians participating in the Expedition, Erin was the only one assigned to an exploration crew. Jake, who was mostly calm and didn't like challenges, was employed as data entry specialist. A perfect fit for his personality, Erin pondered. She never liked his lack of exuberance. Charlie, on the other hand, received the sweetest deal of all, being employed as assistant chef. He was an artist when it came to food, and it didn't take long for the rest of the crew to notice and appreciate his brilliance in the kitchen. However, besides a few sporadic encounters, usually during meetings, their paths hardly ever crossed.

The first few days at camp were mostly spent acclimating and becoming familiar with the attributes of other members of the team. Exploration of Inner Earth was supposed to last ninety days, while the overall Expedition had supplies that could last over four months.

No information was available on whether or not it was safe to live off the land, so each individual had been equipped with dry and smoked food, along with a set of survival weapons: one small knife, a big knife, a gun, a crossbow, and thirty arrows.

Every crew member was given a distinguishing necklace with a serial number on a metal plate, similar to those issued to soldiers. The chain could not be removed manually, and it contained a small device used not only for detection but also for measuring and monitoring values, such as body temperature, heartbeat, blood pressure, and other vital functions.

Each team member was also provided with an 8-point cardinal compass: North – South – East – West – vertical distance from inner core (North and South) – horizontal distance from inner core (East and West). It took Erin a full day to learn how to use the new compass, but in the end she managed to read directions reasonably well.

The earth at Taras was white sand and somewhat hard to the touch, almost like dry clay. The difference in atmospheric pressure and the increased gravity affected the human body more than anyone wanted to admit, causing movements to be slower and more difficult to perform. A distance of 500 feet seemed like a mile, and it was even hard to breathe. Part of their preparation had been learning how to slow down one's heartbeat in order to prevent accelerated aging in the body. In Tromso, Erin and her teammates had undergone intense mental training and many sessions of deep meditation in order to gain control of their vital bodily functions. It still took several days before they were fully accustomed to the new and unusual environment at Taras.

The therapist responsible for their spiritual practices was an eccentric and vociferous person. Despite enjoying the company of unconventional people, Erin had a hard time establishing the same sense of trust that all the other team members had developed toward the clinician, the main reason being that Erin didn't like to be asked such challenging and personal questions as, "How do you plan to control your level of anxiety in situations of intense distress?" or, "If you needed to kill one of your teammates for your own survival, what would you do?" Although Erin knew that such an examination was part of the normal protocol, she didn't like to be forced to think in advance about events that she thought could never happen; hence she avoided being left alone with the therapist. Escape strategies were employed with a variety of odd excuses but always contoured by her most courteous manners.

One afternoon during an outdoor, physical training session, Erin sneezed. That simple act turned out to be quite a revelation. She observed the sound produced by her sternutation reverberating for a long time as if it had a life of its own. The echo would increase and decrease at constant intervals, almost like a vortex, and then all of a sudden it ceased. The same thing did not occur when she shouted. Erin made a few attempts to ask her archery coach about the cause of such an unusual event, but he was too preoccupied to consider anything besides bows and arrows. In the end, remembering Alan's advice, she thought it wise to keep the discovery to herself, hoping that one day she would be able to share the experience with her team.

Eventually the explorers left base camp and began their adventure in earnest, journeying into the even less hospitable Sandy Rings.

The first tour was a one-day excursion for the sole purpose of investigating the ringed terrain. The goal was to reach the top of the Lower Ring and return with samples of sand and potentially other specimens. Without knowing what was ahead, the team walked at a slow pace and safe speed, weighted with their gear. That included heavy backpacks and a variety of supplies to spend the night, if necessary.

Matt was leading the pack, followed by Steve, Erin, Roger, and Rachel at the end.

The geography of the world in front of them had little in common with the one they were leaving, but despite the landscape lacking in interest, it was the expression of something more magical. The sand in the rings was very fine, almost like a white powder. Looking back, Erin could see the base camp, already so far away. Below her lay the dark reservoir of icy waters and lightless entry to Devil's Passage beyond. The contrast of black and white was stark and the view made her shiver. In order to save energy, the team had been told not to talk before arrival, unless necessary. A subterranean adventure such as this took much courage and instilled a deep level of complicity, trust, and harmony between them, perfectly generated without the use or need of language.

During the hike to the top of Lower Ring, the team experienced almost nothing outside of the ordinary. They reached the anticipated destination in less than four hours. The plan was to eat a quick lunch before collecting a few specimens and then return to base camp. Despite the long hike and her fatigue, Erin felt a sense of excitement in being free after so many days of training and preparation. A brief glance at her teammates informed her that it was a groupwide sensation.

The team collected samples of sand from three different areas of the ring, and some rocks found on their way up, which were the only other element recovered besides sand.

Erin's observation on the first day was quite short and essential:

Day 1: departed base camp at 8.00 a.m., arrived at the top of Lower Ring at 11.52 a.m. Collected 3 samples of sand: 1 ounce from base level, 1.3 ounces from median level, and 1.7 ounces from the top level. Collected 2 small rocks, color light gray, total weight 2.74 pounds en route.

The place was so quiet that it felt almost lifeless.

The strange reality triggered in Erin some deep thoughts: If anything were alive, where was it hiding? How could anyone explain the beauty of this kind of landscape to human beings who seem only devoted to excitement? How could anyone describe the grace of being an alien life in an alien world to people who are afraid to be left alone? How could anyone talk about the artistry of stillness and the inspiration found in an absence of colors? How could someone even begin to detail a silent world to a society where the person who makes the greatest noise is often the most celebrated?

Slowly Erin was realizing that there were things that needed to be experienced in person in order to be fully understood and appreciated.

If only she could spot some anomalies, it would be easier to illustrate. It would become easier, she mused, for others to believe.

Despite the fact that her team was preparing for their descent, Erin had no desire to return to camp. But her duty was to follow orders, so she grabbed a handful of sand and stuffed it in her pocket. Perhaps the simple sight of it would be enough to retain the sense of calm and the epiphany she had experienced that afternoon.

Erin knew she would need such comfort, that night especially. She was finally being allowed to see Alan. He had been kept in quarantine since the accident and was still in a coma-induced state. Only a few visitations were allowed for fear of contamination.

It was due to Alan's circumstance that Erin came to realize they were all responsible for each other's lives. The farther one was from a familiar world, the more life seemed to be precious and fragile.

Upon returning to camp, Erin was escorted by a robot to the military hospital, which was nothing more than a small facility located only a few hundred feet from the central tower. The hospital was built in the same fashion as any other building on the base: a gray, concrete floor with white walls, and a ceiling made of polystyrene tiles arranged in a grid-like pattern. The common area in the unit was equipped with plastic chairs and decorated with inexpensive prints on the walls.

Alan was kept in a disposable isolation tent, which was pressurized below the ambient pressure as a safety feature and divided into an anteroom (for physicians and attendants) and a patient chamber. Everyone who had contact with Alan was required to wear personal protection equipment, which had to be tossed and burned each time after use.

Erin was one of the few people allowed to visit Alan, but only for five minutes at a time. From where she stood, there was no noise and no movement, just a complete display of passivity. Alan was clearly paying the price for his audacity, but was he in the process of dying? Was he waiting for a peaceful extinction or was he fighting to stay alive? Those thoughts exhausted Erin more than they allowed her to be wise.

The line between life and death is usually crossed without warning and Erin wasn't ready for a conclusion she didn't want.

She felt stranded in the middle of nowhere after realizing that she could not even bring Alan something as simple as a flower. In her mind, she imagined him flying above the hospital with his usual loud laughter. Perhaps in a country far away, a little kid was crying and praying for an angel, and Alan was responding.

No! That was not what Erin wanted! She felt her anger building up pressure, like steam, and quickly reached a breaking point in her tolerance. Her eyes filled with tears and she felt hollow.

A nurse, who happened to be Megan, entered the room. Her serious face softened into a smile when she saw Erin on the verge of crying. She asked a few simple questions in a gentle, musical voice, and for the rest of the time only listened. After a few minutes, Erin felt relieved. She was given a small energy drink and a big smile before being accompanied out the door where the robot was still waiting. With preprogrammed perfection, the robot escorted Erin to the sleeping quarters and, in a flawless manner, waited till she disappeared inside the building.

CHAPTER 7: LIFE

The samples of sand and rocks gathered during the first Exploration provided no signs of life. There was no organic material found, only crystals and mineral particles.

Maybe it was the slow passing of time or perhaps a sincere interest in geology that Erin didn't know she possessed, but she found herself following Roger's work in the laboratory during his afternoon examination sessions.

By this time Roger had understood that Erin was full of curiosity, but he was still surprised to see, and could not explain, how such a young person could be fascinated with dead rocks and minerals. Considering that the life of a scientist was usually a lonely one, he felt comforted by her interest and company.

On one occasion Roger asked Erin the reason for her passion in such a tedious science as geology. She didn't take long to respond with a statement that surprised him. "I watched a documentary about the oldest known building on Earth, the Cairn of Barnenez in France, which is dated about 4800 B.C. I have always asked myself: If the building is that old, how old are the bricks that made it?"

"That's actually a very good question! Unlike people, one cannot guess the age of a rock by simply looking at it."

Erin picked up a sample of rock and inspected it with her hands, feeling the rough, cold texture. "Isn't that so. How do you determine the age of a rock?"

"The most popular methods are the Law of Superimposition and Radiometric Dating. They are mostly based on common sense but serve as powerful reference points, although they both have their limitations."

"Limitations?" Erin repeated wonderingly.

"Yes. The Law of Superimposition starts with the assumption that unless something happened, the newer sedimentary rock layer would be on top of the older one. The biggest limitation to this approach is that it can only be used in reference to a sequence of rocks deposited in layers. In contrast, Radiometric Dating determines the age of a rock by tracing radioactive impurities incorporated when the material was formed. The problem with this method is that it is only applicable to certain materials."

"Interesting. Have you found anything worth mentioning in the specimens we collected the other day?"

"Not really. I was able to determine an approximate age of half a billion years, which might seem a lot at first. But considering the Earth is 4.6 billion years old, it's not a significant result. I've observed that the materials we gathered have been slightly weathered, and that means well preserved. But no sign of life, anywhere!"

"You seem a little disappointed," Erin noted with an inquisitive glance.

"Well, yes, I truly am. On the surface of the Earth, everywhere there's water, there's also life. And I mean always! After many years of experience, I am facing a new quest that requires a different level of prudence."

"Why so? Prudence and disclosure have never been fellow travelers. Maybe you need to step up your game and decide where you want to stand." Erin's response was short and a little sharp.

Perhaps one of the reasons Roger was intrigued by Erin's presence was her uninvolved way of looking at things, which was something more than a "new pair of eyes." But did he really need to step up his game? No, he felt pretty comfortable with his capacity for reason. He knew he wasn't in it for the money or for recognition. He only wanted to be right! Why was that so hard to understand? After a few hours of fruitless effort, Roger decided it was time to call it a day.

"Maybe tomorrow's excursion will be more successful," he concluded, walking toward the door.

Erin followed him in silence, her mind already marveling at what awaited the next day.

She had almost forgotten about the upcoming mission and it was probably wise to get prepared. Erin waved at Roger and quickly made her way out of the building. She looked up at the sky. It was a flat, monotonous gray, no different from any other day. It was possible that her young mind lacked judgment because Erin never gave importance to the concept of time. But now with the sky always the same color night and day, with neither clouds nor sun, she realized how easy it had been for her to underestimate the ability to tell the hour of the day simply by looking at the changing light on the horizon. It was possible that Roger was not the only one having to face a new challenge or engage a different level of prudence. To her great wonder, Erin actually regretted having said those words.

The second excursion went a step further than the previous one. This time the team planned to reach the top of Sandy Rings, camp for two days, and return to base camp. The total length of the mission was four days.

The terrain had already been approved as fit for driving, and this time the team was provided with four-wheelers to make the ascent a little easier and faster. Despite changes made to the engines, there was no guarantee that the three motorized vehicles would work without complications. Plan B was to continue on foot.

The team was ready to depart at 5 a.m. the following morning. Erin had spent the last few minutes before departing with Alan. With her mind gripped by emotions, she exhaled some breath on the window, creating enough condensation on the glass to draw a heart with her finger and then watched it gradually disappear. That morning, time seemed to be slower than ever, and despite her sadness in leaving her dear friend, Erin was ready to make the necessary sacrifice. Somehow she understood there was a strong glue in the universe linking together people who love each other. Any separation was only temporary. "I will be back," she whispered, knowing that Alan could hear her. A quick good-bye and off she went.

The engines of the four-wheelers sparked into life as Erin was exiting the camp hospital. Roger stared at her from under his helmet. His glance was both that of a loving brother and a jealous boyfriend. Then he winked and closed the visor, making it impossible for Erin to see his face. Both Steve and Matt were lugging a trailer with everybody's backpacks and a few other supplies and equipment. Matt took the lead as usual, and without another word, the team left base camp.

Traveling in tandem, they kept a moderate speed until gradually slowing down as they started the climb up Lower Ring. Erin noticed that their footprints from the previous excursion had drifted away, leaving the path as pristine as if nobody had been there. She had not expected to find anything different, and yet that little detail had the ability to unsettle her. How can something fade away if there is no rain or wind? It seemed to Erin as if everything in that area was reclaiming its original state. For the second time since leaving Ushuaia, she sensed a presence, both threatening yet somehow protective, almost as if someone or something was aware of their intrusion. Despite the tangibility of her feelings, she wasn't ready to share them with the rest of the group.

It took them about an hour to reach the top of Lower Ring and another four hours to arrive at the Sandy Rings summit.

Once on top, the view presented was almost unbelievable. To their amazement, a boundless, glorious, green prairie extended seemingly forever in front of their eyes.

Life!

Green, abundant life!

The prairie lay on a gentle slope, and for as far as they could see, there was nothing but a green, grassy ocean. That simple, surprising view was powerful enough to fire the imagination, and for what seemed to be a very long time, nobody said a word. Roger dismounted his four-wheeler, followed by the others. His legs were wobbling, and he fell to his knees. Placing his trembling hands on the ground, he bowed his head and cried. Erin could hear him quietly praying. She kneeled too, tore a blade of grass and smelled it … it felt and looked just like normal grass. Her lips curved into a smile, and when she looked up in awe, she saw the exalted faces of the others. Joyful shouts erupted in the air. Erin felt like a warrior having just won their first battle.

It took her a minute or two to realize that the sky had changed its glow. It was no longer gray like the one she was getting used to but had now assumed a creamy, yellowish shade, almost like vanilla. Colors were slowly appearing: at first the green grass, now the blond sky … how was that even possible? Erin turned her head toward the side of the sky from where they had come from and noted it was still the usual gray. Nothing had changed. She met Matt's eyes. The smile exchanged between them was a sign of complicity and a commitment to know more.

Eventually the team agreed to set up camp for the night, and it wasn't too long before they decided it was time for some sleep — everyone except Erin. The excitement of the day had overwhelmed her to the point that any residue of fatigue was completely gone. She lay on the grass with her arms crossed behind her head wishing for a shooting star. Her mind was quiet and happy, despite her relentless train of thought.

Why do humans explore?

Looking for an answer, Erin blamed her happy but solitary childhood when every strange, little thing used to set off her imagination. It was in those years that the spark of exploration was first ignited within her, and that fire had never stopped burning ever since.

All of a sudden a rustling noise, almost like a whisper, lifted her out of her memories. Overwhelmed by the uncommonly long day, she ignored the sound and finally considered the possibility of sleep.

The next morning the team decided to advance their exploration. After marking their location with an orange flag, they began to move forward into the unknown.

Besides verbal commands, there was no other form of communication among the team members, so the idea of splitting the group was immediately discarded. There was no trail to follow, but the grass was about six inches tall and perfectly dry, making it easy to navigate the four-wheelers. To everyone's amazement and despite the lack of a breeze, the air was notably fresh. Once again silence prevailed, and the impression of going nowhere soon began to settle in the minds of the fellow explorers. As far as anyone could see, there was nothing besides green grass, but the aspiration was to find diversified species and to determine the possibility of any other forms of life. Gradually the ground started to become wet, making it more difficult and somewhat risky for the vehicles to continue.

Matt, who was leading the team, decided it was safer to stop before getting stuck in the mud. "Let's end it here for today before we go a step too far. We should not expose ourselves to danger."

The most critical decision in any expedition is whether to continue or stop before it's too late. Matt's decision was quickly supported by the other team members, especially Roger; however, he thought it would be interesting to first take some samples of the swampy grounds.

"I agree," said Matt. "We can explore by foot the immediate surroundings. Where there is water, there is life. Let's see if this applies to Inner Earth as well."

Roger seemed almost in a hurry to prove himself right, because he jumped out of the four-wheeler as if he had noticed something unusual. In fact, looking closely, Erin could see a different type of grass, more similar to moss, growing in certain areas of what had become marshland. Roger was already extracting some samples to be preserved in a vial. He seemed very happy, and Erin couldn't resist mentioning the fact. "It looks like you are having the best day of your life!"

He laughed loudly before responding. "Almost! You are not far from the truth! Do you know what this is?"

Roger looked at Erin, who appeared clueless. He smiled, then continued. "This is a lichen, an organism that grows from bacteria and fungi. Although they might seem like a plant, lichens are not plants because they don't have roots that absorb water and nutrients. Some people think lichens are among the oldest living things. Did you know that?"

Roger looked at Erin hoping for a sign of interest, which she expressed in her reply. "It looks like everything in this place is pretty old, from rocks to sand to lichens. I wonder if we will be able to find anything more recent or new."

"Erin, you are missing the point here. When it comes to life, usually it's safe to say that the older it is, the more adapted it is. Adaptation occurs because life has changed many times. See the paradox here? Sometimes old is new and new is old. One only needs to look at things with discernment in order to focus on what is important."

"You're right. In order to live long, one needs to adapt. My grandmother always said that, and she was 102 when she died."

Roger stared at his friend for a moment, once again pleased with her company. "See? I'm not crazy!"

Perhaps the whole team was having as good a time because when Matt asked everyone for their attention, mentioning that they should be making their way back, nobody believed the day had already come to an end. There was no way to read time. Carrying a stopwatch was the only way to determine how many hours had passed.

On the eve of such a productive and fulfilling day, everyone's heart was filled with hope from the realization that a new section in the mapping of Inner Earth had been recorded.

No matter what, Erin, Roger, Matt, Steve, and Rachel were pioneers of the unknown, like those ancient sailors that no one remembers. And just like the ancient sailors, their names would be quickly forgotten.

But the importance of their mission would be remembered for generations to come.

CHAPTER 8: ALAN

The following night, after team Delta had safely returned to base camp, a large celebration was held in Taras.

It was the first since beginning the Expedition.

Although in unconventional surroundings, it was the most organic thing Erin had done since arriving in Inner Earth. There were drinks and food in great abundance, and everyone appeared to be lighthearted and having a good time. Despite there being no explorations planned for the next few days, and regardless of the fact that she was enjoying the conviviality, Erin decided to leave early. She fled without saying a word, seemingly because she didn't want to be asked any questions but mostly because she needed some time alone.

Once outside, she realized how much she loved the gray glimmer of the sky, even if nobody else admired it. She closed her eyes and, stretching her arms wide, took a deep breath of satisfaction. Erin had become accustomed to the enduring grayness and was no longer wishing for darkness or a starry night. There was freedom in such moments of appreciation. She was glad she had left the party.

On her way to the sleeping quarters, the idea to visit Alan unexpectedly crossed her mind. It was a strange feeling, almost a sense of anticipation, a chance that she didn't want to miss. Maybe, by some blessing, she would find him awake and well!

Megan, the nurse on duty, immediately recognized Erin and, without asking anything, guided her toward Alan's chamber with a benevolent smile. He was lying in the usual supine position with his eyes closed and a serene expression on his face. It was heartening to see how Alan still radiated peace after so many days in limbo.

The hospital was quieter than usual, and Erin thought how nice it was to finally have a few moments alone with Alan. Her devotion was rewarded when Megan quietly entered the room and, to Erin's surprise, said, "I am the only one here, since everyone else is attending the party. I need to make a quick stop at the storage department to pick up some supplies. I will be back in less than fifteen minutes. Do you feel comfortable staying here by yourself or should I call someone?"

Erin responded calmly, trying to conceal her enthusiasm. "I'm fine, thank you. Feel free to take all the time you need. I'll wait till you come back. I will be here with Alan."

Megan smiled amicably and gave Erin a small device. "If anything happens, the only thing you need to do is push this red button. It will trigger the alarm and someone will be here in the blink of an eye. But I really hope you don't have to use it."

Erin nodded, delighting in the responsibility she had just been assigned.

With a slightly troubled look on her face, Megan warned her, "Please don't tell anyone. It is against protocol to leave a patient unattended. But I can see you mean no harm and could probably use some time alone with your friend."

"I won't say anything, I promise. Thank you for your trust. Rest assured, it is well-placed."

Megan thought so too and quietly left, closing the door behind her.

Erin sat there in silence trying to attune her heartbeat with the beeping sounds of the machine, the only indication of Alan's continuing existence. The stillness in the room felt unnatural yet comforting at the same time, but despite her contentment in being there, Erin struggled to synchronize her mind with the present moment. A profound sense of sadness dominated her perception of the situation and an image of sorrow engraved her face.

"Why are you so sad, Milady?" The voice broke the silence like thunder in a sunny sky.

At first Erin could have sworn that it was just her imagination talking to her, but when she looked up, she almost screamed. To her amazement, Alan was awake and smiling.

"I missed you, Milady." Alan was sitting on the bed with his arms resting on his legs.

Erin, trying to remember how to breathe and still unable to speak, kept her eyes wide open.

Alan removed the plastic protection surrounding his bed, disconnected himself from the machine, and stepped outside. He looked strong as if he had just woken up from a long slumber.

Erin's disbelief was slowly fading away, and once able to feel her legs again, she finally stood up. Still trying to make sense of everything, she opened the door that separated them and walked closer to Alan, wrapping her arms around her beloved friend. The hug was a simple gesture of affection but strong enough to show how much they cared for each other.

Erin's maternal nature fussed over her buddy sooner than her mind could comprehend. "Alan, you should not detach yourself from the machine unless the doctor tells you to do so."

Alan smiled. His expression transcended every concern, and his whole persona seemed to be surrounded by a timeless, glowing light. "I wasn't sure I would be able to see you again, Milady, but I am happy this moment has finally arrived."

Despite her remaining confusion, Erin was slowly regaining a grasp of her mind. "Alan, I have so many things to tell you ..."

Alan didn't seem surprised by those words. In fact, he grabbed a chair from the corner of the room and placed himself comfortably on it. "We have time, Milady. You can tell me everything. This is why I came here."

Erin was no longer trying to hide her emotions. In fact, she was starting to feel a little more at ease with the situation. It didn't take long for her to begin describing the series of events that had taken place since her arrival in Inner Earth. Her memoir was captivating and not neglectful: beginning with the accident on the vessel, to her initial loss of hope, to the training received, and her mastery in avoiding the intrusive questions posed by the psychologist. Nothing was omitted. What started as a conversation became a monologue, with Erin the only elocutionist. She was particularly enthusiastic in describing their first Exploration to Lower Ring, followed by the second and most rewarding one, during which the team discovered a previously undocumented green prairie, later named Longview Fields.

Alan was listening with patience and empathy, nodding occasionally and expressing astonishment from time to time. Aside from being sincerely captivated, he was genuinely glad that Erin was having such an enjoyable experience in Inner Earth.

"Milady, nothing happens by accident. Remember, every-thing has a meaning. I suggest you value your time here, even if sometimes you might not realize how precious it is, because it won't repeat itself."

The sound of those words took Erin by surprise, and her mind traveled back in time to the ritual she had attended in Ushuaia. The statement made by the shaman was analogous to Alan's remarks: "There are no coincidences."

She felt an urgency to advise Alan, but he courteously interrupted her. "Milady, there are things I need to tell you before my time here expires."

"What do you mean before your time here expires?" Erin's eyes now showed concern. "You're not leaving, are you?"

Uncertainty wasn't generally her gig, but this time she was at a loss for words. Her mind fell silent. The stillness grew deeper until almost unbearable. She was about to begin from where she left off, but Alan stopped her by putting his finger on her lips.

"No worries, Milady. My time here is coming to an end, and I need to make the most of it before I go. There are important things I came here to tell you."

Something within Erin was trying to resist that kind of undesirable information, but a more spiritual element was imploring her to pay attention. She decided to let prudence go and surrendered to the oncoming revelation.

Alan smiled, perhaps aware of the train of thought rushing through her mind. Eventually he continued. "Don't allow your mind to become your tormentor. Let joy soothe you."

It soon became apparent that Erin didn't like discussing transition. Alan's behavior and his words were becoming quite divergent and that was causing her head to spin. Finally, in the midst of her confusion, Erin was able to find strength. "Fine," she murmured, crossing her arms and making herself more comfortable on the chair.

"Very well, Milady. Don't be distracted. There is a reason I am here. I want you to be safe should events outside of your control occur. Keep the map I gave you undisclosed for now. It will become helpful in a plan to survive, and there are high chances you might need it. Once the right time arrives, you will be able to use it. But don't be fooled by the names. They are not always symbolic of the landscape. Instead, they often refer to a terrain which will present a variety of obstacles and dangers. Be careful!"

Erin's uneasiness surged, as did her level of engagement. Perhaps it was a logical reaction, but there was a sort of humility in receiving guidance.

He continued. "Some events must happen, and I want you to be safe."

Alan possessed the natural ability to express dreadful concepts with kindness, something that Erin found rather attractive, especially in a man. Aside from that, she was scared. "What do you mean? Am I going to be in danger?"

"If you listen to what I am about to tell you, you will be fine. Inner Earth is bigger than what you have been told and much different than what you or anyone else in your Expedition can imagine. You will confront some events, beings, and places that you have never experienced before. This might daunt you for a while, but with an open mind and a little bit of knowledge, you won't be harmed."

The way Alan said the last phrase intimidated Erin even further. "I don't understand. I won't be hurt ... what does that mean?"

"The Expedition you have undertaken is not an easy task. I need to warn you that some of the people you trust have a pure intent and an honest desire to stretch the limits of science to the unknown. But there are other entities who have another purpose, less virtuous and benevolent. Your candid and youthful mind, so easily seduced, doesn't give you (yet) the ability of discernment. But you will develop it, and I will help you with that."

Erin felt lost again. She smiled and nodded, but without conviction. "I don't think I understand," she murmured.

"Don't worry, Milady. Your life is the real journey. And when you are the captain of your boat, there is not much advice anyone can give you. But one thing I can say: People consider adversities as if they were the exception, although I tell you, my friend, they are the norm. Ignorance is better than a lie and sailing in darkness is better than having a false light. There will be moments when you will feel so lonely that you will be calling for help in any possible way. In those days you will learn to follow your instinct for guidance. You will discover how to do that, but it will take time and a continuous, conscious effort. Don't ever give up, Milady, not until you have found what matters to your soul! I will be with you every step of the way. Regardless of how things are, remember these words: You will always have a choice."

Despite his voice being gentle and his manner reassuring, Alan's words were hard to hear and made Erin want to pull back. "Okay, I will remember that, Alan. But I still don't understand what you are really trying to tell me ..."

"Persistence is what makes an expedition successful. You must endure and cultivate patience. Have faith. Many things will be revealed to you. Now I can only tell you what you are ready to accept; otherwise it would exhaust you. Useless agitation of the mind doesn't bring you any good, Milady. Trust this old man." Alan's face lightened into a gentle smile.

"You seem to know so much about me. Why don't I have the same impression about you? I thought I was accustomed to your character, and yet I have never felt so blessed to be with you as in this moment. The idea that I might have taken you for granted, even if only for a second, breaks my heart. Will you ever forgive me?"

> *Milady, you are learning so fast,*
> *much more than what I could ask!*
> *This is a very good thing.*
> *It makes me so happy that I could sing!*
> *But I better save my time.*
> *It is more precious than a dime.*
> *Allow me, please, to go ahead,*
> *so I can give you a few more crumbs of bread.*
> *My mission here is almost done,*
> *sure I had a lot of fun.*
> *I hope I made you feel the same,*
> *because this is why I truly came.*
> *And by the time I'm ready to go,*
> *you'll have so much more than you know.*

As usual, Erin felt cuddled by Alan's little doggerel. For a moment, all her fears faded away. Alan paused, giving Erin the opportunity to assimilate the information he had just delivered. Although he was more than pleased with his young friend, he wanted to engage her mind even further.

"Milady, why do you think I am telling all these things to you?"

"Actually, I don't know. Why?"

"This is a question you should ask yourself. Don't you think so, my young fellow?"

Erin was caught by surprise with these remarks. Her face flushed with embarrassment to the point that it was delightful for Alan to watch.

"Tell me, Milady, how much will you be paid for this Expedition?"

"Paid? I am not getting paid for this Exploration. Being here is the reward itself. I thought you knew."

Alan was cheered by Erin's response, so much so that he exclaimed, "I would have you come with me, Milady, but not yet." Then he gave her a long, compassionate look. "Unlike the rest of the crew, you will not be paid at the end of this Expedition, regardless of how it goes. You have accepted the possibility to die for free. Forgive me if I say that everyone else has a different type of commitment. They believe their life is worth something fancy, whether they live or die. Why do you think it has been set up this way? Is it because your life might be worth nothing? You didn't think about any of this, did you?"

Erin's eyes and mouth were petrified in an expression of stunned surprise. "No. Except for a few specialists, I thought everyone was a volunteer. Being part of this Expedition is such a privilege that I thought everyone felt honored and happy just to be here ..."

"A pure intent is a noble and courageous thing to hold. Let me remind you, Milady, that you are the true sailor of this Expedition. Don't forget it. The fine nature of your heart has been noticed."

Erin's disarray grew even more at the sound of those words. The man in front of her was quite different from the Alan she remembered, but peering into his eyes corroborated her understanding that there was something really good about him.

"Let me tell you something, Milady. This Expedition means more than you know. Keep your heart clear and your mind receptive. Most of all, follow your intuition. It will uncover abilities you didn't even know you possessed. When all is clouded around you and there is nothing left but your inner voice, *decide* to follow it. It shouldn't feel like an act of desperation but an opportunity. You will be surprised by what you will be able to do! Choose to be the wind that waves the flag, instead of the flag."

Alan paused, giving Erin one of his good-hearted glances. "We shall meet again, Milady, someday in the future. But before I go …"

Alan opened his hands and there was a clean, folded piece of notepaper. "This is my wish for you, Milady. Hopefully it will remind you of me but, most of all, that it will bring you strength and happiness. You will need both."

How was it possible? Just moments before, Alan's hands were gesticulating and empty. Erin's curiosity, however, was promptly surpassed by her light heart. Her eyes glimmered with watery tears as she found herself caught between joy and the fear of saying good-bye. Needless to say, it was another song:

Milady, there is something great inside of you.
Trust me, even if now you don't have a clue.
The time has arrived for you to know.
So stay the course and be in the flow.
There are many decisions you need to make,
so keep your mind open and wide awake.
If you learn how best to cope,
you will succeed and always find hope.
And if you learn who to trust,
you will not have to bite the dust.
Listen to your beautiful mind.
It will never let you go forward blind.
This adventure can be glorious.
Choose to finish it, be victorious.
Milady, I depart my way from you now.
One last salute and a respectful bow!

By the time Erin had finished reading the song, tears were falling freely onto her cheeks. Perhaps an oddity, but she didn't even hear the door open when Megan entered the room. "I brought you a glass of water with some vitamins. It will boost your mood. I think you need it."

Startled, Erin nearly jumped out of her chair at the sound of Megan's voice. It was utterly unexpected. She looked again at the wrinkled piece of paper in her hands. And then she looked up, in a manner almost too slow to be normal. Alan was inside his chamber, still unconscious. Her mind started to become paranoid. She felt incapable of moving. "I was talking to him just a minute ago ..." she stammered.

Megan thought it was time for Erin to go and kindly invited her to leave the room.

"I'm not crazy ..." As the nurse approached, Erin started to talk loudly, as if in the middle of a heated argument.

There was kindness in Megan's face. Her gentle smile spoke of someone who understood intense suffering. Her eyes communicated a beautiful soul. "I'm sorry for your friend, Erin. I know it is hard to let someone go. Sometimes our imagination tricks us and makes us see or hear things that are not real. I think you will feel better tomorrow after a good night's sleep. And, by the way, thank you for covering for me." Megan winked in a sign of complicity and escorted Erin to the door.

Still confused and incapable of a conscious thought, Erin said good-bye and left. It wasn't just her imagination fooling her, the paper Alan gave her was real! Her mind drifted back to the explosion on the vessel and like in a movie, she replayed a perfect memory of those events. In that snapshot, she remembered having the feeling that somehow she would receive one more song from Alan. Back then, something inside of her already knew. Was this the type of inner knowledge and trust that Alan was referring to? Erin walked toward the sleeping quarters slowly, in a dazed state, keeping her hands inside her pockets. Her mind was still baffled, but this recent event had corroborated what she had long known: Alan had wanted to say good-bye as much as she did.

Erin looked up at the sky and, despite the grayness, she knew it was nighttime. Strange how people seek darkness when they don't have it and wish for light when it is dusk. It occurred to her that it was a part of human nature to always want what isn't there.

"Thank you," she whispered, to the silent and abiding sky. It was when she saw a white flash crossing the horizon, something similar to a falling star, that she knew she had been heard.

Alan was right. She was not alone.

CHAPTER 9: THE ART OF SEEING

It wasn't a surprise when the next day Erin was informed of Alan's passing. She knew he had accomplished what he had come to do.

The medical report stated that the cause of death was a cardiac arrest due to an unknown and incurable infection, but at this point in her journey, Erin knew that there were no coincidences.

There was a small funeral that all the crew attended. Not everyone had a memory to share, but those who did showed how much they were touched by Alan's presence in their lives.

Despite her devotion, Erin chose not to say anything about her beloved friend. She believed there was something private about their friendship, a foundation of trust that didn't need to be shared.

Alan's body would be kept in a refrigerated cell until the end of the Exploration and then returned home in the same vessel as he arrived. Erin wondered whether Alan would have preferred to be buried in Inner Earth instead. Although he was the least lonely person she had ever met, Erin wasn't sure that there really was anyone home waiting for him. She was the vulnerable one. Despite being surrounded by people, she felt truly alone.

At the end of the funeral, the coffin was carried away by four strong men and yet they almost buckled under its weight. Erin noticed a small cross nailed to the top of the steel crate and a few colored, paper flowers assembled in a nice decoration. She wondered if they had been made by Megan, and a nostalgic smile painted her sorrowful face. But it was only when Alan was being taken away that Erin's eyes became glazed with a shiny layer of tears. As she blinked, they drifted down her cheeks.

After the ritual was over, everyone left quietly. The joyful atmosphere that had entranced the crowd only the night before had dimmed to a saddened mood. Death had arrived in Taras like a bullet from behind. It was a reminder to everyone of the real sacrifices of the mission.

It also occurred to Erin that the true nectar of an experience is free of charge and that no sum of money could have saved any of them from the risk of demise.

With sorrow in the core of her being as well as in her mind, she decided to skip lunch that day and opted for a short stroll around the citadel. There were only a few roads to wander and she picked a quiet spot in front of Origo Lake. Erin had previously discovered a secret hollow, not far from the Admiral Q-Oho. It was a cozy and contemplative place, and despite the sinister emanations coming from the facing Devil's Passage, it was one of Erin's favorite spots.

The time of loss was supposed to be a moment of forbearance, but now that the numbness following Alan's fate had passed, grief was already beginning its unforgiving attack. Erin made a conscious effort to filter out that part of reality and, pulling the map he had given her from her jacket, realized she had never taken the time to fully examine it.

The paper was yellow, like an old parchment, but the texture was smooth and new. On the bottom left corner appeared Taras and the Sandy Rings, which continued to the location of the recently named Longview Fields. However, everything else on the map was too blurry to be understood. Strangely, Erin remembered seeing clearly all the details once before, but now it was almost impossible to recognize any other feature besides those she already knew. She checked again to be sure it was not a flaw from a water spill but quickly rejected that hypothesis. Something on the map was different — she was sure of it — as if some of the information had left with Alan. There was nothing exotic in this map, nothing that she wasn't already aware of. At this point, being angry or disappointed wasn't much of an option, so Erin folded the map and put it back inside her coat pocket.

"Value your time here," Alan had said before departing. Erin knew that should she not follow his guidance, all her days in Inner Earth would quickly evaporate like steam from a boiling pot. In spite of her apprehensions, she understood there was a need for calm and patience because, worst of all, she was beginning to experience a lack of self-determination. It was only when she grew tired of her own thoughts that she stumbled onto the most unexpected revelation. Encouraged, she quickly reopened the map and noticed something not perceived before: All through Longview Fields were little black dots. They were now very apparent and mostly concentrated in the area furthest away from Sandy Rings.

Erin wondered about the significance of those small spots. Were they a warning of potential danger? Or maybe an indication on where to find the next clue? Her deepest wish, stronger than a desire to know, was the need for self-validation. The truth was that Erin's confidence was still anchored in a place where she felt safe. It wasn't deep enough. It needed to grow within, to reach that point of raw depth that constitutes the true nature of oneself. To the majority, that simple understanding would have triggered a sort of discontent, but for Erin it became an epiphany! As a general rule, she didn't like to show her emotions, but this moment was different. The smile that illuminated her face hadn't been seen since she was a kid, as she walked faster and faster toward the citadel. All of a sudden her time in Inner Earth wasn't so overwhelming, and the realization gave Erin the determination that nothing could go wrong. It was simply impossible!

As she reached the main tower, she had to remind herself to keep a more reserved composure. After all, there had been her friend's funeral just a few hours earlier. Erin saw Roger in the distance. He walked toward her. She waved and received a big smile and a hug when they met in return.

"I haven't had time to talk to you, Erin, but I'm really sorry for what happened to your friend. I know how much you cared for him. It must be hard for you ..."

Despite a tornado of emotions, Erin tried to appear somber. She felt permeated with a new level of confidence. Alan had left her with a very important gift, something beyond a few songs and a map. She did not respond directly but hugged Roger and asked him for a coffee instead.

Roger knew that coffee in Erin's vocabulary meant she wanted to talk. He really enjoyed the pleasure of her company, so easily consented.

Not far from the main tower was a little coffee bar called the Inner Grounds. It looked more like a small cafeteria where the crew liked to meet and spend time together. It was a place that the psychologist had planned, which was obvious by the walls covered with quotes, such as "good food brings good mood" or "food is a great way of communicating" and "we all need love and chocolate," and many more.

Despite the cafe being full, the noise level was low. Roger greeted a couple of technicians studiously bent over their food and then headed to the only table that was still available. In contempt of fashion was why Erin loved the Inner Grounds' atmosphere, because it gave her a sense of late summer when the colors start to fade and things develop into a gradual peace. The menu was quite simple: no alcohol, a discrete list of soft drinks, coffee, hot chocolate, flavored teas, a selection of sandwiches, and a small variety of pies. It was wholesome and perfect!

From his red eyes, Erin could see that Roger had been crying. Many sentiments had been awakened through Alan's passing and there was nothing meager triggering the emotional response. The rich aroma of coffee interrupted the cycle of melancholy and the two friends spent the next few moments consuming their meals in respectful silence. Reluctantly, Erin had to admit that the psychologist was right: Food held a magic power to generate tranquillity of mind.

"I wanted to share something with you, if you don't mind." Erin was the first to interrupt the silence.

Roger had been waiting for that question all along and felt a renewed spark of enthusiasm at the sound of her words. It wasn't the fact that Erin would confide in him that amused Roger. Being trusted was something he never really cared about. But having confirmation of correctly interpreting a woman's thoughts, that was something worthy of a champion!

"Sure, what's up?" he responded, with an easiness in his tone of voice, perhaps too weak to be natural.

"I don't know how to say this without sounding crazy, but do you have the feeling of being watched sometimes?"

Generally speaking, it wasn't typical for Roger to be caught at a loss for words, but this time Erin's question left him quite unprepared. He cleared his throat in an attempt to gain some time. At the same time, he made a mental note to himself to never take a woman for granted. He finished his last bite and then responded. "Watched? What do you mean by that? Who do you think would be interested in watching us?"

"I'm not sure. I've had this feeling of a conscious presence surrounding me ... meaning us. It's happened only a few times so far, and I can't prove it, by any means. I was wondering if you had had the same impression." Erin stared at Roger as he methodically folded his napkin.

"To be honest, I have not. I know that we are monitored through our devices, and if you really want to know, I think these gadgets keep track of all our conversations, not just our heartbeats. But I am only speculating right now. I wish I could be more helpful ..."

"Oh, but you are! In fact, I think that what you just said is very possible. However, I was referring to something completely different. I feel an invisible presence, almost as if someone or something is aware of us being here. It sounds creepy, I know. I was wondering if the same thing is happening to you."

"No, I have never had that feeling." Roger's expression morphed into contemplation. It wasn't long before he continued.

"Now that I think about it, the other day I was reading some of my old notes about adaptation and I found an interesting article. The author stated that experiencing a sensation of being watched is normal in any new environment. The reason for that is simpler than anyone would imagine. As our brain tries to adjust to the new information, it is possible that it senses something unusual but without actually being able to register it. The element of novelty is what gives you the impression of being watched. In other words, everything is just fine."

Erin stared at Roger unpersuaded, so he continued. "The majority of information processed by our brain is accessed by the subconscious mind. As a matter of fact, we are constantly converting information but are not necessarily aware of it. In new situations, this might give the creepy feeling of something strange or paranormal. I think this fact could explain very well your sense of being watched."

Erin was perplexed. "Is that what science means when they say we don't see with our eyes but with our brain?"

"Yes, that's right! We don't see with our eyes. We see with our brain. People can have good eyesight, but if their visual cortex is damaged and they are unable to see, despite this limitation their brain is still receiving the information through their eyes."

Pretty soon, the tasty food became secondary to the conversation.

"Interesting indeed! But do you think it would also be reasonable to say that our brain sees more than what we are aware of?"

"I'm not sure. What do you mean?"

"Meaning, do you think our brain could have the ability to filter what kind of information we become aware of? In other words, is it possible that some things could be removed before they reach our conscious awareness?"

"You know, Erin, it is possible. We only use a small part of our brain, as everyone knows. To go back to your question, I don't know for sure the answer to that, but I can tell you that the opposite is true. For instance, some recent studies have looked into how visual stimuli invisible to our consciousness can still influence our actions. To be clearer, have you ever heard of the 'blind spot'?"

"Yes, I remember that concept from my driving lessons. It's an area where a person's view is obstructed; right?"

"According to the dictionary, the blind spot is the point of entry to the optic nerve of the retina, insensitive to light. At that spot, a small object can disappear from view. In everyday life, we are not aware of this. Did you know that many people live their entire life not knowing that they have a blind spot?"

"I remember reading something about that a while ago, but I still don't understand how it's even possible!"

"It's quite simple, actually. Our brain uses the information originating from both eyes to create a visual image of the real world. That's called binocular vision. It simply means that every single image we form in our brain is the result of two different views, one from each eye. Thanks to binocular vision, we have the ability to perceive depth."

Erin's attentiveness was independent of her interest in the subject. It was a feature deeply rooted in her nature, a component that Roger found quite strategic and amusing. Her tone of voice was becoming rather persuasive as she started to feel more comfortable in the conversation. "According to what you just said, I must assume that the binocular vision is only possible because we have two eyes; right?" As she said that, Erin covered one of her eyes with her hand.

An amused smile appeared on Roger's face. "People who are blind in one eye have a limited ability to perceive the depth of objects. You are certainly correct, my friend."

"Not too long ago I read a book about the legends of the Cyclops, the giant warriors with a single eye in the center of their forehead. I have just realized that their vision must have been terrible!"

Roger laughed at Erin's ironic but appropriate remark. "Hypothetically, a much smaller but skilled individual could have easily benefited from the poor depth perception of the Cyclops. Sometimes bigger does not mean stronger, you know."

"Sometimes big is small and small is big." Erin looked pensive while remembering the shaman's instructions regarding her need to learn from hummingbirds. Roger was about to pick up from where he left off but was interrupted by an impatient Erin. "Roger, do you have any idea of how good the vision of a hummingbird is?"

"Wow, yes. Hummingbirds have fantastic vision — much better than humans. I'm not sure where your question came from, but I could talk about hummingbirds forever. They are among my favorite animals!"

"Oh, please do, Roger, if you have time, of course."

"I sure do, Erin," said Roger, pulling his chair forward and placing his elbows on the table. "It's believed that hummingbirds can see a feeder three quarters of a mile away. They also have the ability to see into the ultraviolet range. Why do you ask?"

"Oh, nothing. I'm just curious."

Other than Alan, Erin had never had the desire to share with anyone her experience of the ritual in Ushuaia. She had yet to fully understand its significance and didn't want another person's influence to interpret a message intended only for her. "Why do you think vision is so important if it's been stated that we see with our brains and not our eyes?"

"Just think about this: We classify and mark objects in part through visible colors. A red frog is considered poisonous while a green frog is usually harmless. But what if we could see infrared and ultraviolet light? All our categorizations and names of objects would be different. So what we see with our eyes is important. Our brain completes this perception by providing additional information about what we see. For example, it tells us to stay away from the red frog. Another good example would be the Cairn Terrier. It's a type of dog that can be any color except white. As defined by the American Kennel Club, if a Cairn Terrier is born white, it's a different breed called the West

Highland White Terrier. Our labeling of things, including Terriers, would be much different if we had ultraviolet or infrared vision."

"How do you know all these things?" Erin asked.

Roger didn't answer and limited himself to a meek smile, but Erin recognized the strength of his passion for knowledge.

What Roger said next made Erin wonder. "When you are sad, learn something. That's what Merlin taught," he concluded, his expression distant.

The silence that followed was like an antidote, for in that absence of sound, the depth of their conversation was clearly evident. But it didn't last long because soon enough the waiter reminded them that the Inner Grounds was about to close. Once again time had dissolved into nonexistence. They left together without talking. It was the end of a rich day, perhaps too tough for many.

Wandering along the few streets of Taras, Erin noted the absence of shadow, and for the first time she pondered if it was because of her limited vision. Maybe Inner Earth required a higher set of skills in order to be fully appreciated. Maybe there was a changing blue and dark sky above their heads only waiting to be seen. Erin was about to mention something but noticed Roger was absorbed in a world of his own, so she kept quiet instead.

She felt both near and far from the intelligent man walking at her side. How long before their paths would diverge, proceeding onward to new adventures? Soon enough they reached the point where they needed to separate. And saying a simple good-bye, they both walked away without turning around.

Despite the late hour, Erin decided to make a stop at the library. Since her conversation with Roger, her curiosity about hummingbirds had been piqued.

The library was small but fairly well-equipped. There were shelves of books and other piles of manuals leaning against the wall, almost to the ceiling. To her amazement, she located an encyclopedia on animals and, in the chapter regarding winged species, found descriptions of hummingbirds, which Erin pored herself into reading. "Hummingbirds are the only birds that rely solely on their own strength to hover in the air." She read the last few words again. "They rely solely on their own strength." A sense of apprehension took over. It sounded very much like a cautionary note. She continued to read. "Despite their small size, hummingbirds are very aggressive birds. They will regularly attack crows and hawks that infringe upon their territory." Wait, what? A bird that weighs about as much as a penny will attack a hawk? Another confirmation that it was not all about size.

Erin began to feel drained. Her head was filled with different thoughts and "what-ifs." A general sense of drowsiness started to intensify. "Time to leave," she thought.

While returning the encyclopedia to the bookcase, she observed a gentle, glowing, pink light. The glare was mostly concentrated over her hands, but it was also embracing both arms, up to her shoulders. This probably occurs when one's level of exhaustion equates to insanity, she mused. Erin's mind had been working nonstop for the past several days, and it was time to finally surrender to the peace and stillness of slumber.

She left the building quietly. However, walking along the street she identified the same pink glow, this time surrounding people and objects. Erin's eyes followed the light for a moment but, although inviting, she no longer had the energy to process the experience.

"If this doesn't stop, I'll pay a visit to the doctor in the morning." With those words, Erin expressed her last thoughts for the day, already forgetful of what she had just learned.

CHAPTER 10: TEAM SOTIS

Admiral Q-Oho had been anchored at the port of Taras since arrival. It was considered an off-limits area for the majority of the crew, with the exception of a few important people.

Captain Jeff Miller, who was one of the handful who had access to the ship, used to spend a few hours each day in his office inside the vessel, mostly finalizing reports and communicating with the external world.

His routine was somewhat predictable. Every morning at around 8.30 a.m., after the necessary preparations, he would arrive onboard and enter his quarters with a briefcase, only to reappear a few hours later, usually right before lunchtime.

Captain Miller was a very reserved individual; however, his facial expression usually revealed enough to signal whether or not he had had a good day. Because of his calm and somewhat distant presence, he was occasionally approached by a few folks who loved having the opportunity to spend a little time with someone considered a man to be remembered. His manners were serene and always very composed, and he rarely refused to answer questions when interrogated. Whenever he spoke, his voice was courteous and rich but with an agreeable trace of authority. Overall, he was a noble man, disciplined, and of high morals.

Be that as it may, few were the times where he was seen having lunch in the company of other people. To say it in his own words, "Eating is not only about replenishing the body but the opportune time to refresh the spirit as well." This was the reason why he loved to have his meals alone. In his opinion, silly conversations or even work-related discussions were categorically inappropriate during meals.

Nobody knew if he was married or not. Rumor had it that his wife had died a few years prior to the Expedition and, after his loss, he had committed himself to his job, his faith in God, and nothing else. Nonetheless, he never confirmed nor disclaimed such remarks.

This particular day was like many others, with Captain Miller making his way out of the vessel for lunch when a group of operatives — later identified as the Special Operation Team for Interplanetary Security (aka SOTIS) — approached him. A quick briefing ensued, during which he was apprised of some important information.

The group of special agents was comprised of:

- Agent Kelly – SOTIS Inner Earth operations specialist
- Agent Tom Jyrone, better known as TJ – SOTIS interplanetary communication specialist
- Agent Jordan – SOTIS special operations specialist

Kelly, TJ, and Jordan were well known in the Exploration team because of their cold, unwelcoming behavior. Unlike Captain Miller, their formalities transmitted a sour taste, and very few individuals had the pleasure (or the desire) to engage them.

The SOTIS team only reported to the Captain (Mr. Jeff Miller, Jr.) and the Vice Admiral (Mr. Richard A. Windsor). It was rare to see them talking with anyone publicly.

After the agents were dismissed, Captain Miller's face appeared more concerned than usual. He spent the next few hours in his office, onboard Admiral Q-Oho, where he sat in deep silence. It was rare for the Captain to skip lunch, and in his defense he said that important decisions needed to be made.

Due to the nature of the Expedition, every crew member had been informed by the Captain to stand at the ready. The level of trust among the participants was normally high, with senseless alarmism easily rejected. This time, however, a perception of something urgent filled the air. As a matter of protocol, following the meeting with the Captain, the SOTIS team had gained unlimited access to the vessel, a privilege that had never been granted to anyone before. Needless to say, everyone was taken by surprise by the announcement and there was already consternation among the crew.

It so happened that the SOTIS team, equipped with flashlights and backpacks, spent the following night inside the vessel.

"We don't have much time. The job needs to be finished before morning or Miller will become suspicious." It was clear that Kelly held the highest rank among the agents and was most likely the one in charge.

The SOTIS team entered the Captain's office, opened their backpacks, and extracted a few tiny, black mechanisms similar to a little transmission device. Using soundless drills, they cut some small holes in the walls and placed the devices in strategic locations. Despite being wireless, each machine was connected to all the others. Jordan tested the connection to make sure it worked, and after signaling the "okay," the team moved to the next room. They repeated the same procedure in all nine preselected rooms. Twenty-seven devices were installed during the night, with a level of precision worthy of a craftsman. All the openings made in the walls were perfectly camouflaged. The team completed the job just before morning, as planned. The level of stress on their faces was now gone, despite the fact that they had been working on high alert all night.

"Part one of the operation has been concluded successfully. I have already informed the boss." The grin on Kelly's face was almost perverse but also an excellent propeller for the rest of the team. They smirked in return. There was no sound coming from the outside, perhaps a reminder from nature that a certain amount of decorum was necessary.

By the time Captain Miller arrived in the office at his normal hour the next morning, the entire operation was complete. He looked around, searching for something different, but nothing seemed to be out of the ordinary.

"Either these guys are really competent, or things are too normal to be good," he thought. Carrying a slight suspicion and feeling more perturbed than usual, Miller decided to make a phone call to the General of Defense, Mr. David Curtis.

General Curtis was a small man, somehow too short for his build and with a big ego. Everything about him spoke of passion and the love of pleasure, especially when it came to cigars, whiskey, and tennis. Compassion wasn't alien to his character, although he rarely understood how his behavior made others feel. He would never listen to what someone had to say without interrupting, not because he didn't care but because he was born without patience. He was a good friend of Captain Miller.

After a brief introduction and a formal chat, the legitimacy of the operation was confirmed.

"Please let Mr. President know that I have called," Miller said.

"I will meet the President in the Security Room in a couple of hours, and I will deliver your message." By default, General Curtis wasn't hesitant to revolve a conversation around topics that he was most invigorated by, even if that meant switching the talking point to his interests. The shift was usually so abrupt as to appear almost natural. "I want to let you know that Jeremy Howdy has moved to the Wimbledon finals. He will now face the world champion, Seth Logan."

Unimpressed, Miller reacted, "Oh, that's good to hear. I will toast to his success when I return."

"I will not allow you to have fun by yourself. I am always a good buddy when it's time to celebrate a great victory. You should know that."

"Thank you, David. I certainly know you are a great companion. I'll let you go now. You must be very busy."

"I am indeed, my friend. But you know that I always find the time to chat with you. Good-bye now, Jeff. I wish you well."

"Good-bye David. Thank you."

Captain Miller hung up the phone. He felt an uncertain sense of turmoil, accompanied by a strong desire to pray. Without second-guessing himself, he put his hands together and implored the God he knew for guidance and strength.

He was seen departing the vessel at his usual hour but this time his face showed a very pensive attitude.

The SOTIS team ensured him that everything was well under control. It was up to his judgment whether or not to inform the rest of the crew.

Making important decisions had never been a problem for Captain Miller, but this time the situation was different. The setting was unfamiliar. Unpredictable variables were at play and it was essential to limit any useless escalation as much as possible. An eventual extraction could take days, if not weeks, even if it were permissible. In that moment Captain Miller felt he bore the responsibility for all the lives on his ship. The full weight of the Expedition was completely on his shoulders.

With that in mind, he allowed himself a break and a good meal at the cafeteria, placing his troubled thoughts aside. He knew that with a full stomach he would have a calmer and better perception of things. When he was just a young lad, his grandfather used to tell him, "Fight with an empty stomach but think with a full one."

"Why?" he would ask.

"Because people with an empty stomach are more aggressive, and that's beneficial in war. On the other hand, when people have their basic needs taken care of, they can reason better. Never make an important decision with an empty stomach. Chances are you would regret it."

His grandfather was proud to say that he learned everything he knew from nature. "Look at nature when you seek answers," he would repeat time and again. From what Captain Miller had observed so far, Inner Earth displayed little of nature's majesty.

He seated himself across from the cafeteria window and, despite the limited choice of cuisine, enjoyed his food as if he were dining in a fancy, gourmet restaurant. By the time he was done with the meal, he knew what to do. Not surprising, the answer came to his mind without effort. He was ready to command the conference.

That afternoon the sirens long stationed throughout Taras rang for the first time. It was almost a violation of the peace that had reigned until that moment. People were told to immediately relocate to the main tower and wait inside the conference room for further instructions. Erin and Roger found themselves running alongside each other, and in the middle of all the sudden mayhem exchanged a wink.

The room inside the tower was packed with people. A few folks were leaning against the back wall while others sat on the floor, since there were not enough chairs to accommodate them all. Jeff Miller entered the room with his usual self-control and persuasive posture. He looked steadily at the people waiting before him. The SOTIS team — TJ, Kelly, and Jordan — stood behind the Captain forming a human shield with their arms crossed over their chests and their eyes hidden behind black sunglasses.

A gentle smile appeared on Miller's face as he approached the audience.

"Thank you all for coming. I promise I won't take too much of your time, but I have an important announcement to make. Yesterday I had a meeting with these guys you see behind me. By now you all must know they are part of the Special Operation Team responsible for our safety. Please join me in thanking them for their highly valued work." And with that he turned around and applauded the three men. Everyone in the room followed his example.

After a brief pause, Captain Miller continued. "During the briefing, I was informed that our security system has been under attack. There have been some interferences, but fortunately the risk has been neutralized and our security restored. I don't want to bore you with a lot of unnecessary details. I just want you to know that the situation is under control. I expect each of you to make sure your personal device works. This is very important because in the event of an emergency, you will be informed via your device. Additional information will be provided if and when needed. Please take time to review all the safety rules and make sure you strictly follow the protocols you have been given. It is essential, now more than ever. This is all I have to say for the moment, so please enjoy the rest of your afternoon. It is a lovely day out there. I guess we still have the ability to imagine a blue, sunny sky over our heads. I'll be available for the next few minutes for those of you who have questions. Everyone else, thank you again for coming and God bless us all."

Meanwhile, at the White House, the President had just finished his daily briefing with the press. He was on his way back to the Oval Office for more meetings with his cabinet staff when he saw General Curtis waiting. It had been a while since they had last interacted, so the President decided to approach him. "Mr. Curtis, any news regarding our Inner Earth Exploration?"

General Curtis stood to attention, gave the President the military salute, and responded. "Yes, Mr. President, I have just finished talking on the phone with Captain Jeff Miller. Everything is under control, sir. We have found samples of life, as expected, and everything is being fully reported and properly archived. Nothing out of the ordinary, as it is seen."

"Very good, General. I would love to have a full dossier of the findings on my desk no later than tomorrow afternoon."

"Yes, Mr. President, I will have it ready for you first thing tomorrow morning."

General Curtis left the White House and went to lunch. The dossier had already been prepared weeks in advance. Now he was free to enjoy the warm, spring afternoon with no further meetings scheduled for the rest of the day. On his way to the car, a smirk of satisfaction crossed his wrinkled face.

He knew he didn't have to worry because everything was going according to plan.

CHAPTER 11: LOST

The third excursion proved easier than the previous two due to the fact that team Delta had by now become accustomed to the alien environment.

For the most part, fear of the unknown had diminished, as one might imagine. Prudence, however, was not something to be overlooked, and neither was danger.

By virtue of that, when Rachel reported some muscle aches and head pain, she was precluded from participating in the exploration and kept under medical observation. As Rachel watched her team depart in the dry, gray morning, she was shivering, while flashes of heat ran through her blood. The fever was crippling her mind more than it was consuming her body. In that moment discomfort and caution prevented her from the frustration of not being a participant. She said good-bye with a downcast look before clinging back into her blue, wool blanket.

The rest of team Delta packed the last few provisions and left. Despite Rachel's absence, the group's morale was still high. It was always a good day when nobody had to be reminded why they were engaging in such an enterprise.

For a third time the fellow explorers departed with two heavily packed vehicles, in full gear, and well-armed. As with previous trips, they reached the top of Sandy Rings in respectful silence.

Everything was as pristine as usual. The gray sky gradually turning cream was confirmation that they were on the right path.

Additional samples of grass and moss were collected for the purpose of studying possible aging factors in the ecosystem.

All told, Alan's death gave the explorers a deeper appreciation for their own lives but, most of all, it infused the team with a regenerated sense of being on a mission and new reasons to move forward with determination. Every participant knew that survival lay in each other's hands and that they had to live up to the trust their companions placed in them.

Confidence builds in those who have been crushed and are able to bounce back, a type of courage that is hard-won but, once achieved, purges all fear. The determination that develops strength in a person was rooted in each explorer, but especially in Erin. Her secret map revealing the dots fired her spirit to the core. Without generating any suspicion, she quietly attempted to validate the privately received information. But even the use of technical goggles didn't yield a result, and her endeavor to locate anything resembling the mysterious black dots fell short. Longview Fields was impeccably, uniformly green.

Erin's eyes showed disappointment that the others didn't notice.

However, surprises did await. Oddly enough, the team could no longer find the orange flag's position from the previous visit, despite coordinates showing the exact same location. Without too much concern, a new landmark was quickly selected. Erin was more perplexed than the others appeared to be. Again, she had the impression a mysterious force was somehow restoring everything to its original state and condition. Where could the orange flag have gone? In the absence of wind, rain, and animals, what could possibly explain the disappearance? Sharing her feelings with the rest of the team didn't bring solace, as both Roger and Matt agreed there was little to be concerned about with the situation. Maybe the flag was somewhere nearby hidden by tall grass, was their conclusion.

"Let's hope for the best," Roger murmured, without anxiety but lacking conviction in his voice.

Although his words were supposed to be comforting, Erin trusted her own premonitions more than the words or actions of her companions.

Eventually she resolved to drop the disagreement and, getting to her feet, moved away from the group. If she wasn't enjoying the company of others, hopefully she was prepared to spend time alone. Not being understood built a nervous type of energy. "I know something you don't. I have a map," she grumbled, with a note of annoyance, but making sure no one could hear her as she began marching away.

Roger caught up with her suddenly. Behind his masked politeness, she sensed criticism and sadness. "Erin, if you need some time by yourself, that's fine. But we are supposed to stay together. Please stay at a close distance so we don't have to wonder where you are." His voice sounded condescending, like an alarm on a Sunday morning, very undesirable. Erin wasn't angry; she was resentful, which was probably worse. And yet an inner voice suggested she not dwell on her friend. She kept a polite face and stood motionless.

After Roger left her alone, the first thing she did was pull out the map and study it carefully. Everything looked exactly the same, blurry for the most part, but upon further inspection she realized the black dots were missing! There were advantages in being left alone, although it was in moments like this that Erin would have preferred someone to talk to. A battle between doubt and confidence played out in the twists and turns of her mind.

For Erin, it wasn't an easy struggle. A sense of failure gripped her. She let her eyes wander upward. Somehow the emptiness of the sky infused relief. Her restless spirit relaxed and in that moment, to her amazement, she noticed something very different: a new shade of color had appeared in the sky, darker than the already familiar, creamy light. The glare was more like a pale-orange stain and it seemed to be dancing across the sky.

The stream of light was shimmering and expanding, growing and receding, stretching and shrinking. It took a few moments for the new information to register. Wonderment didn't quite capture what Erin was experiencing at that instant.

The rest of the team seemed too distracted to notice something so beautiful and unusual.

"Too much wool has been pulled over our eyes," Erin thought to herself as she returned to the group.

"Did anybody notice the sky?" she exclaimed, in excitement.

The silence that followed surprised Erin because she had expected reactions of amazement. Scanning Roger's face for a clue, all she could perceive was an expression of sympathy. In her pride, Erin didn't trust him.

Roger stood up. "Erin, you seem erratic today. I need to ask, are you feeling okay?"

His compassion was usually a bridge between them, but not this time. Erin took no notice of him. Pointing to the sky she continued. "Don't you see? The color is changing!"

Roger, Matt, and Steve looked at Erin as if she had pulled a dinosaur out of the air. It wasn't the situation that caused Erin's frustration but rather their attitude. She hadn't expected this level of denial from her team. Ignoring their stares, she twitched her mouth in what was intended to be a smile.

Roger looked at the sky again. His face showed perplexity, but he said nothing else.

It suddenly occurred to Erin that she had seen a similar pink-orange glow on the same day as Alan's funeral, several days earlier, after she had stopped by the library.

It didn't take her long to register the connection.

When no one was looking, Erin pulled the map out a second time and, to her great amazement, discovered the black dots were once again visible. She was overjoyed. She had been given the opportunity to possess this map and the ability to perceive what others were apparently unable to see. Erin didn't know how to make sense of everything but she was ready to embrace the responsibility.

Less than half an hour had passed since Erin had reunited with her team. The lighthearted atmosphere was quickly restored, and everyone ended up having a good time, forgetting the brief disruption.

Later, a crackling campfire acted like glue among the group. Hypnotized as she watched the dancing flames unwilling to be contained, Erin thought it was the perfect time for storytelling. Unfortunately, the rest of team Delta had their own ideas.

Steve was vigorously showing the lads some of his photos when all of a sudden his chattering abruptly stopped. His face turned red, then white, as he started pounding his chest with his hand. At first the team thought he was just playing a game, but when a lack of air caused him to start gasping, everyone knew it wasn't a joke.

Desperate, Steve glanced around in search of help, then collapsed on his side with one hand on the grass supporting his weight. Moments later his body met the ground and his eyes closed. A warm, yellow liquid spilled from his mouth.

Without wasting any time, Matt was already on top of Steve, urging him to regain consciousness. Despite none of his attempts producing a positive result, his face showed no concern for himself or fear. That's the reason why he's our leader, thought Erin.

Quickly, the group decided to split. Separating the team was never a good idea, especially since the group was already so small. It was a gamble, but Steve needed to be taken back to camp to receive urgent medical assistance. The rest of the team, Erin and Roger, were to stay behind to complete the assignment, dismantle the tents, and collect all the gear.

Before leaving, Matt gave his two comrades a fair warning. "We are walking a fine line, and at this point anything could go wrong. It is up to you to make the decision to complete the task or to abort the mission."

Then he left in a hurry, transporting Steve's motionless body in the back of his vehicle.

Retreat sounded like failure to Erin and Roger. Had the moment to stop their research arrived? Roger maintained an expression of casual indifference, while Erin, the more frenzied of the two, watched him out of the corner of her eye as they continued their work.

Remaining steady, Roger broke the silence. "Strange how things work. One moment you feel undefeatable and the next you are fighting to stay alive."

Erin moved a little closer to her friend.

Hesitating slightly, Roger continued. "Many explorers have died because they didn't want to stop. I recognize this same urgency inside myself that drives me to want to keep going. When will it be too late to turn around?"

Before them was uncertainty and the unknown; behind them was Taras, no longer in sight but familiar.

Erin met Roger's eyes and recognized the same spark of audacity that she was feeling. Somehow that made her feel comforted, as she remembered Alan's words: "Persistence, this is what it takes." She turned around, managing a quick smile. "I think it's called gold fever."

"That could be infectious," Roger replied, with a grin on his face but without masking the anxiety apparent in his voice.

Erin's enthusiasm was almost contagious as she rallied, "Inner Earth will have its warriors!"

Roger looked around. They had been left with one four-wheeler, two tents, three backpacks, and most of the supplies. In his rush to leave, Matt had left most of the gear behind. The decision to continue was made without speaking, as Roger and Erin began to pack only what was necessary. A second orange flag was planted close to the remaining supplies as a landmark for their return.

It wasn't clear whether the change in magnetism caused the engine to stall or if the mechanical failure might have happened anyway, but when the four-wheeler suddenly stopped, it surprised both Roger and Erin. The interval of lightheartedness had come to a premature end, despite their best intentions.

"I don't understand. The tank is full of fuel and there are no warning lights on the dashboard," but Roger's initial assessment failed to impress, as a gust of smoke blew out from the engine. There was no use in telling Erin that the situation could have been worse. Roger knew a direct approach was the best way to communicate with her, and so he said what they both were afraid to admit. "I don't think I'll be able to fix it. If we decide to continue, it will have to be by foot. I'm sorry, Erin." Roger's voice failed to hide his frustration.

At first neither of them said anything, but Roger was worried. Things he felt he should have done dwelt on his mind. Erin gazed at his face. His expression was burdened by conflicting emotions.

She didn't want the bigger picture to escape them. Despite their vulnerable situation, a thin strand of excitement was still alive in Erin.

"At this point, our best option is to continue. We have enough supplies to last us for at least a week. If we don't find anything within the next 24/48 hours, we can always decide to go back. Our mission was supposed to last for another couple of days anyway. It will be a long walk all the way to Taras and I'm not ready to go back yet. I have a feeling that there is more we need to find. I want to complete this mission."

Erin paused for a moment, waiting for her friend to say something, but he looked pensive and more than a little concerned. Erin had never seen Roger so contemplative. A weak smile crept onto his face, and he left it there, without talking.

Erin continued. "You keep telling me that I am not mature enough, that I need to grow up. I thought being an adult was about being flexible. Maybe I'm not as wise as you would like me to be, but I know that bad things feel bad and good things feel good. And I feel good about keeping going."

For Erin, common sense was a simple thing, but Roger had deeper thoughts running through his mind. "How do you know that good is good? Are our decisions coming from a sense of love and duty for others or are we just thinking of ourselves?"

"I don't know, Roger, but there's only two choices — going back or moving forward. We need to pick one or the other; we cannot pick both."

Eventually Roger responded. "Fine, Erin. I guess your mind is made up. We'll mark this spot very well and move forward on foot. Time seems to follow different rules in this place, so I'll monitor our movements closely to make sure we don't go too far. It's risky, because our compass might or might not work, and our ability to communicate with the rest of the team is very limited. Are you sure you want to keep going?"

"Prudence and discovery don't work well together. We came here to explore something new. Let's not be afraid of the unknown."

Roger knew that going back was the safest choice. He had always been a crusader but never to the point of allowing himself to be harmed. But now when he reflected on all the decisions he had made, he wished he had had the courage to be bolder, to somehow make a difference. He knew that regret would eventually follow, as it usually did during his quiet moments, demanding him to reexamine his choices. The same ambition that was pushing him forward was also asking him to face his fears.

A slight blush appeared in Roger's cheeks as he declared, "Farewell, then, Taras. We shall proceed." And with those words he took the lead and started walking towards the unknown. At that point in the Expedition it was all about trust.

"The new person being born in me might be someone nature will protect," Roger whispered, but not loud enough for Erin to hear.

For the most part, the two explorers ventured into the unknowns of Inner Earth quiet, but happy. The absence of contrast in the landscape was an invitation for them to sink deep within their souls.

The thick silence that accompanied them was peaceful and somehow spoke its own language, but after days of trekking they both arrived at the same conclusion: the Longview Fields were anything but amicable.

Inner Earth was a tough existence, despite being one of the most evocative and beguiling of places. Yet the actualization of their human experience, vulnerable by default, drove them to reach the end of what they could endure. Food and water were running low and there was no room left for miscalculation. Ultimately, after days of challenging endeavor, survival had become their constant obsession. They were lost.

Several more days of aimless wandering, and Erin and Roger came to what appeared to be the twilight of their adventure. Noiseless, with bodies failing to respond, they collapsed on their knees, unable to walk any further. They lay on the ground for what seemed an eternity. Unable to speak, they were keenly aware that their journey by foot had forcefully come to an end, and not in the way they had imagined. The cream-colored sky was the only witness to their fading, mortal existence. Inner Earth no longer seemed so magical after all.

"What do you think will happen to our bodies, once we are dead?" Erin eventually croaked.

Her question saddened Roger more than he wanted to admit. A few tears fell on his cheeks, but he no longer cared about hiding his emotions. "I don't know, Erin. Maybe we will not decompose and will remain here in this place for a very long time."

Erin's laughter was feeble. "Do you mean like the people of Pompei?"

"Yes, something like that. And just like those people, I trust that sooner or later someone will find us. Till then, this place will preserve our bodies."

"Have you ever wondered … maybe we were not supposed to be here. Maybe there was an invisible line that was not meant to be crossed. Maybe, after we die, we will disappear as if we never existed."

"Immortality is about the people who keep living in the minds of their loved ones." Roger's voice was becoming softer, almost hard to hear.

Erin turned her head toward him. "I wish we'd made it back, Roger, but if I could have picked one person to share this experience with, that would have been you. Inner Earth gave us a lot, but now it's time to leave it all behind."

Roger knew that this time, regret would not haunt him.

Erin inhaled a trembling breath. "I could go happily now. This is better than dying alone," she managed to say.

And with those words she closed her eyes, falling unconscious moments before her last breath left her body and her heart gave its final beat.

CHAPTER 12: CLYDE

For Matt, the rush to Taras had been even more terrifying than the accident itself. Once back at base camp, the still senseless body of Steve was immediately rushed to the hospital. Nurse Megan, despite being surprised at what initially appeared to be another fatality, spoke to Matt calmly. Her ability to make an alarming situation to others appear easy and natural was remarkable.

Matt, having been part of the unfolding drama, was questioned about the incident. Sitting on a chair in the doctor's office, he made an effort to keep a temperate attitude while trying to remember as many details as possible about events that preceded Steve's collapse.

"I don't know how to explain what happened." With his head bowed and eyes closed, Matt was striving to revitalize his memory. "Steve was showing the rest of us the pictures he had taken during the day when all of a sudden he appeared to suffer from a lack of air. Then he crashed to the ground. This is all I was able to observe."

The doctor listened and asked questions to collect targeted information. His movements were soft but controlled, his appearance ordinary. To say it in Matt's words, he was a non-threatening person.

"Matt, you are the leader of team Delta and, as such, I expect a full report from you about the circumstances preceding and regarding this incident. You are now dismissed, but please be available for further questioning just in case we need more information. Thank you for your time, Matt. You may now leave."

With those words, Dr. Scott Anderson, who was in charge of the Inner Earth hospital, released Matt but not without ordering a full physical and mental examination. Dr. Anderson seemed to give commands more than requests, and that small detail helped Matt feel more at ease with the situation. It was unusual for Matt to be treated as if he were a child, but even with that prospect he still felt he was in control.

After the full body examination delivered a positive outcome, Matt was allowed to leave the hospital. He was walking with slow steps toward the exit when nurse Megan approached him. She had a note in her hand and gave it to him with just a few words. "Captain Miller wants to see you immediately. He is waiting for you in his office. Good luck, Matt." A somewhat forced smile appeared on her face before she returned to her duties.

Matt nodded in acknowledgment and left the building.

Admiral Q-Oho was anchored majestically at the end of the citadel, making Taras look even smaller than its real size. It was the first time since the ship's arrival that Matt had been invited to enter. And despite his concerns, a slight sense of excitement infused him while heading toward the vessel. Captain Miller's office was on the second level, the last door on the left at the end of a tight corridor.

Matt knocked on the door and a modest voice from the inside instructed him to enter. "Please take a seat, Matt. How are you?"

Matt made himself comfortable in the small but robust chair. "I have seen better days, thank you. How about yourself, sir?"

Miller stared at Matt and sighed. "As one would imagine, things could definitely be better. I think you already know the reason I have convened you here. Unexpected events seem to be occurring more often than predicted these days, and it's my duty to understand why. I have been informed by Dr. Anderson that your state of health is good, and I am relieved to hear that. Unfortunately, I cannot say the same for other members of our crew. We had a fatality just a few days ago, and it is my responsibility to keep unfortunate accidents as few as possible."

"I understand, sir."

"I need to know what happened. What caused this incident? I have a feeling there might be something we are completely missing about this place."

Matt, with his usual calm deliberateness, again related all the events leading up to the incident. This time, however, his mind was clearer and more relaxed, making it easier to recall more details. From the missing marker to the tall grass and the creamy glow of the sky, nothing was left out.

Captain Miller listened attentively and with an open mind. His expression showed occasional signs of concern, especially after Matt had finished relating the journey back to Taras. "You are telling me that two members of our crew, Erin and Roger, have not yet returned from the excursion. Have they been given directions to follow?"

"Sir, the main priority was to bring Steve back safely, and I volunteered to take that responsibility. There was little time to discuss this with the rest of the team, so I entrusted Roger and Erin with the authority to make a decision, but not without a warning about the risks to which they might be exposed."

"Matt, what exactly is the procedure to follow in the event something like this happens?"

"It depends, sir. In the case of unpredictable events, the protocol needs to be adjusted to suit the circumstances."

Captain Miller looked at Matt. His expression was becoming impatient. He didn't say anything further, so Matt continued. "It depends on the supplies, on the level of danger, and the degree of expertise of the members, but ultimately it is up to the individual to make a decision. I assume, sir, that we have followed the basic directives of our written protocol, and I trust the rest of my team made the correct decision."

"It sounds like you are telling me there's a chance that the remaining two team members could have decided to complete the mission before returning to base camp."

"This is accurate, sir. There is, in fact, that possibility."

"But we don't know if what afflicted Steve could also happen to Erin and Roger."

"Sir, you are correct. We can't exclude that."

"Considering the incertitude of the situation, what makes you believe that refusing to give your team the order to abort the mission was a good decision?"

"Sir, we have not come this far only to survive."

Matt's words carried the type of self-regard that is earned with hard work, passion, and commitment. Captain Miller insisted no more.

"Thank you for your time, Matt. I hope you feel better. Please don't forget to prepare a written report of the event."

Once the door closed, Captain Miller was again alone inside the enormous vessel. His mind began to trick him. He felt like Jonah who had been caught by a whale and swallowed in its belly while attempting to run away from God. Legend says that Jonah was trapped there for three days, and during that time he asked God for help. In the end, God had mercy on him and commanded the giant fish to release him.

Never in his life had Captain Miller wished to be released from his duties. But now, for the first time since the beginning of the Expedition, the urge to return home was making its voice heard.

What defines failure? And what defines success? That was a riddle that, even with his fullest dedication, Captain Miller was unable to solve.

Furthermore, the idea of reporting the unpleasant news to the White House was making him nervous and uncomfortable. For the first time insecurity and a sense of abandonment started to slowly creep into Captain Miller's mind. It was hard to feel accountable for things that were beyond his control. The decision to call General Curtis, his beloved and trusted friend, finally settled the matter.

General Curtis was the type of friend who would never fight other people's battles. Yet despite having many of the flaws that took Captain Miller several years to abandon, General Curtis was a good ally.

His voice was loud and almost shrill but his words very friendly when he exclaimed with genuine excitement, "My dear friend, how are you? I am starting to miss your company over here. Your timing is brilliant! I had a meeting with the Prince of Saudi Arabia yesterday and guess what I was gifted? A box of Saudi Arabia Royal Family custom cigars! I am waiting for your return to try them. Some things are better enjoyed with a good buddy. But tell me about you, my friend! What is going on down there?"

At the sound of his jovial voice, the Captain's fears and doubts almost vanished. Consoled, a relieved smile appeared on his face. It took a moment or two for Miller to find the right words to describe the situation without shattering his friend's enthusiasm.

"Things are ... proceeding. I told you yesterday about the new laboratory results. There is a good possibility that this place is not only fit for human inhabitancy but according to the latest findings, it might be rich in resources. I can easily foresee a permanent base here not too far down the road."

"That's great news, my friend! I've always known you were the right man for the job. But I get the feeling there's something bothering you. What's up, my friend?"

"You know me well, indeed. Here is the unfortunate side of the story. Another member of our crew has fallen ill. The causes are still unknown, but he is under medical observation. Also, two other explorers have not yet returned from their mission."

The long pause that followed increased Miller's tension.

"What do you mean 'they have not returned yet'?"

"They have been classified as a missing party. So far, all attempts to establish communication have been unsuccessful. We have been unable to determine their location or their condition. But we are doing everything in our power to try to locate them."

"This is very unfortunate, indeed, and definitely something that we cannot afford. The United States of America is under the spotlight because of this Expedition, especially after all the criticism we have received from our allies, not to mention our enemies. If something goes wrong, it will impact our reputation in the eyes of the world. It is urgent that the missing members are found at any cost, and hopefully alive. If that is not the case, I'm certain we'll be able to come up with some sort of justification."

Captain Miller was shocked at the sound of those words.

"David, we are talking about someone's life here. I'm surprised to hear you speak in such an uncaring manner. We should never put the reputation of an institution ahead of the lives of our people. Every day we are here is a risk to be taken. Please don't forget that!"

"All right. I'm sorry, Jeff. I didn't mean it to come out that way. I was caught unprepared. That's all."

Curtis' voice seemed more pretentious than sorry, but Miller decided to trust his friend's intentions and continued. "I'm seeking your advice. We have been here for 72 days and more than half of our supplies have been consumed. We have limited mobility, considering the unfamiliar circumstances. I have been thinking this over and over and I don't believe it is still safe for us to stay here. We need better equipment. I am asking for your permission to abort the Expedition and to prepare our team for extraction."

"My opinion?" Curtis' voice was becoming more and more aroused. "My opinion is that you stay there and finish the tasks you have been hired to do! We have invested so much time and resources in this Expedition that the idea of not completing the mission is unacceptable at this point. I am here to support you, but I have no intention to accept your request. We all knew this was risky before we started, but that was never a reason not to think big. Has it become an excuse now? I need you as strong and committed as you were before you left, because that is the only Jeff that I know."

Captain Miller maintained his composure like a calm sea, despite being appalled by his friend's tone of voice. He had known General Curtis since high school, and never in his life had he found him so unnerved. It was as if he were afraid of something.

He took a deep breath before replying in a sharp tone. "Farewell, then. I will do my best to recover the missing crew and I will update you shortly. It was a pleasure talking to you, as usual. I wish you a great rest of your day, David."

"Oh, c'mon Jeff, you know that I have only your best interest in mind. I don't want you to quit. This is too important, even for you! Stay the course, and I promise you will thank me later."

"Thank you, David. I will do as you say. Good-bye now." And without waiting for an answer, Captain Miller hung up the phone.

Miller felt fatigued after the conversation with his friend David Curtis. He knew the only thing that could bring peace to his mind was to find Roger and Erin. He was aware that his choice could become a curse or a strength. Hoping for the latter, he began to contemplate a rescue strategy.

His collection of college and high school notes were carried with him everywhere he went. The Captain found it comforting from time to time to read and recall the many dreams that as a young fellow, with an innocent heart, had made him the man he was now.

Oh, how blessed is youth when the heart is relieved of responsibility and concern!

One short quote by E. Joseph Cossman caught his attention: "Obstacles are things a person sees when he takes his eyes off his goal."

He remembered writing it just a few months before graduation, a busy and cheerful time for most of his friends but not for him. His mother had recently died from a sudden heart attack, almost causing him to abandon high school. It was only with intense discipline and a high work ethic that he was able to finish his senior year and graduate with honors. Now, forty years later, Miller was still looking for a reason to keep going.

Someone once explained to him that people keep re-experiencing lessons they have not understood or learned from. To his surprise, the hurtful wound from his adolescence was still open and the need to find closure still pressing. Buried emotions from that distant event needed to be embraced and understood once and for all. The ability to move on requires a mindful intent, not just the skillful art of preoccupation to avoid the problem. Captain Miller was determined to find a solution to his current difficulties, even if it took all night. He had never been the kind of fellow who avoided his duties, but there were still hidden aspects of his subconscious mind that he was unaware of. At some point they had to be addressed or they would continue to affect his behavior, below the level of his awareness.

Having made a decision, Miller contacted the operation room, located on the third floor of the tower.

Clyde was on shift. He was Miller's favorite computer technician. He was responsible for all the monitoring devices and communications between staff members. Clyde was a quiet young man, uncommonly tall and skinny, to the point that those who didn't know him could have suspected an eating disorder. His pale skin was mostly covered in freckles, giving the illusion of a tan, and his big, thick glasses overstated his eyes to almost appear the size of the lens. According to some people, he had a creepy appearance, but he was an honest and trustworthy fellow. His generous nature was only surpassed by his genuine behavior.

Captain Miller had a sincere devotion to Clyde, like the son he had never experienced, and he was always happy to have a reason to get in touch with him.

Clyde responded before the end of the third beep, maintaining his professional attitude. "Operation Team, Clyde speaking."

"My dear Clyde, I have told you many times you don't have to say Operation Team since you are the only one working there. How are you today?"

"Yes, sir. Very good, sir. Am I not supposed to ask you the same question, sir? What can I do for you today, sir?"

"Thank you, Clyde. Your professionalism is valued and quite rare these days. People call me Mr. Miller, which is still a very good way to address your superior, but sir is the correct way. When I was your age, I would have been demoted for using the wrong appellation, so thank you! Well, having said that, I assume you are aware of the situation, are you not?"

Clyde needed a moment to collect himself. A dreadful sense of inadequacy assailed him as his hands began to tremble. Before replying, he cleared his throat. "Sir, you must be referring to the accident that happened to team Delta."

"Yes, precisely. I need to know if you have any information regarding the exact location of our two missing staff members, Miss Erin Palmer and Mr. Roger Wood."

"Unfortunately, no, sir. The signal coming from their devices is very weak and hard to detect. I am in the process of testing a new software that could allow me to magnify and decode the message."

"Can you please be more specific?"

"Sir, the transmission that we are receiving is not clean. It seems … compromised."

"Compromised? How so? Is it because of a device failure?"

"I can't confirm that yet, sir. I am receiving a form of communication that our system is unable to read and analyze. It's unclear whether this is because of a deficiency in our network or because of something else."

"Something else like what, exactly?" Miller's voice was becoming sharp.

"Sir, it's possible that our system has been … hacked!"

What followed was a long silence. Captain Miller's worst fear had just been confirmed, but his position of authority did not allow him to display any weakness. Straightening his shoulders and raising his voice, he ended the call with a simple command: "Find out what is going on and provide me with an update as soon as possible. I will be in my office for the rest of the day. Good-bye, Clyde!"

"I'm on it, sir." But Clyde didn't have time to add further comment because the elongated beep coming from the line indicated that Captain Miller had ended the communication.

Following the briefing with Clyde, Miller immediately alerted the SOTIS team. "Sorry, son. These guys don't have any sense of humor, nor a scrap of patience, but they do need to know what's going on," he thought to himself, after releasing the command.

In no time a meeting between the SOTIS team and Clyde was scheduled.

Clyde had a slight suspicion about the situation but not the evidence to corroborate what he felt. However, he wrote his impressions in his journal, as he customarily did. That was the best way to keep unofficial information to himself without losing track. Clyde was a pretty smart, young man and he knew that sometimes what seems to be unlikely in the beginning can be confirmed once science has the tools to prove it. The invention of the microscope did not create the presence of microorganisms; it only confirmed they existed. "I'm sure there were people believing in the existence of bacteria before they had a way to prove it. Oftentimes, it's science that needs to evolve to the level of intuition, not the other way around. I think Einstein said something like that," he wrote in his journal.

Clyde knew he needed more time to analyze the situation and elaborate an objective answer before informing Captain Miller. The software scan on his computer was proceeding smoothly and nothing on the screen seemed to be out of the ordinary, but there was a sort of low interference, distinguishable as a soft noise, that was interrupting the script at constant intervals. Clyde had never witnessed something like this before.

He remembered his excitement when he was accepted for the three-month mission and how surprised he was to learn he would be the only one managing the entire communication system. Having an outstanding background in cybersecurity and computing information, he was considered the perfect fit for the job. Now he had to live up to his reputation and the role that had been entrusted to him.

The problem was simple and yet hard to identify: Was it a slight electromagnetic interference or something else? If the sound traveled along a channel, it meant there had to be a receiver but also a source. If that were the case, the next question would have to be: *Who* or *what* was the source?

A knock on the door interrupted his train of thought.

"Quiet!" he wanted to shout, but restraining himself pronounced instead, "Come on in."

His voice sounded more hoarse than loud. The door opened and three burly men entered. They were wearing black shades, even in the low light of the laboratory. Clyde was taller than all of them, but their stiff, statuesque posture made them look bigger than their actual size.

"You guys seem to have been born in uniform," Clyde joked, in an effort to ease the tension in the room, but soon realized he was in the presence of government investigators with no sense of humor.

The SOTIS members had no intention of letting him call the shots, and the team proceeded with their formalities and questioning without the slightest response. Clyde listened and cooperated, trying to apply just the right amount of flattery. He knew any sign of insubordination would cause him to lose his badge and potentially his budding career.

Clyde was able to answer all of their inquiries while carefully studying the agents in front of him. He noticed the operative standing on the right running a finger down his Glock with the same expression Clyde would have reserved for a juicy steak. He gulped, suddenly sensing danger. His insecurity didn't diminish when he was asked to follow the SOTIS team to an undisclosed location. Asking for more information about where he was going provided no results, so he thought it best to comply without further argument.

Clyde left his computer running but secured the access and locked the door to his office behind him. He was following the SOTIS team down the tower stairs when all of a sudden something hit him from behind, causing him to lose balance and fall down the stairway. Shocked by the attack and his tumble, Clyde's breathing became a panting gasp. He was alive, his heart beating very fast. He looked at the bloody mess on the ground and realized he was wounded. His head hurt and he had the sensation he was losing his balance and sight. Using both arms, Clyde made an effort to raise himself, but immediately his eyes were covered with a cloth and his arms tied behind his back. Two individuals quickly transported him down the tower, dragging him like a wounded animal. His body in pain, the fear didn't last long before everything went black and silent.

It had been a very long day. By early evening, Captain Miller was surprised and concerned that he had not received any update from Clyde. He had hoped to obtain necessary information by now to plan his rescue strategy, but in the absence of a clear report, it was hard to administer accurate instructions. Frustrated, he decided to visit the tower. Clyde, he thought, was the type of person who could use a surprise once in a while. "That young man is so committed to his job, someone needs to remind him to eat," Miller thought to himself while striding toward the tower.

As soon as he entered the building, the Captain couldn't help but notice an odd, clean smell, very different from the usual odor of concrete typical of the structure. Paying little attention to what he thought was a minor detail, he climbed the stairs leading to Clyde's office, while smiling briefly in anticipation of his favorite employee's astonishment. He found the door locked, which was unusual. Miller knocked on the door. Then straightening up and clearing his voice he ordered, "Clyde! This is Captain Miller. Open the door!" A few seconds went by. No answer. The situation was getting awkward. "Clyde! CLYDE!"

Miller looked down, and through the small gap at the bottom of the door he noticed a faint light, a sign that someone was or had been inside. He glanced at his watch, 8:27 p.m. Had Clyde already left? If so, why? Disappointed, Captain Miller decided to leave. He searched his pockets for something to write on and found a used envelope. Ripping the paper and using the pen he kept in the inside pocket of his vest, he wrote a short note:

"Still waiting for an update. Contact me ASAP – Captain Miller."

Bending down, he pushed the slip of paper under the door, then adjusted his jacket, wiped the dust from his pants, and strode away.

By the time the Captain had reached the end of the corridor, a beep followed by a typed message appeared on Clyde's screen:

NEW FORM OF COMMUNICATION DETECTED
ENCRYPTED MESSAGES (2) RECEIVED
TRANSMISSION DOWNLOADED
OPEN FILE? Y/N

CHAPTER 13: AGOR

Erin felt a strong pressure on her chest followed by an intense heat. Her mind was empty and numb. Gasping for air, she opened her eyes but felt an immediate desire to close them again, as if a bright light were blinding her. She managed to slow her breath to a regular rhythm, as the strain and the warmth in her torso gradually diminished. She moved her fingers gently, and an expression of relief spread across her face when she realized she was still in control of her body. Again, and this time slowly, she opened her eyes. The shadow of what appeared to be an individual loomed directly above her body, looking down at her.

Erin's immediate instinct was to scream, but she couldn't emit any sound. She made an effort to reach for the device on her neck to send a message but, to her dismay, the unit was gone. Her chances of being saved went from 50% to 0% in less than a blink of an eye. Everything, she thought, was about to become a memory.

Her moment of despair was almost too painful to indulge. She was about to protest when the stranger bent its head gently to one side and a smile appeared on its singular face. Using her heels, Erin tried to push herself backward away from the perceived threat but quickly discovered she was missing the necessary strength to perform even such a simple action. The being seemed to understand her uneasiness and, with an unblinking expression, gently rested its hand on Erin's forehead. She couldn't help but notice the unusual length of its fingers!

Presently, a sense of warmth permeated Erin's body, followed by the lessening of her fear and tension. She took time to examine the strange creature in front of her. Its skin was a light green color, tending toward a grayish tone. The long, black hair was gathered in a braid behind its head. Its ears were undersized but unusually pointed, and two large, black, prominent eyes without sclera slanted toward the edge of the peculiar face. The being's mouth was small with thin lips, and its nose was composed of two nostrils on a narrow, aquiline bulge. The top of its scalp appeared larger than the lower portion, and eyebrows were completely missing.

"Who … who … who are you?" Erin almost choked on the words.

The strange entity removed its hand from Erin's head and said softly, "I am Agor, a member of the people of Wasay." The voice was deep, reassuring, and friendly.

"A … A … Agor?" Once again Erin tried to pull herself into a sitting position, but now a mysterious force seemed to be preventing her from getting up. Erin's reaction was immediate and almost explosive. "I can't move! Why? What's happening to me? Where am I?"

She scanned the new surroundings, looking for something familiar, and suddenly remembered. Memories of an earlier moment formed quickly in her mind … Roger. She last recalled being with him but could see no sign of him near her now. She frantically began calling his name until her voice cracked. Aside from gaining the stranger's attention, her efforts produced no results.

Agor patiently allowed the unleashing of Erin's turmoil. Eventually she regained her self-control, as much as her perception of the situation allowed. She stared at Agor again — deciding the entity was male — and searched for something evil to justify her outburst, but all she could perceive was an eerie and loving presence.

"Humans are creatures of habit," Agor said, in response to Erin's disoriented gaze.

Although Erin was still fuming, the rational side of her character attempted to revert to a more composed stance. "Where is Roger?" Erin finally asked, trying to keep her temper to a minimum.

Agor didn't reply but pointed to his right with an elongated finger. At the sight of his long hand, a shiver ran down Erin's spine.

Not too far away, Roger was lying on the ground, motionless. He appeared to be lifeless. Erin's mind went silent. There was nothing left to say. After a few moments of emptiness, something inside began to return her attention outward. A sense of dread and danger increased her tension.

"What did you do to him? Did you kill him?" Horror flew through her as she pronounced the words.

Agor looked at Erin with surprise, then quietly responded. "Your friend is sleeping now and will soon be fine. He seems to be weaker than you and thus needs more time to recover. I decided to help you and your friend, but humans worry about everything. You are now in the land of peace. Please be at peace."

These last words sounded more like a command than a simple appeal and gave Erin the impression she was under a magic spell. A pleasing sensation of harmony and serenity pervaded her consciousness. Agor smiled and continued. "In our world the predominant energy is harmony. You need to learn to be at peace with our world or your body will perish."

Finally, the pressure that was holding Erin to the ground was lifted and she found she was able to stand up. Somehow invigorated, she felt strong and was ready to move on. All of the cuts and wounds accumulated during their aimless wandering were gone! Looking at Agor, who remained on his knees, she asked, not without surprise, "Did you do this? Did you heal me?"

Agor stood up, finally revealing his true size. He had to be over eight feet tall! Despite his benevolent presence, that minor detail intimidated Erin. Eventually he replied, "You and your friend were almost dead when I found you. I understand that your spirit wants to live, so I decided to give you the opportunity to empower your soul."

Despite being quite amused by the way Agor communicated, Erin didn't fully grasp the meaning of his words. She didn't know if she was understanding a different message, but she felt so much better knowing she was alive. Perhaps not the same could be said for Roger, she thought.

"What about Roger? Will he get better?" she asked, pointing to her friend with a gesture of her head.

Agor looked intently at Erin and replied, "Your friend needs to make a choice. His spirit wants to live, but too many fears still remain in his mind. Time will help him decide."

Erin's confusion grew even deeper.

"I don't understand you. I don't understand the words you speak."

"I only say what I can see. Your friend has free will, and I know not what he will choose. The voice of your spirit is very loud and clear, but your friend's volition is as yet unknown. The destiny of your friend is something that I know not."

Defeated in her comprehension of the situation, Erin walked slowly toward Roger. He was lying inert on the ground. His breathing was shallow, accompanied by sudden, deep movements in his chest. Sorrow filled Erin's heart. She wanted Roger to wake up. Reality lay in front of her, but it was like a low quality movie. Her head became foggy again as she sat on the ground and allowed herself to drift into oblivion.

For the entire time, Agor remained nearby in respectful silence. Once the present moment slammed her back to awareness, a sudden realization came to Erin. She turned toward Agor as if she had abruptly become aware of his presence and asked, this time with more conviction, "Who are you? What are you doing here?"

He turned slowly, but without saying a word. Erin continued. "I am an explorer. Our Expedition team has a base not too far from here, I suppose. We lost our way back and ended up being defeated ... but you, where do you come from?"

As if it were the most natural question, Agor quietly responded, "I am Agor, of the people of Wasay. This is my land. I live here."

Erin looked away, before an arrogant smirk appeared on her face. Skepticism didn't adequately describe the way she was feeling.

"Did I hear you correctly? Did you say that you live HERE?" Erin scoffed. "That's impossible! Nobody could live here." Erin's attitude was slightly condescending.

"You are wrong. I live here. My people established themselves here a long time ago before humans arrived on Earth."

"Before humans arrived on Earth? What are you talking about?" Erin's impatient reaction abandoned her quickly as she listened to his next words.

"It is unfortunate that humans know very little about their origins. Doubt and arrogance live freely in the human mind but, sadly, not enough curiosity. Humans don't change, or very little and very slowly."

"Why do you keep calling me 'human'?" At the sound of her own words, Erin's eyes widened.

"I call you human because you are human. Mankind believes they are the only ones, but their sapience is limited and wrong. Humans cannot even wrap their mind around the Milky Way, and yet they think they know everything. I say to you that reality is much bigger than the human understanding. One day your scientists will inform your people that human DNA did not originate from Earth."

Erin felt conflicted to where she almost wanted to pull back. Eventually she spoke again. "Agor, as little as you might approve of us, I am human. And I don't really know what you are talking about, but for me there is nothing more natural and beautiful than being a human being." Erin's arrogant attitude quickly subsided as she walked toward her languishing friend. Moments later she heard Agor enunciating some fathomless words. She turned around and looked at him, forcing a smile, despite her ambivalent feelings.

"This is not a game. Watch!" Agor indicated an area on Longview Fields, known to her team as the prairie. The black dots, the same as Erin had noticed during the second

127

Exploration, were visible again. This time they were bigger and moving at a gradual pace. Agor instructed Erin to come closer. Then his large hand made a slow, circular movement just in front of her vision, creating an invisible screen that provided a magnified view. Erin was now able to see clearly that those dots were, in fact, bison. It took a few stunned moments before the new revelation could sink in, even though it was right in front of her eyes. Her grin faded as she stared at the fields in front of her.

It so happened that Erin had identified the presence of evolved life in Inner Earth and not just bacteria!

"I thought that where I was, no one had walked before." The sudden shift in her reality brought on more emotions than Erin's mind could possibly contain.

Within her inner eye she saw herself returning to Taras with the most astonishing announcement. Feeling so magnificently vainglorius was a very human kind of emotion! Her absorption in self-glory was only interrupted by the sound of Agor's laughter. It was an odd-sounding, spluttering giggle.

Slightly embarrassed, Erin interrupted him. "Are those really buffalos?"

Agor paused before responding. "Yes, those are bison. Many animals live here, as you will eventually find out. We are very close to the buffalo reserve. Buffalos eat grass, and this is a good place for them to find food. Do you follow that logic?"

Erin felt an impulse to walk toward the herd, but after Agor placed his hand on her shoulder, she accepted the gesture as an indication to desist. A sense of relief enshrouded her, as the thought of leaving Roger alone penetrated her mind. Instead, she took advantage of that moment to look around or, as her buddy would have recommended, "to check her surroundings."

On one side the vast green prairie extended as far as the human eye could see, but on the other, just behind her and not visible before, was a much different panorama, the beginning of what appeared to be a thick, gloomy forest. She remembered the map given to her by Alan. Before leaving, he had said one day she would need it. Had that day finally arrived? Thinking again of Alan's passing, she tried to hold back tears as she opened the parchment and, with some amusement, detected that this time even more details were appearing on the map. It was as though Alan's magic map was drawing itself, using Erin's journeying like a pencil. "I don't understand. These attributes weren't here before." Her eyes pleaded with Agor, hoping he could sort out some of her predicament.

"The drawing is correct. We are here," said Agor pointing to the section of the map showing the beginning of the Forest of the Giant Trees.

Erin replied in an impertinent tone of voice, "Last time I checked, there wasn't a forest indicated anywhere on this map."

She scoured the landscape one more time with the extraordinary vision Agor had afforded her. While doing so, she noticed something else. White peaks were appearing just beyond the ancient trees. Her eyes followed their crest and she was stunned to see that the sky above the forest had assumed a different color, a light, bluish tone. In fact, all of the scenery was now stained with bright colors. It was as if the landscape were suddenly becoming alive! Although absorbed in that observation, Erin began to grow aware of the presence of something mysterious, both benevolent and hostile at the same time. Perhaps, she thought, a greater unity inhabited this place, asking only to be aknowledged.

"Your mind is informing you of the reason you are here. Your spirit desires to know more. Remember, the sky is never the limit." After saying that, Agor covered Erin's eyes with his hand and disappeared.

All that Erin felt was a soft breeze move across her face. When she opened her eyes, any despair at being left alone had been outweighed by a greater yearning for adventure.

She now understood there was so much to explore in this place, she could feel it! Realizing Agor was gone should have scared Erin. But to continue an adventure without a known destination was a type of freedom she had never had the pleasure to experience. What lay ahead would bring smiles or tears, but excitement for the unknown was pushing her to know its limits. Not even the bitter realization that Roger had vanished could break Erin's will. Something inside of her had been awakened. A new layer of strength had been aroused.

At this point, having lost all ability to communicate with her team, it was practically impossible for Erin to go back to camp. Resources in Longview Fields were insufficient to survive, as that prospect had already been tested directly on herself and Roger. Her best option was to move forward, hoping to find a more sustaining landscape ahead. Training for *The Last Templar* had made her a pretty good hunter, and the idea of stalking bison wasn't so bad.

Using binoculars, Erin looked back across the prairie. The buffalos were considerably distant but still there. With a brief calculation, she estimated at least two to four hours of walking just to reach a favorable hunting position, but only assuming the bison did not move from their current location. It was too risky to even consider. With a sigh of discouragement, she focused her attention in the opposite direction, toward the forest. A sense of awe settled in her mind, but for the most part it was a desire to know what was on the other side of the unexplored woodland that kept Erin going.

The forest seemed very ancient in all its glory. Giant trees towering over her were serene, peaceful, and majestic. There was no open path through the woods; however, passage was relatively accessible, despite the easy to establish fact that no one had walked on this ground before. Erin proceded slowly and carefully, paying attention to every little detail. The feeling of being an alien in an alien world was aroused again in her mind, taking her back to team Delta's first excursion among the Sandy Rings. She had never thought of herself as an alien form. Despite the fact that Agor may have saved her life, it was still highly speculative to assume that she was welcomed in this place.

With time, having survived on meager rations and moisture found on vegetation, Erin was able to gain more confidence, and that allowed her to observe the terrain in more detail. Alongside the magnificent trees were other gigantic plants of a lighter color and with hulking leaves, almost as big as a small car. One of those leaves could have been used as a tarp in case of rainfall. Everything was enormous, making her feel the smallness of her presence in that place. With the strong desire to prove herself, Erin refused to fall victim to any of her insecurities.

For the most part, the ground was covered with moss and lichens, indicative of wet soil. Erin's hope was to find a creek or a little waterfall. With each passing day, the need for a source of food and water was becoming more urgent.

Again, from her training for *The Last Temlpar*, she knew how to build a good trap without bait. Although she hadn't seen any small creatures, she was becoming desperate. She used a forked stake planted into the ground, sticks, and a rope to set a decent ploy, then patiently waited, hiding not too far away. Hours went by, with no success.

Venturing deeper into the forest, Erin finally found a small bush supporting a yellow-orange fruit, similar to a grape but much larger and with all the berries "glued" together. As a rule, Erin knew not to eat what was unfamiliar, but she determined the risk of starving was higher than the risk of being poisoned, so decided to make an exception. Inside the fruit was a white, soft, jelly pulp, almost transparent, and with a pungeant, nasty smell. It took a lot of courage, but Erin finally sampled the semiliquid content. To her surprise, it tasted like jam! It was the sweetest thing she had eaten in a long time, and in a matter of seconds she felt rejuvenated.

With her morale boosted and her body invigorated, she was eager to move forward. She checked the trap again. Nothing! "Never leave a trap unattended," she mumbled to herself while triggering it with a rock. Despite the severity of the environment, Erin understood the forest deserved her respect and she was willing to honor that sentiment. Eventually she prepared camp for her third night alone and constructed a comfortable lean-to made from the giant leaves. She started a fire using dry lichens found on trees and by rubbing two sticks against each other to create a spark. Her survival skills were very, very good "thanks to *The Last Templar*," she mused, especially for a young lady who grew up in a suburban area. She was definitely becoming proud of her achievements.

Days went by. Erin made her way through the forest eating vegetation and collecting moisture from leaves to quench her thirst. The greatest accomplishment was in becoming positively acquainted with her solitude. The stillness of Inner Earth and the many days of wandering brought Erin to a deeper level of awareness, leading to a complete evacuation of time. The silence of the forest began to develop into an improvised melody.

It was in a similar state of mind that Erin had once seen the glow. Now it was again surrounding her, this time beginning at her feet, then legs, and gradually expanding until her entire body was emitting the same pink-orange glare, with some areas darker than others. With a glint of intuition, Erin hurriedly peeked at the map and found confirmation: The territory beyond the forest was in full display, and it was beautiful! There were rivers and lakes, mountains and fields, but it was like nothing she had ever seen before. Although she assumed that the map could only be interpreted when she was in a particular state of mind, Erin couldn't be certain of the truth of that assumption.

Carefully studying the additional details, Erin noted the closest body of water was Lake Pracon, just outside the forest to the left. She made a mental picture of the specifics before they vanished again. Her curiosity deepened as she contemplated where Agor might have gone. And was Roger there with him? Where was Agor's village located? Unfortunately, nothing on the map, so far, revealed any sign of a settlement — no cities or towns, and absolutely no roads.

As if Agor had heard her thoughts, he made his second appearance to Erin. Startled, she had to stifle a little cry of bewilderment and joy when she saw him. Agor didn't show much emotion in seeing her. He simply approached with a brief but courteous salute. "Good day to you, human visitor, to our land. I see that you live well in nature."

Despite the fact that she didn't like to be called human and wondering how, for the second time, he had found her, Erin forced herself to reply with a simple "hello." In that moment she understood her conditioned vulnerability and a humble "thank you" came out of her mouth, almost by accident. For the first time Erin noticed how skinny he was. The long, maroon cape made the entity look even taller than his eight feet, but no less benevolent.

Agor didn't wait long before announcing, "My people are aware of your presence here."

"Did you tell them?"

"No. My people know who is here. My people are aware of your Expedition and of the city your people constructed."

"Do you mean Taras?"

"The name is not important. My people sent a warning message to your people. Most of the humans who have arrived here are good, but there are some entities who have bad intent and no honesty. My people don't want humans here."

"You told me before that this is a land of peace. Why then are your people so defiant toward human beings?"

"Humans are creatures of habit and they evolve little and too slowly. At this moment in our evolution, my people are far more spiritually and technologically evolved than humans. Inviting this diversity cannot be productive for my people, nor for human entities. If we allow humans to come here, they will soon ask my people to accommodate their human needs and beliefs. This would not be sustainable for us and cannot be allowed. My people are in charge of protecting this land, and the peace long established in this place cannot be preserved if we allow intolerant and entitled people to enter. My people have been here for eons, before even humans came to this Earth. At this point in time, my people say no to human incursion."

"Human incursion? We are only here to explore Inner Earth. We mean no harm to you or anyone else. Our Expedition is supposed to leave soon."

"You mean well. You know that you are a temporary visitor to Inner Earth. Once your Exploration is over, you will go back home. But some people in your group have another purpose. They want to change this place permanently to accommodate their needs and system of beliefs. Most of your people, including some of your leaders, are not aware of that. This makes bad people more powerful and good people more in danger."

Erin was puzzled by what she was hearing. "If you don't want us here, why did you save me? You could have let me die."

Agor had no intention of being manipulated by Erin. "I don't like to repeat myself. But humans listen not, so I will say it once again. I saved you and your friend. Your spirit wanted to live and expand. Your friend is still in fear of losing his life. At this moment your friend is back at the village with your people. If you respect our land, you alone will be allowed to visit and expand here. My people and I respect your innocence and free will but only if you honor our sovereignity and our place."

"I still don't understand. You just told me that humans are not welcomed here and now you are telling me that I have an opportunity to grow if I stay here." The more Erin reflected upon the words, the more her head was spinning, producing further questions rather than answers.

"You have free will. You can stay here or you can go back to your people. If you decide to go back, you need to tell your leaders to leave because humans are not welcomed here at this time."

It was hard for Erin to follow Agor's train of thought. Mixed with relief knowing that Roger was back in Taras, a rising, emotional intensity was creating an inner turmoil hard to restrain. The desire to shout grew stronger in Erin. She managed, however, to stay calm and subdue the impulse in order to show Agor that humans did have the ability to be decent people.

Suddenly Erin felt fragile and irrelevant and turned on her feet and walked away. For some reason she felt robbed in her soul — shattered, really. Was it because she was given sudden insight into the real purpose behind the Expedition? Her heart was beating with good intent but her mind was being starved for a reason to endure. Should she try to go back, or continue forward into the unknown? Then losing her self-control, she burst into hysterical sobs and fell on her knees, covering her face with both hands. The pain that flowed through her was palpable, and she didn't struggle to keep her tears silent.

Agor felt compassion because he knew she was being genuine and had been under intense strain. He looked at her with kindness in his eyes, then jabbed his finger into Erin's forehead. Whispering a few words in an incomprehensible language, he waited until she composed herself again. Shortly the sobbing stopped and Erin cleaned her face, with hair now mingled in tears and dirt.

"This isn't fair," she said, still perturbed.

"Maybe this doesn't seem fair to you, but humans have been given a choice. It would be easier for you to think that great things are done by great people. Humans make this mistake, always. It would be safer for your spirit to think in terms of preservation. But I am here to tell you something different.

"Great humans are mediocre people before becoming great. They can be boring, arrogant, dull. Not perfect. Not perfect at all! Masterful humans are common people in the beginning. Change starts with a dream. Don't be fooled into thinking that those who are younger, older, smarter, stronger, richer, can do things better than you. Don't compare yourself to others, and don't think you might be less than other people. The human mind, when faced with responsibilities, searches for easy ways out. It happens all the time. But I repeat myself: Great entities are common people just like you, often isolated, hated, excluded. The strength to rise comes from within. A noble purpose is all that it takes. An ordinary human does something extraordinary and all others will benefit from it. This is how common entities become great people. You can live your life like a mediocre human being or you can decide to become a great individual, a true leader. The choice belongs to you."

Erin felt a little uncomfortable but Agor's warm smile removed every residue of embarrassment.

"Know that you have free will. It is a God-given right. Know that you are loved, and hold the bigger picture. Many years ago we saved humans from self-destruction because we saw their potential and a better future for mankind. You ask why I saved you. I saved you because I saw your potential. Follow your inner voice. My people believed in humans a long time ago. Now it is time for humans to believe in themselves. Imagine what entities could do if they knew they were loved."

Erin looked at Agor with a curious expression, but she was shocked when she heard his next words.

"SunAlaka, I need to warn you of a potential danger to your life. Some vile individuals in your city are planning atrocious things, putting everyone in danger. If you go back now, your life will be in jeopardy. I saved you from the risk of peril. Contemplate my words, if you will."

"How do you know about SunAlaka? I have never told anyone except Alan." Erin lowered her head, trying to hide the fact that her eyes were again coated with a thin blanket of tears. The memory of her friend still brought pain, but she had no desire to explain the reason for her anguish.

Agor allowed a few moments of silence. Then he continued. "It is very dangerous if you go back now, SunAlaka. If you believe the truth of my words, you are welcomed to stay here. I will show you Inner Earth, and you will be safe. There is a reason that you are here now. One day I will tell you more, but right now your heart is still closed and your mind disturbed."

Crushed by the weight of her own dilemma, Erin was fighting an inner battle for truth. Once again she had to make a choice about something she knew nothing about. *"Do you believe?"* asked the shaman. A broader reality was beginning to unfold, but it was the pink light that appeared in front of her eyes and surrounded Agor that gave Erin the ultimate faith she needed to decide her destiny. With a few simple words she announced. "Show me this place. I want to know more."

CHAPTER 14: RULES OF ENGAGEMENT

Inner Earth was a boundless and magical place and it didn't take long for Erin to realize that simple fact. Even in her wildest dreams, she would never have imagined such magnitude or such artistry.

After Erin made the decision to stay, Agor guided her out of the forest. As they made their way through the woodland, it became noticeable that what had been timberland in the beginning was developing more into a tropical forest except, curiously, there had been no rainfall since her arrival. They walked together among the massive trees, moving safely through gigantic, carnivorous plants and even waded across several small — if small could be said — waterways.

At last, after what seemed to be hours of walking, they reached the edge of the forest.

The view was spectacular! Just in front of them was an immense, lush valley. Agor assured Erin that the breathtaking landscape was only a small part of the bountiful nature of Inner Earth. At the bottom of the canyon was a round-shaped lake surrounded by a few, scattered trees. To the right it was possible to see distant white peaks and on the left more fields with occassional blue spots. Those were lakes, Agor explained. Erin had the impression she had almost been born into a new world. It was so different compared to Taras, or the colorless Sandy Rings, and even the green, grassy Longview Fields. Here everything was abnormally bright and luminous. Erin was stunned by what was appearing in front of her eyes. Yet the most amazing sight still awaited her.

"You live in a beautiful place," she said to Agor, casting her eyes around to appreciate the breathtaking landscape.

He didn't respond but looked forward, gazing at something in the distance. Then indicating the farthest point on the horizon, he said, "My people live there, beyond the Rusty Mountains."

Erin squinted, searching for the Rusty Mountains but couldn't spot them. "I don't see them."

"They be far, far away," was Agor's short reply.

He again took the lead and started walking downhill toward the bottom of the valley. They followed a little trail, and all over the hillside she saw beautiful, colorful flowers. Some of them Erin had never seen before: giant pink bells with yellow stigma and blue anthers, white and red roses almost as big as a basketball, and never-ending, multicolored flower gardens. Erin stopped to pick an enchanting, blue blossom and placed it in her hair. She laughed, as it was so big that it served as a hat. For most of the way, they walked in silence. Agor didn't seem to touch the ground with his feet. To Erin, he appeared to be walking suspended in air, but that oddity was kept secret by the length of his cape.

Large butterflies flitted across the horizon and disappeared in the blue sky. A flock of white birds passed over Erin's head and landed on the shores of the lake. No time seemed to have passed when suddenly Erin realized they were already at the bottom of the hill. Looking back toward the forest, she saw the steep slope and was surprised it had taken so little time to arrive at the base of the valley. It was as if time had been frozen. Erin had the impression that all things in Inner Earth, including space and time, followed their own set of rules, independent from the effects of human observation. As that may be, one of the most evident aspects of Inner Earth was that everything was bigger — perhaps enormous would be a better way to describe it.

Although Agor never introduced Erin to his people, he spent a lot of time showing her the fascinating surroundings. Sometimes he would make his appearance by materializing in front of Erin or alarming her even more by showing up riding a giant eagle.

Giant eagles, as he explained to Erin on one occasion, were domesticated animals used by the people of Inner Earth for travel. They lived at the top of White Peaks, as the mountains were called, the same mountains Erin had spotted beyond the forest days before. Agor's personal eagle was named Pepecus. The first time Erin saw Pepecus, she almost succumbed in her fear of the majestic animal. It was at least twice as tall as herself, and Erin was not a short person. The width of its wings would have easily reached over twenty feet.

It took a lot of training for Erin to be able to mount Pepecus and feel comfortable riding the beast. Despite Agor's insistence, Erin never learned to ride an eagle by herself. She only agreed to short trips with Agor leading the raptor in front of her. She did, however, master quite well and rather quickly the skill to call an eagle. It was accomplished by emitting a loud sound with a guttural voice, which she had no problem mimicking, although hers was much different from Agor's soft command in his perplexing language. Despite her fear of flying on eagles, Erin was almost mesmerized by the beautiful view of the landscape that was afforded her while in the air. From above, everything seemed a little smaller, making Erin feel more acclimated. Most of the time her tiny size, compared to everything else, caused her to feel vulnerable.

On one occasion she asked Agor if everything was bigger or if her size had diminished after entering the forest. "The mind is like water. It seeks its own level. The body follows the mind," was the only answer he provided, which became just another riddle to Erin.

During her time with Agor, Erin learned how to procure nourishing food, mostly from edible vegetation. Occasionally she would hunt giant ants, which were the smallest creatures among Inner Earth's fauna, even though they could easily reach the dimension of an adult squirrel.

"Remember to thank nature for its life force before you kill an animal or eat a plant. All food is a gift from nature," was Agor's only remark on food.

139

It still wasn't clear to Erin why Agor would be so ambitious in showing her the territory of Inner Earth, while at the same time telling her that humans were not welcomed there, but she was certainly enjoying the experience and the time she was gifted. "I will show you the animals that live here," he said one day, and without further discussion led her on a long ride soaring over prairie, lakes, and valleys in that magical place called Inner Earth.

"Look over there," Agor pointed down to some giant beavers lingering near the Mystic River. "Those are ancient, giant beavers, extinct in your world but still alive in ours. They look small from up here, but they can be very tall, over eight feet in human measurement." Erin didn't have time to comment because Pepecus veered abruptly, causing her to almost lose her balance. She reminded herself to stay focused and tightened her clasp around Agor's waist. Not too far from the giant beavers were groups of prehistoric lizards dozing in the lazy day. The primordial armadillo was a very solitary animal, often hiding in the bushes around the lake. It wasn't easy to spot, but when she saw it, Erin felt a sort of camaraderie with the strange animal because of its singular behavior. Not to say that Erin loved being by herself as much as the ancient critter, but she was, in fact, also venturing alone in that alien territory.

"What's his name?" she asked Agor, indicating the giant armadillo.

"Glyptodon. He is a nice creature but does not like company." On the other side of the Mystic River, there were mostly woolly mammoths and prehistoric elephants, beautiful and big, with long tusks and massive trunks.

There were pastures, mountains, forests, and lakes inhabited with prehistoric animals, considered extinct by current, human science. With the exception of dinosaurs, most still lived in Inner Earth. Many of the ancient creatures belonged to the Ice Age, but others did not. What was even more surprising was that they all lived in complete harmony with each other. There were predators, of course, even though most of them followed a vegetarian diet.

One day Agor took Erin to the shores of the lake and did something curious. He said he needed to talk. They were standing under a giant oak and Erin started to feel a little stressed.

"I have to leave to take care of things with my people. You will be alone for a while. But before I go, I want to warn you of dangers you don't know."

Erin's eyes shifted to the side, trying to hide her sudden concern. Behind her straight face was disappointment and more than a little surprise.

Agor continued. "Keep your mind alert and your spirit calm and you will be fine. There are things you don't understand that can cause you harm. Once you familiarize yourself with this new information, it will no longer be unsafe for you to remain here. Many entities live in Inner Earth and not all are friendly, not because they are bad but because it is their nature to be that way. You need to learn how to know them. Remember, you are a guest here. It is your responsibility to conform to their environment. This is their territory. This is their home. Do not expect them to change for you. If you follow my advice, you will be fine."

Despite nothing in her face betraying fear, Erin knew that the tide had turned. She tried to say something, but words were simply not escaping her mouth. So she waited for Agor to continue, and he did.

"There are animals you need to stay away from. They are predators and can kill you. Observe but don't engage. They look like big dogs and cats. They are very tall with large teeth, and you have no training to face them — not yet, not now. There are also big lizards and giant snakes. My advice is that you stay away from them because they eat human flesh."

This unexpected news was the worst, Erin thought to herself. Being with Agor was like resting on a couch in front of a fire, while outside the storm was raging. She could handle the frightening truth while with him, but then? Erin started to doubt she had made the right choice by staying in Inner Earth, but he didn't allow her to linger over those doubts.

"I want to show you where they live, so you can be prepared. Do you have a map?"

Again caught by surprise, and without reply, Erin took out the map she had received from Alan. With another large dose of amazement, Erin realized that the map was now showing many more details clearly and perfectly. She held it reverently in her hands for a few moments, appreciating the value of that precious gift. Then with pride, she handed the parchment to Agor.

"You will need this," were his first words. Then using the tip of his left finger, he started to write something on the side of the paper. From where she was standing, that's all Erin could see, but it was enough to dissipate the fear and cause her heart to slow to its regular beat.

Before giving back the map, Agor folded it, using extreme care, and then holding it with both hands returned it to Erin. "You can study that later. For now, there are a few more things I need to tell you. I think we need to sit down."

Wordless, her mind again blank, Erin stared at him with concern and a little curiosity. In the end, she did as asked and took a seat near Agor. The lake was as flat as a mirror, not even a ripple, and from the surrounding trees came no sound, no movement of branches, and no birds were singing. The sky was reflected in the blue water. Agor seemed to enjoy the view as much as Erin because for what seemed a long time, he didn't say anything. A sensation of eternity pervaded Erin as if the moment had always been written in her book of life and was a part of her destiny.

"Entities have asked me about you. They are curious. I said you will meet them. Before you encounter them, I need to warn you. They don't look like humans, and they are much different from me. They are — how do you say this in your language — original."

Erin was taking shallow breaths, careful not to make a sound, but her curiosity was elevated. Strangely, she now felt a pure sense of peace.

"I have always liked genuine things," she replied with nonchalance, trying to appear as level-headed as possible.

"They wouldn't be happy if you call them things. They are entities," corrected Agor. "When I go back to my people, I will see what I can do for you to meet them. They are very curious because they have never seen a human person before. The majority are very old entities, and if you are wise, you can learn a lot just by listening."

"How old?" Erin asked

"Very old; they never die. They are the guardians of Inner Earth because they know everything about this place, although they have never been outside of here. I am much younger but, unlike them, have traveled to other places."

"How old are you, Agor?"

"We don't count years, but to answer your question I would be 417 in the human counting of time."

"417?" Erin was once again shocked. "You look like 30!"

"Time follows different laws here. My people are very old. One day, if you choose, you can become like my people. Dedication, effort, and patience will take you to your destination."

An inclination toward wonder began to burst into Erin's mind, as she turned her stare away from Agor.

He resumed. "In your world, young people want speed and old people want to slow things down. Humans rarely live in the present moment. This is sad because in human time, life is very short. If you learn to master time, every minute spent in Inner Earth will be given back to you later."

Erin gave Agor a long, innocent gaze.

After a thoughtful pause, he then continued. "You need to learn to trust yourself if you want to meet the spirits of the forest. It will be your choice to engage them because they are happy to just observe you. When in the forest, pay attention to movements, changes of light, sounds. It is very important that you listen to your intuition because it will tell you and prepare you for what is ahead. Human intuition lives in the future. Doubt and fear live in the past. Understand you what I say?"

Any appearance of confusion had vanished from Erin's face, and it was then that for the first time she thought of Agor as a creature of her own kind. "Yes," said Erin.

"Your intuition will be challenged, your trust tested," continued Agor. And without even conceding a glance, he said, "Do not despair. This remains a friendly place if you watch it with pure eyes. What you learn here will stay with you forever. Do not succumb to misery."

Erin's eyes were fixed upon the horizon, and her face, despite wearing a tired look, was serene and composed.

He continued. "The spirits of the forest are not the only creatures you will encounter. There are also the entities of the water, called mermaids in your tongue but here are known as nymphs." Agor stopped for a moment, giving Erin the chance to say something but she was still musing over his last words, so he went on. "Nymphs live close to the water. They are unable to speak but have the ability to read the past and the future of every living thing. If you learn how to communicate with them, they might be willing to help you."

"How do I learn to communicate with them?"

"This is for you to find out. My people have the ability to talk telepathically, but humans have not yet developed that skill. You have more than you know. The second part of your journey starts now. Remember, I saved you for a reason. There are no coincidences."

His words reminded Erin of the shaman's predictions, so her next question surged spontaneously. "Are there humming-birds here?"

Agor smiled before replying. "SunAlaka, learn to reconcile. Hold the bigger picture. How big is a small bird in a gigantic world? Why were you given the name SunAlaka?"

"It was because ..." Erin seemed to stumble on her words. "I was told that small is big and big is small."

"Sometimes, yes. Sometimes that can be true," Agor interrupted Erin, correcting her once again.

"I have been told that in order to survive this journey, I need to be like a hummingbird. I was just hoping you could help me sort things out."

"You have more than you know. Hold the bigger picture."

Agor repeated those words slowly and intentionally, as if they held a key to the answer. Erin, however, did not feel rescued from her confusion.

"You did not answer my question. Are there hummingbirds in Inner Earth or not?"

"Even if there were, your eyes would not be able to recognize them."

"Why? What? You are wrong. I would be able to recognize them."

Agor smiled again and looked at Erin with a fatherly expression. "No, you wouldn't. You cannot put new wine in an old bottle. Change your way of perceiving things and you will see them."

"That's not helpful." One of the best conversations Erin had ever had with Agor just a few minutes before was now starting to distress her.

"Questions are good for the spirit, but it is never a good idea to rush the answer. Time and patience will tell you everything if you are wise. I told you all you need now to continue your journey and be safe. Do you understand, SunAlaka?"

"My name is Erin, not SunAlaka." A defiant attitude was taking hold of the delicate peace of mind she had just experienced. It wasn't unusual for Erin to change her mood when things didn't go her way, but this time she caught herself in the process of this change in her demeanor. She didn't like what was being revealed about her character, as she perceived it as a tremendous sign of weakness. Erin had never thought of herself in this way. Biting her lower lip, she made an inward attempt at resolve, but her pride was a large impediment to the idea of becoming humble. It was as if there were two parts to her: one was pulled by gravity toward a previous mind-set and old patterns of behavior and the other was simply watching. She felt separate from her own identity. The consensus that had kept her together all these years was crumbling in front of her eyes. What was happening?

Reality was falling apart. A sense of detachment, accompanied by an intense desire to revert to a previous, familiar, known way of being, was dueled by the urgency to replace the old with the new. Was Erin becoming aware of her first step to evolving as SunAlaka? Was it possible that the hummingbird was simply a mental concept that had to be born inside of her? "Questions are good for the spirit," Agor said. In the birth pangs of the moment, Erin had to admit that he was right.

"I don't like the idea of you leaving. I don't think I'm ready to remain here by myself. What if your people find me and kill me? How can I protect myself?"

Agor was looking at the horizon and appeared unusually distant. After several minutes of stillness, he finally broke the silence. "My people know that you are here. They have no intention to harm you. You are the only one who can harm yourself, if you choose to. You have the power of free will, and now you have more knowledge. That gives you choices."

"I don't understand. Why are you telling me that your people have no intention to hurt me and at the same time you say my life could be in danger?"

"My people don't want humans here because humans are creatures of habit. They change little and very slowly. Most of the time they change not. You have been given a choice between proving your strength in the unknown or returning to old habits. One path leads to life; the other one leads to death. Small choices create destiny. Choosing your destiny is a big thing but it is made by small decisions. What you select for yourself now will determine your future. There is no end to the journey. You have free will."

"Small things make perfection, but perfection is not a small thing." Erin was finally starting to catch up with Agor's line of thought.

"Wise contemplation, my friend. I have hope for you."

A few more pleasant days went by after the heady conversation at the shores of the lake. Before leaving, Agor had decided to spend a little more time with Erin, helping her develop the confidence she would need to confront the next and most important chapter in her life. Agor was aware of Erin's fragility. The vulnerability of a human being, coupled with innocence and good intent, was something he believed did not deserve to be punished.

It wasn't hard for Erin to adapt to the new environment. Nature here was beautiful and, most delightful of all, there was a harmony that was hard to describe. Everything was at peace, and only after such a short while being in this place, Erin was already feeling the effects of that unanimity on her state of mind. She was no longer angry, no longer worried, and no longer in fear. The tranquillity gave her the certitude that everything would be fine.

One time Erin asked Agor why Inner Earth was filled with prehistoric animals, and his reply was quite amusing. "Before these animals became extinct in your world, we decided to bring them here. They were given an opportunity to continue their evolution because living inside a planet is always safer than being on the exterior."

Needless to say, the explanation left Erin more baffled than clear, but at least she was getting used to her new friend's unusual communications. It reminded her of a favorite teaching method used by Buddhist masters during the twelfth and thirteenth centuries called a koan.

Erin was very passionate about Oriental culture and had been given the opportunity to study some of its spiritual teachings during one of her trips to India. Koans were riddles that required students to change their thinking paradigms in order to provide the solution to the puzzle. By applying a new logic to a known problem, the students were given the opportunity to challenge their old thinking patterns. Because of this background, it wasn't hard for Erin to understand that she needed to develop an open mind in order to see things on her own.

Once again Agor seemed to have read her mind when he made a comment that gave the impression he was following her train of thought. "You are learning fast. New wine cannot be put in old bottles. If you become clear, your intuition will be a strong voice and that will change your vision. When you change your vision, you understand how many things humans have missed throughout history. Humans have been lied to about everything. Nothing you know is true. Humans have lived inside an artificial world created by entities with low energy and selfish intent. When humans wake up as a collective, they will be able to see the truth beyond the lies, the light beyond the shadows. Critical thinking is the greatest threat to tyranny. People who think for themselves cannot be controlled. The process of human awakening has already started and cannot be stopped. We are here to assist in that transition."

"Transition? Transition to what?" Erin wondered.

"To a new era, when humans will remember their origins and will finally be able to express their divinity."

Eventually the morning of Agor's departure arrived. He made his last appearance riding Pepecus, but this time something was quite different. Both the eagle and Agor were dressed for battle, wearing leather armor and a shiny helmet with a long, golden feather on top. Something about that image scared Erin but, despite her newly acquired confidence, she did not venture to ask.

"The day has arrived," she lowered her head trying to hide her emotions but was immediately released from her burden by an attentive Agor.

"You will be fine, SunAlaka. Remember what I said. Remember the bigger picture. I will be with you in your dreams, in your thoughts. Learn to trust your intuition. It will guide you."

"I am scared, Agor. I don't want you to go. I don't think I'm ready for this."

"SunAlaka, you have more than you know."

"I wish I didn't have to go through this."

"At a certain point in life, you must ask yourself what are you willing to die for."

"I don't want to die. That was not the deal. I didn't stay here to die. I DON'T WANT TO DIE!" Erin shouted.

"You will not die but you will find the meaning of life in what is most important to you. I must ask you again: What are you willing to die for, SunAlaka? If you answer this question, you will know why you live."

"I am not willing to die! For anyone! For nothing!"

"Then ask yourself what are you willing to lose everything for? You made that choice when you accepted the spot in the Expedition. SunAlaka, are you aware? Ask yourself what are you willing to lose everything for? You must find the answer inside yourself in order to keep going."

Agor's last words struck Erin like lightning out of the blue. Oddly enough, she had never thought deeply of her commitment in that way. But now Agor was pointing out her courage in making that choice and challenging her with a question she had never asked herself: Why had she been willing to risk everything? What for?

Questions are good for the soul.

You have more than you know.

Hold the bigger picture.

Learn to reconcile.

"This will take a while," murmured Erin, hoping not to be heard.

"I have a gift for you, my friend." Agor searched in his pockets and pulled out a leather necklace with a green stone.

"Oh, this is beautiful, Agor. Thank you." Erin was surprised, nevertheless.

The stone was emitting a soft, green light while Agor held it in his hands.

"This stone will glow when you are safe. It will become deep emerald when you are in danger."

Erin was sincerely moved by the precious gift, despite an unsettling alertness. "What do I do when it stops glowing?"

"I taught you how to survive. Use the skills you have learned and don't let your guard down. The gem will tell you when you need to change something. Sometimes small changes can make a big difference."

"A change of direction ..."

"A change of direction will take you to a different destination."

Pepecus ambled slowly toward them. Agor placed his hand on the shoulder of the huge creature, and before departing asserted, "You are not alone, SunAlaka. We shall meet again!" And without further comment or looking back, he mounted the eagle and flew away.

Erin watched her friend become nothing more than a tiny dot in the sky, then disappear before her eyes. Holding the stone tightly in her hand, she closed her eyes and, more than making a wish, she recited a prayer asking for guidance and protection. Her sincerity was expressed by her tears. The answer to her invocation was the brightness of the stone glowing in her hand.

She was not alone.

Someone out there was aware of her presence.

Someone was listening.

POSTSCRIPT: ANIMALS OF INNER EARTH
(as imprinted by Agor on the map)

- Eight-foot-tall giant beaver, otherwise known as Castoroides. First appearance during the Ice Age, lives near the five lakes (Lake Marmud, Lake Tumira, Lake Temer, Lake Bolesco, Lake Pracon) and the river (Mystic River). Feeds on grass; not dangerous.
- The woolly rhinoceros, also known as Coelodonta, with thick fur and two large horns on its nose. Inhabits the right side of the river (Mystic River). Feeds on plants and grass; not dangerous.
- The giant armadillo, named Glyptodon, about eleven feet long. Solitary animal, found in the forest and in proximity of lakes. Not dangerous; feeds on plants and giant ants.
- Large carnivorous mammals, such as the Hyaenodons, with a long skull and doglike body. Carnivore. Used in war to attack animals. They live outside of the forest and around lakes. Do not approach.
- The ancestor of the elephant, the mastodon, and the mammoths, with long tusks and trunk. The mastodon does not have hair, while the mammoth has long hair. They both feed on plants and grass; not dangerous.
- The prehistoric lizard called Megalania. Big as a crocodile, eats meat, used for war by people in Inner Earth. Do not approach. Found close to the river (Mystic River), especially on its left bank.
- The prehistoric kangaroo and marsupials. Their diet consists of meat or plants (eaten by giant lizards). Do not approach.
- Several prehistoric catlike animals with extended canine teeth. Normally used for combat, they eat meat. Do not approach.
- The woolly mammoth, a prehistoric member of the elephant family. Friendly animal but approach with caution.

- Large snakes, like Titanoboa, over forty-three feet long. They live in the river (Mystic River) and on its shores. Do not approach. They eat meat.
- Ancient Thunderbirds; very similar to giant eagles but only found deep inside Inner Earth. Hardly approachable, their only duty is to protect the city of Aldora from intruders.

CHAPTER 15: SECOND CHANCES

Clyde woke up, but without comfort. The pain was deep and warm in his head and not at all pleasant. The place was pitch-black, but soon he realized his eyes were covered with blinders. All of his body was hurting. He had always suffered from genetic afflictions, but this was different. Conscious enough to recognize that something had happened to him but not yet sufficiently perceptive to understand how, Clyde tried to recall what led to such a state. His last memory was of working on a report in the lab and then leaving with the SOTIS team. Apparently, nothing out of the ordinary. Fear set in, and his efforts to scream resulted only in a dull sound. "Help … help … please help."

But it was only his mind being loud. Attempting to provide some relief to sore muscles, he started moving his legs from side to side. In that simple action, his foot hit what seemed to be a wall beside him. Hands bound, he used his extremities as a support until he was finally able to push himself up into a sitting position. That major task almost drained all the energy he had left but was at least sufficient to alleviate the blood circulation and mitigate some of the pain. It was then that he became aware of an intense thirst. Passing his tongue over his lips, he realized how dehydrated he was. Nothing made sense. The fear for his life caused his heartbeat to accelerate to a point where he again lost consciousness.

He woke in delirium a few hours later without any concept of time but feeling slightly stronger. Clyde knew he could not afford to faint again, so this time his main intent was to remain calm and move cautiously. His head was bombarded with strong pulsations, as if being hit by a hammer at intervals of two to three seconds. Oh, no! He was about to be sick. His body reacted to the thought before he could even elaborate on the meaning, and Clyde soon found himself on his side spewing. The smell was repulsive. No! He had to move away from it. Motivated, and with all the strength left in his skinny body, Clyde moved a few feet to the right. As his heart started to slow down again, he noticed a little thread of light coming from the corner of his blindfolds. If only he could remove them to see where he was …

Scraping his head up and down against the wall, Clyde tried to budge the blindfolds from his eyes just enough to see. It cost him a few scratches on the side of his face but at least now he had some vision, although his field of view was limited. He looked around, attempting to adjust his eyes to the soft light in the environment. The room was rectangular, empty, and dusty. There was a metal door on the opposite side from where he was sitting.

Dank and sinister, the place reminded Clyde of the wine cellar in his grandfather's basement. He used to hide there when he was asked to do something he didn't want to do. Clyde was never a confrontational person. His favorite tactic was to remove himself from the situation to avoid taking a stance. His father, a successful businessman, never liked that particular aspect of his son's personality and used to tell him, *"You need to have more piss and vinegar if you want to be respected in life,"* to which Clyde would respond with a quick nodding of his head just to end the conversation and then usually scuttled away. Oh, how much he wished he had listened to his beloved father!

After a few minutes of self-reflection, Clyde decided it was time to do something. But what? Besides the metal door, there were no other exits, and his ability to move was still critically limited. A brief check of his body assured him there were no serious wounds, but the blood on the floor revealed he had suffered some laceration. Despite that evidence and his weakened stomach, he felt his strength slowly returning, and that gave him a sense of control that he had rarely experienced. Being called *"the nerd guy"* can be flattering when in a protected environment but also a curse if used as an excuse to prevent physical fortification.

Clyde's self-indulging contemplation was swiftly interrupted by the sound of steps approaching from the other side of the metal door, causing him to refocus on the present. There were voices. Probably three or four people were outside talking. In the midst of their conversation, he could recognize a woman's reassuring voice. A smile brightened his injured face. The door suddenly slammed open and to his great relief the hospital nurse, Megan, followed by a much calmer Dr. Anderson, ran toward him.

"Oh, my God! What happened to you?" was the only thing that made sense to Clyde in the bustle of the moment. He didn't have any time to respond because he was immediately overwhelmed by a burst of IVs, lights in his eyes, and frantic questions like, "How many fingers do you see? What's your name? Which year are we in now?"

From his position, Clyde was able to see one of the SOTIS members calmly talking to Dr. Anderson, stationed just behind the nurse. His arm was bandaged but his face was still covered with bruises.

"Megan ..." Clyde felt he was about to collapse again. "Megan, I am happy ... I am happy to see you."

The nurse was performing the usual primary care without paying much attention to what seemed to be a raving patient. Nurse Megan took a syringe and while piercing Clyde's forearm she said quietly, "You will be fine, Mr. Clyde. Just close your eyes and count to ten."

Megan's face started to slowly vanish until all went black — once again.

Clyde woke up a few hours later at the citadel's hospital. "I'm still alive," was the only thing he could ponder, and a small spark of joy reinvigorated him. That little burst of energy was better than any drug, he thought. Not that Clyde was a regular consumer of narcotics, by any means.

It didn't take long before Megan entered the room to check on him. Her smile was the best thing Clyde had seen in a long time.

"Mr. Clyde, it looks like you are feeling better."

"Oh, yeah, I feel much better."

Megan walked closer to him and while checking his vitals she exclaimed, "You don't have to worry. There was nothing serious. Just a couple of bruises, and it looks like your wound is healing fast. We should be able to dismiss you tonight. Do you have any questions or concerns or is there anything I could give you to make you feel better?"

Oh, the angelic sound of that voice! The close vicinity of her face with its flawless, white skin, bright green eyes, and soft, curly, red hair was taking every ounce of breath from Clyde's lungs. "I could love you forever," he thought, and in the same instant she turned and caught his elated eyes.

"Mr. Clyde! Are you okay?" The nurse was calling him back to reality.

Feeling a deep sense of embarrassment, he cleared his voice before answering "Oh, yes, yes … yes … I feel great, actually! Thank you … Megan; right?" That was a silly question because he obviously knew her name.

"Yes, Megan," the nurse responded, pointing to her badge.

"I don't remember anything. Can you tell me what happened?"

Megan was now writing some data on the chart at the end of the bed and smiled with the same reassuring expression that he loved so much.

"That is perfectly normal. You will be able to remember more details as time goes by. It looks like you were leaving your office with some members of the SOTIS team when all of a sudden a change in the magnetic field caused you to lose consciousness and fall down the stairs. Another member of the SOTIS team suffered from some light injuries, while the other two agents remained unharmed."

Something was strange about the nurse's story. "I remember waking up in a room by myself with blinders on my eyes and both my arms and legs tied up. Do you know why?"

The nurse took a few steps toward the bed and while adjusting the blanket she softly responded, "It looks like the change in the electromagnetic field triggered an attack of seizures. You had to be temporarily restrained by the officers in order to prevent additional injuries to yourself or others."

That was odd. Clyde had never had seizures before. "Seizures?"

"Yes, it is not unusual that a change in the magnetic field causes hyperactivity in the temporal lobe, leading to seizures in susceptible people. It happens all the time, rest assured."

"Oh ... okay. I must be a vulnerable person then."

"I would say responsive. It's a better way to look at it."

Clyde noticed a light blush in Megan's cheeks. For some reason that made him happy. "How long before you guys came to my rescue?"

"Rescue? Ah ... not too long, probably less than twenty minutes. SOTIS was very efficient in coming here immediately and informing us of the accident. You'll be okay in a couple of hours, and if the doctor agrees, we will be able to send you on your way in a short while."

She walked toward the door and before leaving, turned one more time. "You can always call me if you need anything, but I suggest you take your time and rest."

The redness in her cheeks was still evident.

As soon as she left, the room felt empty. Clyde smiled softly. The air was sweet and there was no rush. His world had been cast anew and he was enjoying every moment of it. Was it the effect of the medicine or a ticket to ride his second chance? A carousel of thoughts started to play in Clyde's mind, demanding attention instead of allowing the body to rest. Eventually everything became nonsense and that was the time to let go. Clyde fell into a deep slumber.

A gentle pat on his shoulder woke him up. He had no idea how long he had slept, but it felt like ages. His body was still recovering from all the stress of the last turn of events, and his mind was heavy, almost gloomy. With an effort and a deep groan, Clyde reluctantly opened his eyes. It took a few moments before he was able to put into focus what was in front of him — or better, who was in front of him. The surprise was such that Clyde almost jumped out of bed.

"Mister Miller … Captain! Sir! Sir! Good morning, sir!" He almost choked on his own drool.

"Clyde, for God's sake. Son, please relax. You don't have to get all out of shape for me. I just heard the news and I came by to see how you are doing. I wanted to make sure you are receiving the best care. Are you, son?"

"Sir, yes, sir, very good care, sir." Megan's face reappeared on the screen of his mind and he couldn't hide a timid smile.

"It certainly looks like it." Mr. Miller was old enough to understand the conflict of emotion going on in that young heart. "Farewell, Clyde. I will be on my way then. I am very pleased to see that your recovery is fast and smooth. Better if you rest now, son."

"Yes, sir, and you are not disturbing me, sir. I'll be on my feet in a couple of hours and will go back to my office as soon as they allow me to."

"Well, well, well. Take your time, son. I want you on the job when your mind is clear; not sooner. Do you copy that?"

"Absolutely, sir!"

"Good."

Mr. Miller had a sort of paternal affection for Clyde because he reminded him of when he was young. He had high expectations from him for the same reason.

Before leaving, Miller gave Clyde the military salute, but as he was about to open the door, he paused. He turned around and walked toward the middle of the room and then stopped. He looked pensive. His hand was over his mouth and he glanced in midair. After a few seconds of what seemed to be a decision-making moment, he volunteered, "Not to put any rush on you, son, but Roger has returned. I will meet with him later today. As it appears right now, there is no news of Erin. I just wanted you to know."

"What? Roger has returned but not Erin? How is that even possible?" Clyde's eyes were wide open.

"Son, this is a question for me to answer and I am about to find out. But I will need you to check Roger's tracking device for possible signs of abuse or misuse. But, of course, not now. Not now. Please take your time to recover because when you go back to your office, you'll have your work cut out for you."

"Yes, sir, understood, sir."

This time the Captain left the room without turning around or saying anything else.

Clyde looked at the clock on the wall. It was 5:57 in the afternoon. It was then that he realized he had been sleeping for almost a full day. And with no clear memory of what had happened, he felt a strong desire to know. While sipping his tea, Clyde allowed himself to indulge in some brief reflection. The uncertainty surrounding the circumstances triggered a desire for reconciliation, a heartfelt passion for meaning. "Later," he thought, as he again slid into a more comfortable position and allowed himself to drift back to sleep.

In the meantime, Captain Miller was already striding along the narrow streets of Taras. There were no people, which was rather unusual. The meeting with Roger was scheduled at the Inner Grounds Café. The assumption was that a slice of pie and a hot chocolate were always a good incentive, especially in stressful situations.

As usual, the cafeteria was overpowered with the strong aroma of coffee, even that late in the day, something that reminded Miller of winter Sunday mornings and home. Miller picked the most discrete table and unzipped his jacket. Roger came in right after. He looked overwhelmed by a profound sadness. Fatigue was engraved on his worn face. The two men stood for a few moments looking at each other without saying a word, Roger waiting for a command and Captain Miller hoping for a formal salute. In the end, it was the Captain who took control of the situation.

"Please sit down, Roger. I assume that you have a lot to tell me."

"Yes, sir, I do." Roger covered his face with both hands, trying to disguise his internal anguish.

The waitress arrived immediately to take the order. She knew that Captain Miller was usually in a hurry and she loved to be tipped well, something that he would gladly do but only if he was pleased with the service.

"What happened?" Miller asked, skipping all the formal introductions.

Roger felt uneasy in his chair, but more than anything he was just sad. "Should I start from the beginning?"

"Please," which sounded more like an order than a request.

"After Matt left, Erin and I decided to move forward. We both felt strong, supplies were abundant, and we didn't think there was a good reason to abort the Expedition. We knew the risk we were taking but also the importance of the mission. With our time here in Inner Earth running short, we made the decision to take the chance and keep going. But after a few hours of riding our four-wheeler, the engine stopped. I'm not a mechanic, but my basic knowledge suggested that I check the tank for fuel and the oil levels. They both seemed to be okay. I have no idea why the motor stopped running. At that point we had to make another choice: turn around or keep going. Once again we both decided to continue, but just for a few hours."

Captain Miller gave Roger a look of admonition. "This is what they call the gold fever. 'More gold has been mined from the thoughts of men than has been taken from the earth,' a quote from Napoleon Hill that says it all. While I truly appreciate your hard work and dedication to this Expedition, I have to reprimand you for the lack of awareness and strategy. Especially you! Erin is just a civilian, nothing more than an intern, for heaven's sake!"

Miller paused for a second, shaking his head as a sign of his disappointment. "Please continue," he said.

Roger was starting to feel the awkwardness of the situation. What just a few minutes ago seemed to be heroic now assumed the colors of a futile action. "Everything around us pointed to the fact that the habitat was conducive for more species of life, and we wanted to prove our theory." But his attempts to recover from the embarrassment of the situation fell short.

The Captain was a hard man to impress. "Roger, this is not a place to test new theories without the support of a team."

"I know that, sir. But our level of optimism was high, and our sense of adventure nullified prudence."

"You both clearly overlooked the risks involved. People are supposed to have survival instincts, for God's sake!" This time Miller raised his voice but immediately recomposed himself after realizing that a public place was not the optimal setting for such a display of emotion. He looked at Roger, searching for a spark of rationality while crossing his fingers to restrain his frustration.

Mortified, Roger continued. "Sir, there is more ..." His face looked traumatized.

"Please, go ahead."

"After a few hours of useless effort, we decided it was time to return to base camp. However, all the landmarks we left behind us were gone. All of them!"

"What do you mean 'they were gone'?"

"Gone! Our compass stopped working and we had no way to find our way back. We wandered for an undefined amount of time and I have no idea if we moved forward, backward, or in circles. All that I can say is that after what seemed to be days and not hours, our reserves were near finished and so was our energy."

Roger took a deep breath and a long pause. He was humiliated, frozen to the spot, but eventually he continued. "Erin became weaker and weaker. We both felt exhausted and collapsed. I don't know how long we were in that state, but when

I woke up I felt much stronger, almost as if my energy had been somehow replenished during my sleep. All my wounds were healed. But the most surprising thing of all is that I found myself just outside of Taras."

The Captain couldn't believe what he was hearing. His manner became subdued.

"And how did you get there?"

"I can't explain it, sir. I looked around and there was no sign of Erin. She had just disappeared."

"What do you mean disappeared?"

"I mean … she was not with me. The whole situation is unorthodox, sir, and I have no way to explain what happened from the engine stopping, to losing the markers, to waking up near Taras, to the disappearance of Erin. I have no idea how this is even possible."

Despite a strong physique and powerful presence, in that moment Roger looked more like an empty shell, almost a shadow. Captain Miller decided to show compassion. Somehow life had chosen to keep Roger alive, and Miller ruled to honor the unpredictable mystery of life.

"This must be the day for second chances," he thought, while allowing a faint smile to emerge on his drained face.

"Roger, you are lucky to be alive."

A few tears drifted from Roger's eyes. "Yes, I know, Captain."

"Having said that, our next goal is to find Erin. What do you think happened to her? Did she lose her mind and run away? I can't find a logical explanation. Anyhow, having you here will make things much easier. There are only a few weeks left of this Expedition, and we need to accelerate our extraction procedure. We need to come up with a good plan to find and rescue our missing member, Erin. We cannot afford any more causalities."

"What if …"

"We don't succeed?" Captain Miller interrupted Roger.

"Then we will fail. But I don't like to think of it this way. We will do everything in our power to ensure a favorable outcome to this Expedition. And, by the way, there is no time to waste."

Miller called the waitress with a gesture of his hand, and without asking for a bill handed over a generous amount of money before zipping his jacket and striding toward the door. Roger followed him like a dog that had just found his master after being lost, his depth of gratitude compounded by his sorrow for Erin. In that moment he realized how much he missed her.

Once outside, Captain Miller addressed Roger one more time. "Roger, I'm going to Clyde's office. I was wondering if you would like to come along."

"Absolutely, sir. I'd be happy to."

And without more talking, the two men headed toward the tower. As they arrived outside Clyde's office, they found the door ajar and the lights turned off. This was not the way the Captain remembered leaving that place. However, nothing inside the office seemed out of the ordinary: All the computers were off, a pile of documents was placed on top of the desk, and some crumpled papers were left just outside the trash bin. Captain Miller looked for the note he had slipped under the door but couldn't find it. "Someone has been here," he whispered.

"Excuse me?" Roger asked, without lifting his eyes from some handwritten notes he was trying to decipher.

"The last time I was here, the door was locked and the light inside was on. I left a note under the door for Clyde, but now I can't find it. I can only assume one possible conclusion: Someone has been here."

"Probably Clyde."

"No, it is very unlikely. When I left the hospital, he was still very weak. I doubt he would have had the strength to walk over here just to shut the lights off."

"So what are you saying?"

"I DON'T KNOW." Captain Miller emphasized each word impatiently. "But I will find out. Actually, since you are here,

YOU are going to find out. I am aware of your past investigative experience. As of now, this is your new assignment."

"My new assignment? Sir, I have plenty to do in the laboratory! Also, I'm a scientist. I don't think I would be the right person for this task."

"I suppose you're right, why would you be? I will ask Clyde to find out. Instead, I need your help with planning the rescue mission. We need to locate and extract our civilian, Erin."

Captain Miller took another look at the room searching for any kind of clue, but there was nothing suspicious, only the sloppy, half-organized clutter of Clyde.

Less than half an hour later, Miller, Parker (the surveyor), Roger, Matt, and the SOTIS team were gathered in the Captain's office to discuss a rescue strategy.

The Captain initiated the meeting. "By now you must all be aware of the urgency of the situation: One of our members, Erin, is missing. According to Roger, she went missing after they both collapsed during the last excursion. Both Roger and Erin are members of team Delta, which seems to have incurred the most amount of trouble. Currently two other members of team Delta, Steve and Rachel, are still under medical observation. Do you have an update about Steve's condition, Matt?"

"Yes, sir. Steve is doing much better. It looks like what caused his fainting was a deficiency in vitamin D. He will be kept under observation for a few more days and then released. The doctor, however, recommends that he should not be taking part in any further explorations.

"As for Rachel, her situation is much different. Dr. Anderson has mentioned that she is showing symptoms of an intestinal disorder, similar to poisoning, but there are also signs of an acute respiratory viral infection. For now, the medical staff doesn't want to take any risks in determining what's wrong. Unfortunately, Rachel is still hospitalized. At this point team Delta is three members short, Captain."

"Thank you, Matt. I am not planning any additional excursions after this one. Our last mission will be to find and rescue Erin. Once this task is completed, our entire Expedition will get ready to exit Inner Earth and return home."

An audible sigh of relief pervaded the room, but nobody dared say anything. A missing member was an obvious sign that their job was not over.

"Agent TJ, what is the situation with the drones?" Captain Miller was now calling on Tom Jyrone, a member of SOTIS and expert in operations management.

"Not good, sir. Our experimental drones don't have the battery necessary to fly for more than sixty minutes, sir. The recharging process is still very slow, due to the different magnetic field."

"What do you recommend?"

"I recommend we leave the drones, sir. Their use is limited, and they could become a liability if we take them with us."

"More good news!" said Captain Miller, with a sarcastic smile on his face. "At this point we have only our resources to rely on."

TJ nodded in a sign of consent. "If I may, sir, that would be the best tactic to use overall."

But Captain Miller wasn't impressed with the lack of equipment. To him, it felt like an undertaking had been fractured. It was, however, his duty as the most authoritative person on the Expedition to find an alternative.

"That's the best we can do, I suppose. How many four-wheelers do we have at our disposal, Matt?"

"Four fully functional machines, sir. Two more currently under maintenance could be made available. The rest are in repair."

"Four's good enough. I'd suggest taking all of them. That would leave the rest of us here in Taras with two four-wheelers. These days, one never knows …"

A contained laughter followed his jest. It was the release of weeks of anxiety but also the sign of adaptation to a profoundly unpredictable environment. Captain Miller continued. "Roger, do you think you will be able to lead the team to the last known location before you and Erin lost consciousness?"

"I'm not certain I can, sir, but will do my very best."

"That's good enough. Could you elaborate some details, please?"

"Certainly, sir. It would take us at least a full day to reach the top of Sandy Rings and the beginning of Longview Fields. At that point the environment changes drastically."

"Can you be more specific?"

"Well, the main challenge in the prairie is the lack of reference points. In addition to that, the grass is extremely tall and it's hard to see what's ahead. Without a good compass it is impossible to know which direction to follow."

"I suppose you are all equipped with an 8-point cardinal compass. However, the main issue is a different one. We don't know Erin's location. Her tracking device has been somehow deactivated."

A murmur swept through the room.

"Agent Kelly, agent Jordan, do you think we'll be able to find Erin regardless?"

Agent Kelly responded, "Sir, in the absence of the tracking device, the chances of extraction are reduced to less than 15%. I'm sorry, sir. At this point I would argue about the efficiency of this mission."

"What exactly is your point, agent Kelly?"

"Sir, I'm not sure it would be worth risking the life of six other people to find one person when we have no idea where she is. The territory in Inner Earth is for the most part unexplored, and the level of unpredictable, unknown events is very high, sir."

"I am aware of that, agent Kelly. But I cannot call this Expedition unless I know we did everything we could to find our lost member. I am responsible for each and every one of you."

Matt, who had the most experience in terms of expedition and survival tactics, took his turn to say something.

"If I may, sir, I suggest we make the attempt to rescue Erin. The chances of finding her might be slim but the risk that something happens to us is also low at this point. I believe it is well worth the effort, sir."

"Very well, then. I propose we vote. All in favor of the rescue mission, raise your hand."

Everyone except the three SOTIS members showed favor in the mission. The majority had agreed.

Captain Miller, not without a look of surprise crossing his face, decreed, "We will move forward with the extraction." Feeling the pressure that such an important decision was having on his team, he added, "I want to let you know that I am proud of all of you. Regardless of how this Expedition ends, we shall return home victorious."

The seven men in the room looked at each other with commitment as if an invisible thread connected them together.

"Gentlemen, this is our last mission. Make it count! I want you all assembled within the hour, fully equipped, and ready to depart Taras."

"Yes, sir!" was the unanimous response before everyone disbanded.

Captain Miller was the only one remaining. The solitary silence was the perfect time to pray.

Chapter 16: Tselby

The creature could not have been taller than two feet.

The brown color of its skin made it look like a sort of primate, but upon closer inspection it was quite different, much more like a miniature entity. Erin moved slightly, trying to gain a better view of the small being, and in doing so a branch snapped under her feet. The creature turned its head towards the origin of the sound and she could see its glowing, green eyes.

Holding her breath, Erin pulled the string of her bow and aimed — schhwaff! The arrow hit the bark of the tree behind it. "Dammit!" she exclaimed, but was instantly captivated by the fast movements of the entity. In less than a fraction of a second, the thing was standing on top of a tall tree. It was now looking down directly at Erin, who was not even trying to hide anymore. She reloaded the bow and aimed at the creature. But again it jumped to a nearby tree, defying all gravitational laws. It looked as if it were flying. Having nothing left to lose, Erin shouted, "Who are you?" but in return received only the disquieting silence of the forest.

Holding her loaded bow at her side, Erin took a few steps toward the tree where the creature was hiding, trying to be as quiet as possible. She looked up, searching for those green, sparkling eyes, but there was no sign of them. It appeared that the critter had vanished. Lowering her vigilance, Erin decided to retrieve the arrow from the trunk of the tree and was surprised to see how deep it went. A spark of self-congratulation uplifted her spirit. But just when she thought the hunt was over, the creature jumped down from its cache and started to run away. Erin quickly put the arrow in the quiver, the bow across her shoulders, and went on the chase. Its ability to leap across the giant roots of trees, over bushes, and through plants was almost inconceivable, but Erin didn't quit. It was only when her foot tripped on a large rock, causing her to fly through the air and then forcefully hit the ground, that she decided to surrender.

"Stooooooop!!" she yelled at the escaping critter with all the energy she still had remaining. But all that was left of its presence was the rustle of some moving branches. Defeated, Erin stood up and shook the dust from her clothes. Drops of sweat trickled down her face, pasting her hair to her cheeks. Still reeling from the exertion, Erin decided to move on, now without haste but nevertheless hoping for some better luck.

The forest seemed remarkably quiet, almost as if the trees and bushes were holding their breath. Erin, who had grown fairly accustomed to the new environment by now, found the unusual stillness strange and almost alarming. Although the green, glowing stone on her neck confirmed she was not in any danger, her sense of caution rose again. She felt as if she were being watched by thousands of eyes, and in her mind she could almost see them springing out from behind the giant trees and peering through the bushes.

All of a sudden a multitude of lights appeared in front of her, dancing, shifting, and swirling before her eyes and all around her. The lights were all white, most of them very small, with a few as large as a basketball. They seemed to have some sort of intelligence, because their movements were highly synchronized, resembling a school of fish. After a few minutes, the lights started to assume the shape of a tunnel, as if it were an invitation to follow. Erin, semi-entranced, pursued the path that was opening in front of her and entered the tunnel of lights. Everything else disappeared: the forest, the giant trees. Everything faded away. There were only Erin and the tunnel of lights.

As quickly as they appeared, the lights vanished, now transmuted into a sphere of multicolored shades. Erin found herself in the middle of a pulsating, vibrating, flashy orb. She looked around trying to make sense of what was happening when she saw a ray of green light emerge from the sphere and bond directly with the stone Agor had given her. After what seemed an eternity, the orb slowly dissolved until there was nothing but the darkness of the forest. Erin stood there, motionless.

What had just happened? Then a vibration, almost like a note, demanded her attention. It was coming from the branch of a tree. The green eyes were staring at her. The creature was back!

Something had changed because the old impulse to grab her bow was immediately dismissed and replaced with a desire to know the entity. From her favorable position, Erin was now able to take a good look at it. The skin of the being was brown and wrinkled, similar to bark, and from the top of the head were some antenna-like protrusions covered in what resembled green bubbles.

"Hello," Erin pronounced shyly, but the creature did not respond.

Embarrassed by her earlier attitude to hunt the entity, Erin searched for a means of eventual repair. The creature jumped down from the tree and took a few steps toward Erin. Trying to keep her breathing slow and quiet, in spite of her heart beating so fast it might burst, Erin recoiled.

The being took another step forward and this time Erin stalled in position. Reaching out toward her, the entity placed its hand on Erin's abdomen and what seemed like a grin appeared on its face.

"Human, beautiful," were the only words it pronounced.

Astonished, Erin limited her reaction to a hesitant smile. Words had left her. The strange entity emitted a guttural sound, sort of a congenial remark, then removed its hand from Erin's body and smiled. As it did that, Erin noticed its eyes light up. Somewhat confused, she remained silent and observant. Finally, the creature slowly moved a few steps back, giving Erin some space to loosen up.

At last Erin's voice came back with a few simple words. "Who are you?" was all she was capable of asking.

The entity seemed flattered by the question. "What an interesting query. I have never thought about that. Let me consider that for a moment."

It then placed a finger to its temple and started to emit a buzzing sound, while all of the antenna-looking hair began to vibrate, almost like the feelers on a cricket.

Baffled, after a minute or two, Erin continued. "Do you at least have a name?"

"I have many names, but today my name is Tselby. To answer your previous question, I would need more time."

"That's okay. I didn't mean to give you so much trouble. So today your name is Tselby. What about tomorrow?"

"Tomorrow is another day."

Erin nodded impatiently, then added, "Let's try this. How should I call you, in general?"

"Oh, you should have asked me! You can call me Tselby."

Erin didn't know if the creature was making fun of her or if it had some limited ability to comprehend. She sighed. "All right, then, I will call you Tselby."

"Oh, what a wonderful idea!" The entity smiled again and its eyes lit up.

Erin felt pranked. "Yuck. Okay, Tselby. My name is Erin, always Erin."

"I like your name, Always Erin."

Erin rolled her eyes backward, then replied, "Always is not my name. It means all the time. My name is only Erin."

The creature grinned before saying, "I am sorry about that, Only Erin. I thought you said Always. Please accept my sympathy."

"That's fine. Wait, sympathy for what?"

The entity looked surprised. "Oh ... For being always only Erin. It must be hard to handle."

Erin didn't know if she was exasperated or amused by the odd character, but in the end all she could do was burst into laughter. Her tension had finally been released. The being joined her cheerful outburst, and once again its eyes began to glow a phosphorescent green. That disturbing detail almost ended her amusement. "You know you look creepy; right?"

"Oh, thank you."

"Actually, it was not meant to be a compliment, but good for you that you took it that way."

"I have added the adjective 'creepy' to my list of personal attributes. I am happy when I can be more than what I thought of myself. Oh, the wonder of human eyes!"

"Tselby, you really are something else. Are you always this way?" By this time Erin had decided Tselby must be a guy.

"Am I always something else? That's another great question. Let me contemplate that for a moment," and in saying that, Tselby again placed a finger to his temple and started to emit the same buzzing sound while his hair began to vibrate.

"That's okay. Please forget what I just said," Erin interrupted Tselby.

Finally at ease, Erin adjusted her clothing, and in doing so the green stone emerged from under her shirt. Tselby's eyes started to glow as he looked at the necklace, and as he did so, the stone began to emit a fluorescent light. Tselby emitted a guttural sound while gazing at the stone, almost like a secret communication. "Human, you have been sent to me."

"What?"

"Human, you are the one I was waiting for."

"Why do you say that? What does it mean?"

"The stone is the key that unlocks the door to greater knowledge."

Erin was again confused, even more so than before. "This necklace was given to me by Agor. He told me it would help me stay on the safe path."

"Yes, and you are on a safe path. There is no danger here in Inner Earth except the ones you bring with you: your thoughts, your fears, your doubts. The stone reminds you to keep your focus on what matters. You found what you were looking for."

"And what would that be?"

Tselby stretched his neck, trying to appear taller, and with a solemn tone of voice replied, "Me."

Erin's enthusiasm and expectations plummeted as fast as a roller-coaster ride, but she was at least entertained that such a modest creature, smallest among the giants she had witnessed in Inner Earth, held so high a level of confidence and self-esteem. An amused smile illuminated her face before she asked, "Well, Tselby, why would you be the one I am looking for?"

Tselby's eyes started to glow again. Now Erin understood it was a sign of joy. Then he responded, "I am here to show you your next step."

"My next step?"

"Yes. This is part of the plan. You have been led here by us, one by one — first Alan, then Agor, and now me."

Erin was shocked by these words. Tears filled her eyes. The emotion was too intense to contain. "Alan? You know Alan?"

"Yes, Alan was part of the plan."

"Which plan are you talking about?"

"The answer to that question will be revealed drop by drop. Patience and curiosity lead to knowledge."

"Everything sounds weird to me."

"That's why you need patience. You have interest but need to develop fortitude."

"Tselby, may I ask you a question?"

"Questions are welcome."

"Are you one of those Agor called the guardians of Inner Earth?"

"That would be correct."

"Wow, so you never die?"

"That would also be correct." Tselby paused for a second, then seeing Erin's bewildered expression continued. "I was never born; therefore, I don't die. There are many of us, and we were all created from the resin of the trees many years ago, but we are not trees."

"So you are not the oldest creature here? Are the trees the oldest creatures here?"

"Trees are older than us, but we are the guardians of this place and the keepers of trees."

"WOW!" Erin was speechless. "This is all new to me. Agor told me I could meet you, but I never thought I would. Now that you are here, there are so many things I'd like to ask you."

"Questions are good. Time is good."

"What can you tell me about Alan? How did you know him if you have never been outside of Inner Earth? Or at least this is what Agor said ..."

"Agor is correct. I have never been outside of Inner Earth. My people and I are the guardians of Inner Earth. But that does not mean I don't know what is going on outside of here. As for Alan, he was not from this time. He came from the future. He was a time-traveler."

"I ... I ... don't understand." Erin was shaking her head, looking really confused. She paused for a moment, pondering what to say next. "Now that you mention it, I remember Alan telling me that he had nobody to go home to." Erin looked perplexed. "I thought time-traveling was a hoax."

"No, time-traveling is real. Your government has been using it for a long time."

"Our government? This is crazy. I don't believe it!"

"Here I say it again: Interest, fortitude, and perseverance will bring you knowledge. Before you come to any conclusion, you should consider all the facts, not just the ones that make you feel comfortable. Are you willing to advance?"

"Yes, sorry. I'd like to continue. Tell me more about Alan. I miss him so much! He was probably the truest friend I ever had."

"True friendship is a rare and precious thing indeed, and just like loyalty, it should never be abused or taken for granted. Children are so spontaneous when they ask each other, 'Do you want to be my friend?' But then when they become adults, they forget the sincerity embedded in those words and they pollute the most beautiful of all things — love. That's why you don't have many friends. True friends are an extraordinary treasure. If you ever find one, don't take it for granted."

"You are so right! Alan showed me what true friendship looks like."

"Alan was a time-traveler. He defeated the laws of time and space. He was not a limited person and therefore he was able to give you a taste of what is eternal. A word of advice from an old fellow: Never expect everlasting things from transitory people. True friendship is immortal."

"I have never thought of friendship in these terms. The way you talk about it makes it look so important and precious."

"Because it truly is! Going back to Alan, his loyalty to you was so high that he was willing to die for you, and he did."

"What? No, no, no … this is wrong! He died from an explosion and I had nothing to do with that. Why are you saying those things to me?"

"Have you never died for someone?"

"What are you talking about? I am not dead! How can I have died for someone if I am still alive?"

"In a more figurative meaning, have you never been willing to die for someone? In other words, have you never gone out of your way to benefit someone else, even if that cost you losing something important to you?"

Those words struck Erin like lightning that split the darkness. The memory of Jessica surfaced once again, this time accompanied with the awareness of her selfish actions. If Erin were to be honest, the answer to Tselby's question was no. On the contrary, she had a lifelong history of putting herself first.

Tselby continued. "What if I told you that Alan traveled to your time just to meet you and deliver a message to you? He knew the risks of what he was doing but he did it anyway."

"Are you telling me that Alan knew about the explosion before it happened?"

"Yes, he knew."

"But then it doesn't make sense. Why didn't he try to stop it? Why would he be willing to put his life at risk for me?"

"Some things have to come to pass for other things to happen. By dying, he sealed a bond with you forever, and with that he gained your trust. His message to you could only have been accepted with faith and trust. He taught you what love, in the form of friendship, looks like. Trust, loyalty, and love: qualities that humans often forget or take for granted. By doing what he did, he gave you the most truthful demonstration of friendship and loyalty one can ever ask for, and that was more important to him than preserving himself. Priorities change when one connects with what is eternal."

"And this was his message to me. I shall never forget it."

"In part, it was. But he also left you with a map of an unknown place. This was to give you meaning and direction, but most of all it gave you hope and, at times, confidence. Alan's message is invaluable, but you need to elaborate and understand it within yourself."

Erin lowered her head. A new level of self-awareness had permeated her mind. Her eyes became glazed with tears, and as she blinked, they drifted down her cheeks profusely. It was a sincere but silent weeping. Out of respect, Tselby paused for a moment knowing that an important revelation was taking place in Erin's mind.

Erin was now shaking as her crying became more uncontrollable and intense. From an outsider's perspective, it appeared as if her whole body was trying to expel something poisonous and ancient. After the outpouring was over, Erin regained her self-control. Her remorse was visible in her dejected face and red eyes. With her mouth still coated with tears, Erin finally whispered, "I am good. Sorry."

"Your soul remembers," was Tselby's short reply.

Erin dried her eyes with her hands and allowed a meek smile to appear. "I guess it does."

"Make your experience here worthwhile, because it cost you something as valuable as friendship." With those words, Tselby sealed an important step for Erin.

She wiped her nose using her shirtsleeve. Then after brushing her hands on the back of her pants, she added, "Do you think I will be able to see Alan again? Just to thank him?"

Tselby's eyes radiated again, knowing the impact his words would have on Erin. "He is already aware, but I'll see what I can do."

As to be predicted, Erin couldn't hold back her joy. Her face became bright again.

"Thank you, Tselby!" she blurted, then almost shouting, "You need to tell me about my next steps!"

Tselby, enchanted by her genuine enthusiasm, beamed and concluded, "I just told you an important one. There will be more, but not today. You have a lot to contemplate. Take your time. Your green stone will guide you to me when you are ready for the next step. I salute you, human." And without waiting for Erin's response, he jumped on a tree and disappeared shortly after.

With a reborn lightness of being, Erin playfully pulled her bow and pretended to fire an arrow at her new friend. "T'chi!" she whispered, imitating the sound of an arrow being shot from a recurve bow. "I got you this time, Tselby." Then she turned away, determined to make the best of her journey.

She owed it to Alan. She owed it to Jessica. She even realized she owed it to her team. But, most of all, she knew she owed it to herself.

CHAPTER 17: THE GREEN STONE

Days went by since the encounter with Tselby, but in spite of her efforts and good intent, Erin was never again able to convene with the extraordinary entity. Rather than becoming sad or anxious, a different form of sentiment started to settle in — doubt. Maybe Tselby was just a weird creature that liked to fabricate stories just for the fun of it. Perhaps he was the fruit of her imagination, created by her mind in a situation of challenge and deprivation. Or maybe Tselby was real and it was she, Erin, who was not ready to see him again. But it didn't matter anymore because despite cherishing the rich contemplations about the value of friendship and loyalty that Tselby had initiated, Erin was left with a handful of ambiguities and unanswered questions.

There was no doubt that Inner Earth was the most beautiful place she had ever been, and the harmony was palpable with every breath. But something was missing in Erin: a reason to stay. After several more days of journeying seemingly without purpose, the day arrived when she decided it was finally time to return to Taras. With new knowledge and her solo experience, she thought of herself as a richer person and certainly stronger. She couldn't wait to see her friends. She could even bring herself to believe that Roger was looking forward to seeing her.

While gathering her belongings and preparing to say good-bye to this marvelous place, a curious thought came to her mind, just a simple contemplation, something that she hadn't pondered before: how odd it was that the guardian of Inner Earth was also the smallest creature. One would think a defender of such a magnificent world would be more impressive in stature or at least have a more dominant-looking appearance. And then the words surfaced again, like a refrain in her mind, *"Sometimes small is big and big is small."* Was everything that was happening to her supposed to be an allegory for "being like a hummingbird"? Was that her quest? The train of thought stopped Erin from what she was doing for a moment or two, but the stronger desire to see her team tugged at her mind, and after lifting the backpack onto her shoulders, she set out for Taras.

There was something charming about Erin's journey. The different landscapes she encountered were stunningly beautiful — place names glamorous, and even conversations, whether real or imagined, had been extraordinary — but perhaps the most enchanting was the excitement of being on an adventure that had come in search of her.

With a new level of confidence born out of her adaptation to the once unknown environment, Erin now ventured with boldness and determination. The geography of the mysterious world she had first entered had not changed and still presented many thrills. There were high, windy mountain passes followed by deep valleys and gloomy passageways under dormant volcanoes. Some places were less hospitable, others warmly inviting, but there was one location Erin wished she had seen. On the other side of the five lakes beyond the forest and mountains lay the great city of Aldora, home to the Wasay people of whom Algor was a part. Access to the city of Aldora, he had said, was protected by thunderbirds and giant eagles which became angry and combative if they sensed the approach of an intruder. The city represented to Erin an off-limits destination in a way that was more than just a feeling. Agor had confirmed this awareness in Erin by way of more than one of his riddling conversations.

Leaving her unfulfilled wish behind, Erin turned to the path that led toward Longview Fields. Once there, she would make her way to Sandy Rings and then, finally, Taras. With her more advanced knowledge and skills, she knew this time she would find her way. But there was one major obstacle: the Majestic River, a major affluent of the Mystic River that she had previously crossed on the back of Pepecus. Agor had informed her of the potential dangers, so she proceeded cautiously. She was fully aware of the presence of several dangerous animals, including giant crocodiles, as had been noted on her map.

Agor had warned Erin against bathing or drinking from the river because it carried the mermaid's spell and would make those who touched the water amnesic. The animals of Inner Earth were not only immune to the enchantment but they could benefit from it in strength and energy.

Despite the impressive view, the place was utterly desolate and perilous with huge rocks placed on top of each other forming giant towers where animals could find refuge and protection. A few sporadic trees were scattered here and there with no particular pattern. Erin needed a way to bridge the river without touching the water. That task was no small undertaking, but she was determined to succeed.

After analyzing all possibilities, Erin concluded that the best way to safely cross the river was by attaching a rope to each side and then fording to the other end. Using a boomerang, she would have to secure the rope to a branch on both banks. Erin knew she had only one chance to do it right without the animals becoming aware of her presence. After hours of meticulous preparation, she was finally ready to climb the towering rocks. It was the time of day when the animals were mostly sleeping, hopefully the perfect window.

Once on top, the view was breathtaking. The colors of the meadow were vibrant, and the river looked like a silver ribbon winding through a field of multicolored, flashy gems. Above, the sky was an expression of every shade, with waves of orange and intense pink melting together and dancing harmoniously. Erin stood in awe as a deep sense of gratitude suffused her whole being and tears of joy flowed down her cheeks. A part of her didn't want to leave, but there was another deeper side that wanted to return home. She had to move forward. Erin knew she was on a mission. Her survival training and being alone in unknown territory was complete. Ultimately, she had accomplished the task and now she was ready to go home.

Time, she knew, was unmerciful and so were the creatures sleeping below.

Holding the boomerang in front of her, Erin focused on the tree on the other side of the river. "This is it. I have only one shot," she thought before firing. Erin threw the boomerang with all her strength, watching the string attached sail behind it. She followed the landing with her eyes, holding her breath and hoping for a successful result. But that was not the case. The boomerang hit the tree, then fell into the water after bouncing on the ground, and floated downstream.

Erin stood immobile, trying to disguise herself among the rocks as the stone on her neck began to glow, but it was too late. A herd of large, prehistoric kangaroos had become aware of her presence and a few had already started to jump toward her. Erin had no place to go. In the meantime, the abrupt movement of the kangaroos had warned other animals, and the peaceful harmony a few minutes prior had transformed into a chaotic, frightening turmoil. Erin pulled her bow and loaded it, ready for the attack, her mind focused and her breathing steady.

"Screeech." A loud sound, like a shrill, piercing cry was getting closer and closer, followed by other squelching and rumbling noises. The beast, now in full view, was at least twelve feet tall and just a few steps away from Erin. Trembling with terror, Erin shot the first arrow, which hit the beast in its chest, close to the heart. Blood spilled everywhere, but the animal didn't seem hurt. Instead, it became even angrier. Erin reloaded as fast as she could, but the kangaroo anticipated her moves and continued bounding toward her, causing the ground to shake.

Attempting to avoid the deadly attack, Erin fell from the tower of rocks but was able to grab hold of a protuberance. She had only seconds before her hands lost the grip. In that moment a state of total peace infused her being as if something was telling her everything would be okay. Trusting her intuition, Erin closed her eyes and focused her thoughts on the green stone, asking for help and protection. A ray of green light emanated from the gem and before she even realized it, a large shadow appeared on the horizon. It took Erin a few moments to understand what was happening, but a flash of bliss infused her when she realized it was Pepecus! The giant eagle veered suddenly, grabbed Erin by the shoulders with its claws just as she was about to fall, and soared away. Erin's heart rejoiced. She was safe!

Pepecus glided over gently rolling hills, woods, creeks, and lakes, but it was only when the magnificent creature put her down gently that Erin became aware of Agor's presence riding the eagle.

Gratitude and delight gushed spontaneously. "Agor! You saved my life. Pepecus, thank you!"

The tribute didn't faze Agor. "This is not the first time ..."

Her astonishment prompted Erin to ask. "Agor, when I focused on the green stone, did I somehow call you?"

"Thoughts are images, and they are visible to me. I am aware of them," Agor explained in a strong but gentle tone.

"Did the stone make any difference then?"

"Not to me. But it did to you."

"How did you know?"

"Humans are like little children. They never do what one asks."

Yes, Agor was right, for after a moment or so, the same realization came to Erin. "And you had to come up with a way to trick me ..." This expanded insight brought Erin great comfort.

"A little talisman helped you the first time. Now you know you don't need one. It will all be in here," Agor replied, while touching his temple with his finger.

Erin removed the necklace and held it in her hands, feeling smug in her being. "I will keep it as a memory."

"Do remember the experience."

"I will never forget," she murmured gratefully.

It was not long before Agor continued. "I know you are now ready to go back to your village."

Before she could start thinking, a spark of surprise filled her eyes. She had never imagined the moment to say good-bye to Agor would come in this way, but she knew it was something that had to occur. Her parting words made her sad and yet proud at the same time. "Inner Earth has changed me, and as much as I enjoyed the beauty of this place, I feel I have reached the limit of what I am capable of enduring. I will never be able to look at my life in the same way, and for this I am grateful. I understand my life has purpose, and had I not been pushed to the limits of what I knew to be possible, I would have never known how strong I can be. It is also true that I could never have comprehended my task in so short a period of time, but now I am ready to go back to my people. I feel a deeper meaning to my life rising inside of me."

"I will make sure you return safely to your people. All of the time you spent here will be given back to you, as I promised. Inner Earth taught you to be a traveler. Keep the same outlook on life when you return to the upper world. Cherish your wisdom and don't forget what you accomplished here. The time will come when we will make our presence known again."

"When will you make your presence known again?" Erin repeated in a tone of amazement.

"It is going to be a long story. Are you ready?"

CHAPTER 18: THE GODS OF AADAU

"Are you ready?"

"Yes," Erin replied.

Erin's attitude was truer than any words. As she grew tense inside, anxious to listen but saddened by the thought of leaving behind Agor and Inner Earth, she began to unleash her personal tumult. Her attention was scattered, filled with nervous anticipation.

"How do we do this? Do I hold my questions till the end or do I just ask as you go? I mean, how long do you think this is going to take? Because I have questions, lots of them." Erin was talking more with her hands than with her mouth. "Maybe I should write them down so I don't forget. I don't mean to complicate things, and this is why I prefer to ask you now. So tell me, what do you want me to do?" Her posture was upright and rigid.

Agor, with his calm and passionless way of being, waited for Erin's apparent anxiety attack to be over. Then he quietly stated, "I suggest that you be ready."

Erin adjusted her body to a more comfortable position, took a few deep breaths, and sat there waiting motionless for Agor to go on.

"Are you ready now?" he queried again.

When she finally thought she was ready to listen, she replied, "Yes, I am."

Agor smiled but without looking at her. "Humans act like little children. They don't like to listen. They always believe they have something more important to say."

Erin swallowed, embarrassed. She waited reticently, hoping for Agor to continue, but he didn't. The silence was louder than any noise and Erin was becoming tense again. On the other hand,

Agor seemed to be perfectly at ease. Erin cleared her throat, looking at Agor out of the corner of her eye in search of a glimpse of sympathy or consideration. After what seemed an endless moment, he finally proceeded. "Your presence."

"My presence?"

"Bring your presence here."

Erin immediately realized how much her focus had been scattered and made a determined effort to concentrate.

Agor seemed pleased with her attempt, because he finally looked at her. "Good," he said. Then after moving his gaze to the horizon, he queried, "Did you have a good time here?"

Such a simple question but it calmed Erin's inner storm to a gentle breeze. "Yes, a very good time, thank you." She added cheerfully, "I was able to meet one of the guardians of Inner Earth. His name was Tselby."

The satisfied look on Agor's face was an indicator he already knew. "That was an important step for you. Did you learn?"

"Yes, I learned a lot. I didn't know that Alan was a time-traveler. I was very surprised to hear that he chose to die for me. There are so many things I thought I knew, but now I realize how much I have been missing." There was no bailing out from Erin's feeling of humility. The embarrassment was evident in the expression of mild bashfulness on her face.

"It is all a matter of choices. But before there can be a choice, there must be information. Knowledge gives choices, choices allow freedom, freedom brings truth. This is why I wanted to talk to you. I want to give you more knowledge so that you can have greater choices in finding the truth, if you so choose."

"I have never been able to express how much I truly appreciate what you are doing for me." Erin's gratitude was utterly sincere.

"Choose not to be a victim of your own nature. Bring back your presence. Your soul wants to listen while your mind is asking to be rescued. The first and most important choice you need to make is this: Are you ready?"

"Yes, I am. I thought I was." But it didn't take long for Erin to realize how easy it was for her to lose focus. Agor was asking her to make a conscious effort to stay present, something more than the simple decision to be ready. Even in the absence of words, Agor was still teaching.

"Do you understand?"

With a more self-aware and humble attitude, Erin eventually whispered a feeble "yes," indicating to Agor that she was finally prepared to listen.

"Many years ago in this part of the Galaxy, there was a planet a little bigger than Jupiter. It was called Aadau, and it was home to a great civilization, the Munya. The Munya were people who knew how to live in peace with each other, and they did it for thousands of years. Their spiritual evolution was equal to their technological progress, and their advancement was second to none.

"The Munya were people with a great heart and a superior intelligence. They didn't know war and agony because they never experienced those realities, and that was their only weakness. Their society was structured in a way that the young ones would spend the first hundred years of their lives going to school and learning. Yes, they were a very long-lived people but not immortal. The only thing preventing them from becoming immortal was a lack of awareness that something was still unknown to them. As the illustrious scientists that they were, with expertise and insight that expanded to every level of life, they didn't know what things they had yet to know. That dilemma, accompanied with a great desire for immortality, became of immense interest to the people of Munya. So intent was the involvement that a council of wise men was called to discuss the issue, but after years of deliberation and controversy they could not come to a common answer. The worst form of doubt started to settle in the hearts of the people. It was a subtle kind of disbelief because no one even noticed.

"Unaware of the nature of the events that had been instigated, a few began to detach themselves from the rest of the Munya. Harshness grew in their hearts and anger colonized their minds, followed by the fear of being rejected. You see, a much deeper transformation was taking place, something profoundly unsettling. Families and friends went to war with one another until each were consumed in their beliefs. In less than a century the great civilization of Munya began a relentless decline. On one side there were the wise men who wanted to preserve the traditions of the Munya and everything that made their civilization so prosperous and grand for thousands of years. On the other were those who thought that the Munya were never great because they never reached immortality. Criticizing every aspect of life, they ended up losing patience, faith, and trust in what IS.

"It took many years before the slump turned into a separation, a separation of heart, mind, values, and spirit. Mothers were separated from their sons, fathers from their daughters, teachers from their students, and employers from their workers. Beware, I am not talking about a physical separation. I am referring to a loss of harmony. The disengagement didn't stop there. It continued until the people of Munya, one of the greatest civilizations that ever lived, separated themselves from nature and their own divinity. What was once one became two, what was two became four, and what was four became eight. Women were pitched against men, young against old, black against white, rich against poor. It was a never-ending, downward spiral of self-deception. For the first time they experienced war and agony, something never known to them.

"The whole Galaxy was witnessing the collapse of the Gods of Aadau. The grieving and imploring were so intense that other parts of the Galaxy became aware of the situation on Planet Aadau and decided to have mercy on the people of Munya. More evolved deities, who had already gone through what the people of Munya were experiencing, agreed to intervene and infused them with their breath of peace and strength. With time, the people of Munya realized that both sides had only one common enemy, and it wasn't what they thought. It was not because of the men or the women, it was not because of the young or the old, the poor or the rich, the white or the black, the few or the many. It was one single, common enemy — fear and doubt — but most of all the loss of connection to their divinity. Those feelings led them to live in segregation from each other and their true nature.

"Slowly most of the people of Munya were able to not only put aside their diversity but to celebrate their uniqueness. Peace was restored in their hearts. What were many returned to one and what was divided became whole again. The people of Munya were able to experience the only thing that had been unknown to them — separation. And by becoming aware of it, they were finally able to overcome mortality."

Erin held her breath in astonishment before she was able to say anything. "Agor, it's a beautiful story."

Agor did not respond right away. His nostalgic stare was more explanatory than words, but eventually he continued. "My people and I are descendants of the civilization of Munya."

Erin was speechless. There was a long pause before she added, "What happened to them and Planet Aadau?"

"Both are still there. The planet is mostly invisible to the human eye, but those who know can still see it at times. Why do you think I told you this story? By now you should know that everything has a meaning."

Erin did not respond. Had her thoughts been visible, they would have appeared like a myriad of chaotic lights coming together to just one conclusion. "It is just a story till someone gives it meaning."

"Reality is no longer objective when bent to serve oneself. There is a need for honesty, so let's start moving in the right direction. You are not the only one to receive the message I am about to give you. With the technology now available in your world, information is easily accessible and available to everyone. The decision to know remains yours. How much you choose to know is entirely up to you, but it will make a difference in your life." Agor paused briefly before resuming. "Some of the things you have learned here brought you discomfort but, in the end, it was all right. Do you think so too?"

Erin nodded in a sign of agreement before pronouncing a subdued "Yes."

"Truth can be painful. This is why some people don't like to hear it. If the new information doesn't fit their old paradigm, they label it as false or conspiratorial. This is what your scientists call 'cognitive dissonance.' But as terrible as it might be, knowledge will bring truth, and truth will always give you freedom. I am not here to tell you what to believe. I am here to share some information with you so you can make a choice. Every entity, regardless of its level of evolution, deserves the opportunity to make choices. Do you understand? My people decided to intervene in order to help the human race a long time ago. Did you know that some of the people who live on this Earth today are not originally from here? They are survivors from the destruction of Mars. Soon your scientists will be able to demonstrate that human DNA does not originate from this planet."

It occurred to Erin that this statement had to be more than a dream, but one part of her was not willing to play along. "What are you talking about? The survivors of the destruction of Mars? What destruction?"

"Not so fast. Human beings have been conditioned to never question what they are told to believe. They have trusted that everything that has been said or taught to them is in their best interest. But what if this wasn't true? What if the people you have been told to trust the most are the ones who deceived you the greatest? A few good entities in your world began to have a suspicion that something wasn't right, and they understood the importance of personal research. It's unbelievable what you can find when you investigate for yourself. Don't you agree?"

That was a tough question for Erin, but Agor solved her difficulty by continuing. "Mars was once very similar to Earth, a beautiful planet. It was destroyed by a war fomented by greed and the desire for power."

"This is not the first time I've heard something like that." Erin commented after searching her memory banks for an answer to Agor's previous statement. "I know that there is the presence of methane on Mars. On Earth most of the methane in the atmosphere is produced by living beings. Some of my friends still don't believe it, but I cannot exclude the presence of life on Mars."

"Much information has been kept hidden from humanity. There was an intentional effort to do so. Information has been used to manipulate people, not to free them."

"My friend Roger said something very similar. He told me that there are scientists in the business of discovering but others are in the business of hiding."

"Your friend Roger is correct. Your government already knows about Inner Earth and about my people. Your Exploration has a different purpose than what you have been told."

"Trust me, our goal is pretty noble. We are here to expand our presence inside the planet and to look for any form of life, new or old. We mean no harm. I am not sure I can follow you. What would be the real purpose then?"

"Power and control and, ultimately, destruction."

"I know pretty much everyone in this Expedition, and I can assure you that there isn't a single soul among us that came here to conquer or dominate anyone else."

"Most people in your Expedition are ignorant of the true agenda of the mission. They are being used under false pretenses. How do you convince someone to do something they would never do?"

"I don't know. By not telling them the truth, I suppose."

"By asking them to do something that they agree with while hiding the real intent. Sometimes a good reward goes a long way."

"It's not that I don't trust you, Agor, but this is so hard for me to believe. Everything in this Expedition seems legit to me."

"Think about opportunity. Assume for a moment that what I told you was true. Would you have participated in this project if you had known that the true intent was to destroy this beautiful place?"

"Of course not! I would never have accepted. I am not a mean person!" There was distaste in Erin's voice.

"There is your answer. What was the attraction for you? What were you made to believe you would gain by partaking?"

"Unlike most of my fellow explorers, I won the spot in this Expedition. It came to me as a surprise because I didn't ask for it. What convinced me to accept was the privilege to participate in something that only a few people were given the opportunity to experience and the hope that this adventure would help me in the future."

"You were given the illusion that you would benefit from it."

"Yes, that is what I thought. My idea was to make it work and to get the most out of it to empower my future life and career."

"The information given to you led you to think that way. But didn't anyone tell you that you were going to die?"

"Going to die?" Erin's eyes were wide open, taking in more light than normal. "No. I mean, yes. We were informed of the potential risks. But they told us that the chance of something going terribly wrong was slim."

"What if I told you that the people who sent you here don't care if you live or die? Your life means nothing to them. Some of your people are going to pay a great price for this Exploration. From our standpoint it is evident that too many human beings have already paid. Too many souls have already been sacrificed. When you hold the bigger picture, you can see clearly what is really going on. And then what do you do? Do you ignore the situation or do you intervene? Does intervention prevent free will? What do you think the best choice would be? If it were up to you, what would you do?"

"If you say that humans are like little children, if it is true that we have been lied to, if knowledge brings power and freedom — if all of what you said is true — then I would never walk away. I would be doing just what you are doing, trying to inform people about their situation, let people know that they are not in good hands. Is this what your people have decided to do?"

"One step at a time. Information is crucial. To answer your question, let's go back to Mars."

"Back to Mars? It sounds like the title of a movie."

"Not too far in the future, travel to Mars will become a reality for the human race, but first you need to know what happened to Mars. Mars was destroyed by nuclear weapons. Entire civilizations who lived on Mars were completely wiped out. The planet became unfit for life due to the resulting high radiation. Some of your scientists have found the presence of particles in the atmosphere around Mars that are very similar to those found in the hydrogen bombs used on Earth."

"Wait, what? Are you now telling me that Mars was once inhabited?"

"Before it was destroyed, it was very similar to Earth. Humans used to live there. After the destruction of Mars, my people decided to intervene. The seed of humanity was preserved and replanted here on this planet. The human race was in desperate need of a new opportunity. From our point of view, humans are beautiful creatures. They have incredible DNA. You now understand why I say that humans are not originally from Earth. They are here because they were given the opportunity to start over."

"I like this game! Let's keep pretending that what you are saying is true. What happened next? Why were we given a second opportunity?"

"When left alone, humans are beautiful creatures. But they had been living under tyranny for too long. Humans deserved a chance to utterly evolve, to express their divinity in full. We brought them to this planet. This is not a game. Unfortunately, the same entities responsible for the destruction of Mars now needed a planet to live on. They saw that Earth was full of resources and decided to come here also."

"Aren't we lucky?" said Erin, a tone of disgust in her voice.

"Humans are spiritually inexperienced and therefore easy to seduce. These entities, on the other hand, are very evolved in technology but extremely poor in spirit. All that they know and want is power and control. While promising mechanical evolution, they slowly infiltrated your world. Their plan was to conquer from within with deception and disguise. They manipulated the information in their favor. Some of your leaders were given a choice by the intruders: comply with their evil intent or be removed from positions of power. Their demand was absolute control over the human race in exchange for unlimited wealth and untouchable power."

"Absolute control over the human race? I don't think this would ever be possible. Humans would never allow that to happen."

"You really think so? It didn't happen overnight. It was a long-planned dream for the conspirators, and it was perpetrated very slowly. Nobody, except those who submitted, had reason to know. These entities thrive in darkness. Humanity needs light in order to evolve. Their design was to weaken everything that made a human being strong: body, mind, and spirit. Those who knew were removed, persecuted, or, worse, killed. They had the perfect plan to hide a terrible secret in full sight."

"This is really frightening," whispered Erin. Fear was now running in her veins, although she managed to keep her emotions in check.

"Some of your people never stopped knowing. They never walked away from their spirit. Have you noticed that some races of people have something in common? They all look at the same stars for answers. They remember where they came from."

"Do you mean the Egyptians, the Mayans, and all those ancient civilizations?"

"Pay attention. Ancient civilizations used the stars to know when to plant a seed and when to harvest. They gave names to constellations. They told stories about the Gods, the heroes, and the mythological creatures. Do you think it was just for entertainment? No, it was done with the intent to preserve culture and history. Some of your people never forgot their true origins and their divine nature."

"Most of these ancient populations are gone. There is little left; just some memories of them remain."

"They had to be eliminated because they posed a threat."

"Was this part of their plan of domination too?"

"Yes. Those entities don't want humans to remember their true nature as divine beings. Humans are more powerful than what they have been conditioned to believe. This is why it is such a big deal for them that history and traditions be deleted. They know the truth can be found in the past. They created division to weaken your people, and under the false name of 'inclusion' and 'compassion' they forced everyone to fit under the same standard. Every residue of culture, tradition, national identity, and individuality has to be erased in order for them to take control. Hold the bigger picture, SunAlaka. Do you start to understand?"

"What you are saying is starting to make sense. The agenda of globalism has been instilled in our minds and forced on us against our own will. I am beginning to understand how it was never about the future of humanity. It was all about THEIR future."

"Yes, it was only about their survival. But there is hope. All of this can be stopped and reversed. Some humans are starting to ask good questions and their prayers are being heard. We decided to intervene to prevent the use of powerful weapons of mass destruction. The same weapons that destroyed Mars were about to be used again. But this time it will not be permitted."

"Are you referring to nuclear weapons?"

"Nuclear energy is a powerful form of energy but very dangerous when it falls in the hands of the wrong people. We will not allow this planet to be destroyed. Humans did not discover the secret of nuclear energy. It was given to them by these entities in exchange for DNA, power, and control. Benevolent creatures would never give nuclear weapons to little children. The same entities responsible for the destruction of Mars wouldn't have any problem using the same weapons to destroy Earth. Such is their desire for power, control, and planetary domination. You might ask yourself why. The spiritual evolution of these entities hasn't ever moved past power and control. This is their stage right now. They have no emotions.

"Just to give you an example, have you noticed how fast technological evolution has occurred in the past hundred years in your time? That type of progress was induced; it wasn't spontaneous. A technological evolution that does not develop with spiritual growth is not natural. The progress of humanity needs to be both metaphysical and scientific in order to be instinctive and durable. You understand?"

"You're absolutely right! We went from the steam train to the supersonic jet in less than fifty years. I have always found that very odd. I have been wondering how that could have happened, and now you are providing me with unexpected insights."

"Advanced technology was given as a form of payment, you see? They used reward as an enticement. Isn't that what adults give to little children when they want them to do something?"

Erin didn't respond, but she knew this meant trouble.

Agor observed her reaction, then went on. "During the last century in your time, an alien contact was made by nonbenevolent entities. Your government at that meeting was offered technology and personal enrichment in exchange for control over the human race. It worked well for them. A secret covenant was signed, and from that moment on the infiltration started. With the exception of a few, most of your rulers in the last several decades were strategically placed under the illusion of being fairly elected. The era of lies and deception started when some of your leaders betrayed their own people, their own country, for the sake of personal interest and empowerment. But it was only when their game started to involve innocent children and nuclear weapons that we decided to intervene. It had gone too far to be allowed to continue."

"What do you mean?"

"We made our presence known to those who wanted truth and freedom and left them with a choice. We provided them with information and disclosure. They restlessly worked behind the curtains in resistance. It was a silent war. They allowed the wicked individuals to have their dream for a while. It had to be so. The presence of the good warriors was kept hidden from the public so they would not pose a threat. We started to groom select people who would eventually become leaders in your time. There was a need for us to do that because humanity was at stake again. In the most recent years, a great number of wicked people have been removed from their positions of power, but the battle continues. The big question is how do you reveal something that is so serious and unbelievable to people who have lived in a fabricated reality for decades without creating panic in the masses? We had only one chance to do this, and it was important to do it right. My role is to inform you of what is really going on in your world. You too will soon have a part in all of this."

"It is really hard for me now to wrap my mind around what you just told me. But what saddens me the most is to think that humans are so stupid."

"Not stupid — inexperienced. Although some people can be stupid, for the most part humans are beautiful creatures of God, and when they finally awaken and bloom, their potentials will be unlimited. It will be wonderful to watch."

"That is reassuring. How did we get this far in the game?"

"Humans are like children, easily seduced. They lack spiritual maturity. When everything goes well, they get complacent and they stop seeking."

"All that technological progress made us feel like everything was going well, that we were really going

197

somewhere. The Internet, the computers, all the technological advancements were just a disguise to distract us from what was really going on behind our back. Is that true, Agor?"

"You learn fast. These entities took control over the information, the education, and the political system. They created fake idols for humans to follow and immorality to dishonor their spirit. They lowered the expectations of human beings with the creation of poverty, diseases, economic decline, wars, and useless taxes. Their supreme goal was to take away all of your freedoms, little by little. It was only when they threatened to use nuclear power that we had to put our foot down. A nuclear explosion would have a ripple effect on the whole universe, not just on this planet. They were never permitted to use nuclear power for control and destruction. We warned them, but they didn't listen."

"So they are like little children too — in a way, I mean."

"Little children are innocent. Innocent people can be forgiven. If you keep making the same mistake after you know, that becomes willful intention. They have lost the privilege to be called innocent children."

"All of this wasn't supposed to happen; right?"

"It is happening in front of your eyes. You have been asking questions, and now you are being given some answers. I am here presenting you with more information so you can find the truth on your own. But this is not enough. Many people have died because of the truth, and more people will die for the same reason. I need to warn you about some individuals in your Expedition. They are not who they appear to be. They don't have good intentions."

"Who are they? Can you tell me?"

"If you keep your eyes open, you will be able to find out when you go back to your people. I want to alert you so you will be prepared for what lies ahead. You will be exposed to things that you have never seen before. The information I am giving you will help you to make sense of things that right now you cannot comprehend. Hold the bigger picture — always. Keep your focus steady and you will find a way. And, remember, many things had to happen."

"You are scaring me now. What is about to happen to me?"

"You have been protected up to this point. There is a reason for that. But don't think you are the only one. We protect the people who are willing to see and move forward. This doesn't mean everyone, even if everybody has a part. Be gentle with yourself and allow your heart and spirit to guide you."

"But you are not answering my question. You said you would tell me my next steps. How am I supposed to know what to do?"

"Time is not linear. Some events cannot be predicted with precision. Don't lose control of what is important. You have more than you know."

Agor took a few steps away from Erin, leaving her struggling to make sense of all her conflicted thinking. She had the impression he was about to leave, but he suddenly conveyed, "You need to trust, SunAlaka. What do you believe? The answer to this question will show you which path to follow. The choice will be yours."

Agor was now standing in front of her, his eyes filled with compassion and understanding. "The next time I see you, there will be little or no time for talking. All I needed to tell you has been said. But there is one more thing, something I want to give you."

While pronouncing the words, Agor made a circular gesture with his arms in the space in front of him and a golden arrow appeared in his hands. Amazement didn't quite cover what Erin was feeling. She stood there in awe waiting for the next clue.

"This arrow is for you. There will be a time when you will need to use it. Remember, it can only be fired once. The moment will be clear to you when that time has arrived. You will know without a doubt. When you fire it, make sure your mind is clear because this arrow will determine your future."

Erin received the arrow from Agor. The golden treasure was bigger than a normal arrow, and instead of goose feathers, it was adorned with the feathers of eagles. It was truly breathtaking. A flash of purple light pierced the sky in half, developing into a myriad of colors more vibrant and intense than ever before. The significance of the moment was sealed in the magic of that brilliant sky.

Agor looked upward and declared, "Never forget this heaven when you return home. Whether you are far away from here or if you find yourself in the midst of a stormy night, remember this sky. Remember the gracious sky of Inner Earth and know that the northern lights originate from the heart of the Earth. They are a gift from nature, a message of hope for humanity, and a promise that this planet will never be destroyed."

Filled with joy, Erin took one last glance at Agor, just before he vanished from sight. Her heart fell silent but, in her being, Erin found enough faith to whisper, "I promise."

CHAPTER 19: BETRAYAL

The phone rang three times. A sluggish voice responded, "Yeah ..."

Agent TJ of the SOTIS team hung up. Looking at his mates, Kelly and Jordan, he asserted, not without a hint of consternation, "He's still alive."

The three members of the SOTIS team looked at each other, apparently confused. Jordan was the first to speak. "Something must have changed, and we haven't been informed yet. We must proceed with our plan. Call him again and find out what's going on."

The other two fellows nodded. TJ hesitated for a moment, then dialed the number again. The phone rang three times, just like the previous call.

"Hello, who's this?" The voice at the other end of the line sounded annoyed.

"TJ reporting, sir."

"TJ! Do you have any idea what time it is here? It's the middle of the night! I hope you have something important to tell me to continue disturbing me at this hour." General Curtis was almost fumbling over the phone.

"Yes, sir. There is an update. We will proceed with the extraction of the civilian. After that, the Expedition will be aborted. It has been decided." TJ's voice was calm.

"Decided by whom?" General Curtis cleared his voice.

"The Captain, Jeff Miller, sir."

The line went silent for a few seconds. Then General Curtis proclaimed, yawning, "Oh, that poor friend of mine! I wish I could be more honest with him."

"We tried to prevent this development, just as you instructed us, sir."

"I know, I know … that's fine." General Curtis paused, as he pondered the next thing to say. "Never mind. The plan is still in place. We just need to resort to option B, which I like better anyway. There will be a slight adjustment in the operation, but we will still succeed as planned. Has the device been set?"

"Yes, sir, the device has been installed without problems. We performed an efficiency test and it resulted positive. Everything is in place. We stand at the ready, sir."

"Very well. I will inform my upper managers. Our next conversation will carry more instructions and it will happen soon. Anything else?"

"No, sir,"

"Excellent! I am going back to bed now. I have a busy day ahead. Good night, gentlemen!"

TJ hung up the receiver and looked at his fellows for a clue. "Why is he still alive? Wasn't he supposed to be terminated by now?"

Kelly added, "We can't trust him. His friendship with Miller is too dangerous. But we have no other choice than to use him as a mediator for now, at least until he is replaced."

TJ and Jordan, who were becoming increasingly anxious about the delicate situation, agreed.

In the meantime, the remainder of the rescue team, comprised of the most expert men in the Expedition — Parker, Roger, and Matt — were getting ready by taking inventory of all the gear they needed. Supplies of food, water, weapons, and ammunition were at the top of the list. Each of them would carry a backpack. The plan was to stay together, but everybody was supposed to be willing and capable of surviving on their own, if anything went wrong or if the situation required. Roger was the first to note that the SOTIS team was still missing and asked, "Where is the rest of the group?"

Matt, the man with the greatest amount of expertise in exploration, wasn't impressed. However, he knew that often the best operators exhibit what to others might appear as unorthodox behavior. His patience had been tested multiple times over the years, and for as much as he agreed with Roger, he didn't want to be distracted. Roger looked around, disturbed by this lack of consideration and still hoping someone could give him an answer. "Really? Anyone know? WOW!" But the only response he obtained was a baffled expression from Parker.

The atmosphere was tense, obviously. Despite the majority having decided to carry out the rescue mission, everyone had been well aware of the risks that it posed to those involved.

Roger, however, was not having it. "Guys, I know everyone is worried about this operation but if we don't even stick together, we will fail. Is anyone wondering where the rest of the team is? I thought we were supposed to be responsible for each other, not having to baby-sit one another!"

Finally Matt, the man better known as "the few-words fellow," looked over at Roger and voiced his thoughts. "Just do what you need to do and stop worrying about them. We will be leaving in an hour as scheduled. Those who are ready will go; the others will stay behind. Three people are enough to rescue one person."

Because of his highly organized personality, it was hard for Roger to condone such irresponsible behavior. "How about our commitment to be one for all, all for one? Does it matter at all to them?"

This time Parker decided to intervene. "Roger, you never liked those guys from the first day you met them on the vessel. You told me you didn't trust the fact that they were speaking a foreign language. The best thing to do now is to focus on what needs to be done because no matter what, we are going to rescue Erin. Let's stay together, at least what is left of us."

Roger gave up on his protest, but the awkward situation only increased his skepticism toward the SOTIS team. It was hard for him to admit that he was really missing Erin, and in his heart he was hoping that everyone had the same desire to find her.

Parker, Matt and Roger spent the next half hour busy without talking, and by the time they were scheduled to leave, the team was ready. The missing SOTIS members had not shown up. Nobody knew where they were, but the unspoken assumption was that nothing would delay their departure. Roger was growing impatient but managed to keep his exasperation inside. Thoughts about Erin completely engulfed him.

5:58 …. ticktock …. 5:59 …. ticktock …….. 6 o'clock.

Surprising to some, more anticipated by others, the SOTIS team was a definite no-show. Roger, Parker, and Matt looked at each other without trying to hide their disappointment. Despite words of tolerance, everyone had hoped that the SOTIS team would make an appearance. The fact was that they hadn't. Nobody was talking. There was no time to discuss. The orders given by Captain Miller were clear: Leave at 6 p.m. Delays were not admissible, except under force majeure.

Perhaps it was his affection for Erin or simply by reason of a higher set of morals that he thought he possessed, but it was in that moment that the SOTIS team became labeled "persona non grata" by Roger.

Matt, with the resilience of an old warrior, gave the signal that it was time to go. Roger and Parker put on their helmets, and the three of them were on their way. There were no good-byes, no final instructions to be given, only the desire to find Erin and the determination to return with her to Taras.

Captain Miller, who was walking toward Taras, arrived at the citadel in time to see the cloud of dust left behind by the vehicles.

In a room on the Admiral Q-Oho, not too far from Captain Miller's office, Jordan, Kelly, and TJ were having a good time drinking whiskey and smoking cigars. They had nothing to worry about because everything was going according to "their" plan. The only thing they had to do was wait for the authorization to proceed. The key word had yet to be pronounced, but the moment to spring into action was approaching fast.

"To Miller!" exclaimed TJ, while lifting his glass. "Thank you for your service, sssssiiiiiiiiiiiirrrrrr. You will be remembered, sssssiiiirrrr!"

Jordan and Kelly exploded in laughter. "You don't say? I kind of like that guy."

"Oh, Miss Jordan is being sentimental ... Hahahaha!" Kelly and TJ were making fun of their mate.

"I'm wondering what those fools think they're going to find. What's her name? Erin? Ahahah!" TJ poured himself another glass of bourbon.

"It doesn't matter. All of them will soon be history. Let them chase their dreams while they can. It will be the last thing they'll do."

With a pretentious smile on his face, Kelly closed his eyes and leaned on his chair while blowing smoke rings with his cigar. The moment he had been waiting for all his life was about to arrive, and a feeling of dominance and accomplishment pervaded him. He was a man with nothing left to lose, and that made him a most dangerous enemy.

TJ and Jordan looked at Kelly. His diabolic energy was almost palpable. They knew he was the strongest among them, and a sense of power mixed with the fear of subservience penetrated every fiber of their beings. It wasn't exactly a sensation of pleasure, rather something more like rivalry.

Meanwhile Captain Miller had arrived at the hospital. He thought it was a good idea to check on Clyde. From the doorway of his room, Miller was happy to see the young man enjoying a cranberry jelly in the company of his nurse, Megan. Even though it was part of the job requirement for a nurse to be friendly with their patients, Miller had the impression that there was something more going on between Clyde and Megan. He took advantage of the fact that his presence was still unnoticed and stood at the door watching the unfolding of a delicate interaction before making his arrival known. Eventually he cleared his voice and, with an innocent, polite attitude, made his entry into the room.

What followed next was quite predictable. Megan excused herself with the pretext of having something else to do, and Clyde almost had a coughing attack at the sight of his boss.

Captain Miller waited patiently while deciding whether or not to address the situation with his favorite employee. It was part of the contract that personal relationships between members of the Expedition were not allowed, and Clyde was supposed to know that as part of his commitment. There was, however, a more affectionate aspect in Captain Miller's relationship with the fellow, and he was inclined toward compassion for the young man painfully embarrassed in front of him. After hesitating for a few moments, Captain Miller decided to break the silence.

"Clyde!" he shouted, with his usual authoritative voice. Immediately after, lowering his tone, he added, "I am pleased to see that your recovery is proceeding smoothly. It looks like you have been receiving … uh … first-class care here. How are you feeling, son?"

Clyde, who had been at the clinic for just over a day, was feeling much better. Part of that was thanks to the professional and attentive supervision of the staff, especially the nurse. He was ready to go back to work but not prepared quite yet to detach himself from Megan's caring treatment. Without thinking twice, he stood to attention to greet the Captain, demonstrating without words the degree of his improvement.

"Sir! I am doing very well. Thank you for asking, sir!" Clyde was sincerely flattered by Captain Miller's interest, and he didn't want to take advantage of his patience. "I am ready to go back to work, sir."

Captain Miller smiled in genuine satisfaction. "I am pleased to hear that, son. I would like to take advantage of this moment to have a quick briefing, if that's all right with you."

Clyde was not expecting this sudden call to duty but found himself actually delighted by the request.

"Yes, sir, sure. We can have a meeting now, sir." He scanned the room, looking for something to sit on and found it beside his bed.

"Sir, please take this," he motioned, while handing the chair to Captain Miller.

"Thank you, Clyde. This is kind of you." Captain Miller opened his jacket before sitting.

Clyde took a spot on the edge of the bed. With his arms resting on his legs, he was ready to listen.

"Clyde, I went to your office with Roger and I found the door ajar. The lights were off and everything inside seemed to be in order. But there was just one little thing that caught my attention. Yesterday when you were ... when you had the seizure, I slipped a note under your door. I was asking you to call me back. I remember finding the door locked, and from the gap underneath, the lights inside appeared to be on. Do you remember what happened prior to your accident?"

To his surprising satisfaction, Clyde remembered and smiled. "Yes, yes! I do remember, sir! I received a visit from the SOTIS members, and they told me that our surveillance system had been under attack. They said I needed to follow them for some security reasons. I remember very well locking my computer as well as the door, sir. As for the lights, I usually leave my desk lamp on. It makes me feel like someone is there."

"Good. That's what I thought, Clyde. My impression is that someone else had access to your office while you were gone. Do you know who that could be?"

Clyde rolled his eyes trying to remember, but he found the situation quite strange.

"No, sir. I am the only one allowed access to my office. The spare key is kept inside the safe on the Admiral Q-Oho, sir. When I left the office, I placed the keys in the same place I usually keep them, inside my pocket."

"You're right, Clyde. I forgot about the spare key in the safe. I will check it the next time I go there. Do you still have the clothing you were wearing when you were ... had your seizure attack?"

Clyde scanned the room with his eyes and walked toward the single-door wardrobe in the corner of the room. He opened the closet door and found a small plastic bag containing his clothing from the day before. But after checking all the pants' pockets, he had to confirm that the key was missing. Somehow he had to explain that to his boss. Clyde looked and looked again but the result was unchanged: no key. Crushed, he turned around and while looking at his Captain, he whispered in a somber voice, "I'm sorry, sir, but I am afraid I have lost my key."

Captain Miller, however, was not surprised. "I don't think you lost your key, Clyde. I have a feeling that someone stole it from you. Do you have any idea who would do something like that and, more importantly, why?"

"No, sir. I don't understand why someone would want to have access to my office. I don't deal with classified information; the people in the laboratory do. I am only managing the intercommunication network. Between you and me, sir, my job can be pretty boring at times."

"Yes, I know, Clyde, and this is what makes the situation even stranger."

"Do you have an opinion, sir, if I may ask?"

"I do, but I am not certain yet. There are a few things I want to verify with you first. Do you mind going with me to your office, if the doctors are okay with that?"

Right at that moment Megan entered the room with a glass of tea and, overhearing the last part of the conversation, said, "I don't think there will be a problem with that. The results of the last lab tests show nothing wrong and the doctor believes Mr. Clyde is well enough to leave the hospital. A full recovery will take about a few days up to a week, but there is no reason for him to stay here. We should be able to proceed with his dismissal right away. I was about to bring some discharge instructions. If any of the symptoms reappear, like fever, shortness of breath, or dizziness, or if you notice any change, please let us know. Otherwise you should be fine, Mr. Clyde. The doctor prescribed you only one medicine to take twice a day before meals. But, more important, drink plenty of water. You were a little dehydrated when we brought you here. That alone can cause severe headaches." A sympathetic smile appeared on Megan's face as she stood in the doorway.

Clyde and Captain Miller looked at Megan with amazement. How long had she been there? Megan perceived the astonishment in their faces because she quickly added, "Oh, don't worry. I just overheard the last part of your conversation. I wasn't snooping." Her cheeks turned red as she walked toward Clyde, handing him some papers to sign.

Clyde was the first one to come to her defense. "Oh, don't worry, Megan. You are fine." But after the glance Miller gave him, he realized it was not his job to say that. Embarrassed, he kept silent.

Captain Miller, referring to Megan, concluded, "As Clyde said, there is no problem, Megan."

Megan smiled timidly, and without saying a word and after a brief look at Clyde, exited the room.

In less than five minutes, Clyde and the Captain were on their way to the office. The tower was located just a few blocks past the hospital between the Inner Grounds Café and the main convention center. The roads in Taras were quiet. A few residents walked by waving at Captain Miller and attempted to start a conversation, but he quickly dismissed them with a gesture of his hand.

Once inside the main entrance, the smell of bleach was still perceivable, even if much less than before. Clyde didn't seem to notice, so Captain Miller chose not to mention it. The door to Clyde's office was closed but unlocked, the lights turned off. A sense of "being home" swept over Clyde as he stared at his workstation. Immediately he turned the computer on and waited for the program to start. The usual password was accepted, and nothing seemed out of the ordinary. After a few minutes of inspection, Clyde said, "Everything here seems the same, except that it looks cleaner."

That little clue bothered Captain Miller. It was obvious that someone had come and cleaned the place, but why? He decided to keep his speculation to himself and simply asked, "Do you notice if anything is missing or if it has been misplaced?"

Before answering, Clyde moved some piles of documents, checked inside the drawers of his desk, even inspected the trash bin, but he couldn't find anything unusual.

"No, everything seems okay." But then he added, almost immediately, "Wait ... my journal!"

Clyde began searching frantically among the files and books piled on his desk. "It was here! I kept it here." His voice was infused with an element of desperation. He looked at Captain Miller, almost in tears. "My journal is missing, sir."

"Your journal?" Captain Miller wasn't sure of the importance of Clyde's statement.

"My journal, sir. I keep all my observations there. I wrote all my comments about the situation regarding our communication, including my unofficial conclusions with reference to Roger and Erin's poor device reception. Now it's gone! I'm afraid, sir, this is very bad news."

Clyde appeared to be highly distraught, and from an outside perspective, one would have thought he was shaking.

"Okay, Clyde, please get ahold of yourself. I will help you find your journal. How did ... uh ... What does it look like?"

"Yellow cover, small size, about eight inches in length. I don't see it!" Clyde covered his face with both hands, perhaps in an attempt to hide his despair.

Captain Miller started looking around, but he had to admit that he could see nothing that reminded him of a yellow diary. His concern grew larger. He didn't want to say, but it seemed clear to him that the whole situation was starting to look like an act of sabotage: the door ajar, the smell of bleach, the lost message, and now the missing yellow journal. Was it all intentional? And, if so, why? Just when the moment seemed to be the most troubling since Clyde's dismissal from the hospital, an abrupt, ringing sound like a computer-generated tone called for the attention of the two men in the room.

Beep - beep - beep. Clyde turned his attention to the monitor in front of him just in time to see a single line in small, white characters appear on the blue screen:

FILE DELETION COMPLETE

A few more beeps followed immediately after, and at the bottom of the panel, another message popped up. This last one appeared to have been received somewhat later than the previous:

NEW ENCRYPTED COMMUNICATION DETECTED
MESSAGES RECEIVED: 1
DOWNLOAD FILE? Y/N

Since the beginning of the Expedition, neither Clyde nor the Captain had ever seen a message like that. They looked at each other confused, without exactly knowing what to do. Captain Miller, hoping for a quick solution, was the first to break the silence. "Can you download the file?"

"Sure I can, sir. The problem is that I have no way of knowing if this is a virus. In my experience this looks more like a hacking attempt than anything else. Our communication with the external world follows different channels, sir. This format is completely new to me and considering the most recent attempts to compromise our security, I find it quite suspicious."

"I agree, Clyde. The security of this operation is my most important concern." He paused for a few seconds before continuing. "What would the damage be if this was a hacker attack?"

Clyde didn't take long to reply. "We would be looking not only at software contamination and physical damage but, more important, security breaches, sir."

"What do you suggest, Clyde?"

"I suggest we find the source of this message before making any decision. I will need some time, but I am sure I can manage." Clyde didn't finish his sentence because he was already typing at a speed that Captain Miller didn't even think was possible. The atmosphere was silent and filled with expectation.

"I can assume that this message has been kept opaque to all the intermediate transit points, making it directed to the Expedition only. The next question would be: Am I the only one who received it?"

Captain Miller checked his portable computer device, but he could not find any trace of encoded messages. "It looks like a personal message to you, Clyde. Someone is trying to communicate with you."

Suddenly Clyde remembered something. "Sir, when I was scanning the software to analyze the lack of signal from the devices, I remember there was a sort of low interposing sound that was interrupting the script at constant intervals. It looked like a soft noise, barely perceivable. I was about to check it out when the SOTIS team arrived and I had to stop. I have a feeling that this message might have something to do with that interference."

A smile of satisfaction appeared on Miller's face. His trust in Clyde was well-placed. He was not only a very detailed and productive employee but he had a sensitivity that only few people possessed and a mind honest enough to follow his intuitions.

"How long would you need to check it out?"

Clyde looked at his computer and, swinging his head right and left, he responded, "A couple of hours would be enough to have an idea of what I can do. Maybe less, if I am lucky."

"Perfect, Clyde. I leave you to your duties, and please let me know if you need anything."

"Yes, sir!" Clyde was already immersed in his investigation when he heard Miller asking something unexpected. "Clyde, I hope you don't mind me asking, but ... do you carry a gun?" was the abrupt question.

"A gun? Like ... a gun, sir?"

"Yes, a gun!"

Clyde not only didn't carry a gun; he was committed to staying as far away from one as possible. His insecurity grew rapidly. The quandary of his mind was clearly palpable in his words, "N-n-no, sir. I do not have … I never carry a gun." His hands were already sweating.

"You should carry one, especially now." Captain Miller's voice was calm and steady.

"I – I – I have no idea how to operate one, sir. It was never part of my qualifications, sir."

"I know, Clyde. I am not blaming you for that. I know this might sound simplistic to you, but the quickest lesson I can give you is this: Aim at the target, keep your wrist steady, and pull the trigger. I know this is not much, but it is all that we can afford in this moment."

Captain Miller searched inside his jacket and handed Clyde a small handgun.

Clyde took it and inspected the weapon in his hands.

Captain Miller continued. "It's a Ruger SP101. It's a small pistol used for self-defense, the same one my wife …" Captain Miller lowered his head and paused for a moment. "The same one that my wife used to carry in her purse. It's not hard to use, and you cannot go wrong with this when it comes to shooting capabilities."

Clyde, however, was still confused. "Why would I need a gun, sir?"

"For your safety Clyde. There is something odd about this situation and I don't want you to get in trouble. And, remember, it is always better to have one and not need it than to need one and not have it."

"Yes, sir!" Clyde was holding the gun with the same fervor a vampire would hold a cross. His voice was shaking when he said, "How does it work?"

Captain Miller walked closer and patiently showed Clyde how to operate a gun. "This pistol holds five rounds. It should be enough."

"E – enough for what, sir?"

"To defend yourself, Clyde, but I sincerely hope you don't have to use it."

"I sincerely hope the same, sir."

"In any case, keep it handy."

"Handy? Handy meaning on my person, sir? I sure will, sir!"

"One last thing, Clyde."

Captain Miller stopped for a moment before continuing. He knew the fragility of the young man sitting in front of him and didn't want to cause him panic, but certain things needed to be said. A layer of tears was forming in his eyes, so he hurried to say, "Don't use it unless your life is in danger."

Immediately after, he lowered his head, hiding the drops that were starting to drift down his cheeks. His emotions took him back to his seventh wedding anniversary fifteen years earlier. It was the end of a long day at work and one of the last days of winter. Miller was proud of the surprise he had prepared for his wife: a Cartier diamond ring, one of her long overdue wishes. At the last minute, however, he decided to add something unusual, something that Molly didn't ask for and did not expect — a small pistol for self-defense. His choice was a silver Ruger SP101. His hope was that she would accept the bizarre present with understanding. During the previous weeks, a strange feeling of being watched didn't allow him to sleep well at night.

In the darkness of the night, the red and blue lights were all that he could see. A few police cars and an ambulance were parked in front of his house. Rushing into his home, he was blocked by a policeman. "Sorry, sir, you need to stay here."

"I live here. What's going on? Let me go!" he shouted, struggling.

When he was finally able to free himself from the cop, he ran inside the house. More detectives, including undercover agents, were standing in the hallway taking pictures and sharing information.

"What happened?" His words were loud. But he didn't need an explanation because all of a sudden came a shattering realization: His wife was lying on the floor motionless in a pool of blood. Tears mixed with desperation were not enough to define the grief of the moment.

Molly had been shot by an intruder, was the first report by the police.

"We are going to do everything possible to save her," was the short statement from the paramedics.

Molly was rushed to the hospital where she died a few hours later. She was seven weeks pregnant, the doctor told him.

He was going to be a father!

He never used the pistol that was intended for his wife, never until now, when he decided to give it to Clyde in memory of the son he never had.

Clyde was standing immobile, with the pistol in his hands, conflicted. Thoughts were forming in his head almost uncontrollably. A sense of duty and awareness transported him, placing his whole being in the space between friend and enemy. In the midst of internal chaos, a sense of strength quietly rose. It was a battle of fear versus faith, and it needed to be fought.

Before leaving, Captain Miller gave Clyde another long look and in that moment of gratitude, reflection, and humility, a silent prayer formed in his mind spontaneously.

"Thank you," were the only words he was able to whisper.

Without making any sound, he left.

Back in his office on the Q-Oho Captain Miller pulled his Bible out of his desk drawer and opened it randomly. The verse that appeared in front of his eyes was a perfect allegory for the present situation:

> *"Finally, be strong in the Lord and in his mighty power. Put on the full armor of God, so that you can take your stand against the devil's schemes. For our struggle is not against flesh and blood, but against the rulers, against the authorities, against the powers of this dark world and against the spiritual forces of evil in the heavenly realms. Therefore put on the full armor of God, so that*

when the day of evil comes, you may be able to stand your ground, and after you have done everything, to stand. Stand firm then, with the belt of truth buckled around your waist, with the breastplate of righteousness in place, and with your feet fitted with the readiness that comes from the gospel of peace. In addition to all this, take up the shield of faith, with which you can extinguish all the flaming arrows of the evil one. Take the helmet of salvation and the sword of the Spirit, which is the word of God.

"And pray in the Spirit on all occasions with all kinds of prayers and requests. With this in mind, be alert and always keep on praying for all the Lord's people. Pray also for me, that whenever I speak, words may be given me so that I will fearlessly make known the mystery of the gospel, for which I am an ambassador in chains. Pray that I may declare it fearlessly, as I should."

— Ephesians 6:10-20

CHAPTER 20: "WHERE LIGHT MEETS SHADOW"

Now that Agor was gone, Erin was left with the golden arrow and a lot to ponder. Being troubled was nothing new to her. But this time she wondered should she intervene or leave her complicated thoughts alone. Despite all the renewed insecurities and the unrest stirring in her mind, she decided to keep building her strength. She had been given an opportunity, as had many others before her. Some people engaged their journey; others refused. And there were those who turned their head to the other side and procrastinated. After all, it was only a matter of choice and free will.

Against the counsel of Agor and despite the increased danger while returning to Taras, Erin decided to navigate the river with the hope of encountering some of the mystical creatures who were known to live in the water.

The greatest river in Inner Earth was the Mystic River. Originating in the Rusty Mountains, its meandering waters flowed into the five lakes, proceeded through the Forest of the Giant Trees, and made its way underground beneath Longview Fields before finally cascading into the deep, dark waters of Origo Lake. It took Erin a few days to construct a small canoe. She was proud to apply some of the skills learned during the game *The Last Templar*.

The most noble creatures of the river were mermaids. Recalling the folk tales recounted by Tselby, Erin understood that the Wasay people created the mermaids from a species of ancient dolphins and subsequently enslaved them. It was only when the Wasay evolved spiritually that the mermaids were set free. They were, however, deprived of the ability to talk, and their only way to communicate was through dreams or telepathically. The mermaids were known for their aptitude to see the past and forecast the future. It was also said that the mermaids were better seen in a certain place, "where light meets shadow." Erin could never understand the meaning of the statement.

The river was, for the most part, wide and navigable with sporadic inlets used by Erin as areas for rest. By this time she had become accustomed to the strange environment and proficient in her regular engagement with the creatures of Inner Earth, including some of the animals who possessed the ability to communicate. Among her new friends were Magusta, the little orc, Pefy, the woodpecker, and Quinon, the giant green frog. But none of them had ever seen the mermaids or knew what a place called "where light meets shadow" was. That detail was almost disheartening to Erin, who was sincerely hoping to encounter the mystical water creatures before returning to Taras.

She was told by Tselby that they usually gave a sign prior to making their appearance, almost as an invitation to meet. Could the voice she heard on the vessel, just before entering Devil's Passage, be their signal to her to anticipate a future interaction? Erin didn't know but hoped that her intuition was correct. However, after a few days of navigation, she abandoned her hope of finding "where light meets shadow" and seeing the nymphs. She was approaching the final stretch of her journey, leaving the majestic White Peaks behind and skirting along the last edges of the Forest of the Giant Trees.

It was there that a thick dew, more like a heavy fog, wrapped her surroundings like a blanket. It became hard to see, and Erin had to rely on her instincts in order to move forward safely. The vegetation in the area was also unwieldy and more similar to badlands rather than a forest. Enormous water plants with gigantic leaves sprang up from every direction, making paddling extremely difficult.

Despite the increasing adversity, Erin's courage was bolstered. It was her last night of navigating the Mystic River, and according to the map and her calculations, she would reach the waterfalls in a few hours. Once there, she would have to proceed overland by foot, as she had been warned by Agor not to touch the water. The underground tunnel was too dangerous to even consider. A sense of familiarity pervaded Erin, because this was the part of the forest she knew well. Not too long ago, as an apprentice learning how to survive in the unique environment of Inner Earth, she had spent many days and nights in the area hunting and searching for food. It was also the memorable place where she had met Agor for the first time. So much had occurred since she was last there. But as she had learned during her journeying, time in Inner Earth held a different meaning. It wasn't linear but more like a vibrational frequency, Agor had told her.

Drained after many hours of paddling but happy to have arrived at a location intimate to her and filled with good memories, Erin decided to stop. She was looking for a suitable place to dock her raft when all of a sudden lights appeared in front of her, slowly spinning in circles and revolving outward. As they rotated, a vacuum started to appear inside the circle of lights. It looked as if the glare was eating up the fog, creating a window of visibility, otherwise impossible.

In a short while Erin was able to find a cozy spot to moor the canoe, and as she did, the lights disappeared allowing the fog to return. More exhausted than enchanted, Erin made herself a comfortable bed using giant leaves provided by the water plants, quickly started a fire for protection, and in less than no time she was already asleep.

Her dreams took her back to the water. Erin saw herself paddling the Mystic River with the same canoe she had built a few days prior. It was a beautiful, sunny day and the air was filled with the fragrance of roses and wildflowers. Flocks of birds were crossing the horizon like migrating thoughts. The destination she sought in her dream was that mysterious place called "where light meets shadow," but there was no way to know where or what that location was.

Along the shores of the river, animals were quenching their thirst in the warm, sleepy afternoon. Some of the leaves on the trees were already showing their first autumnal blush, and a lazy breeze was gently moving the golden wheat in the meadow. Gradually a soft gust began to increase in intensity until transformed into a strong wind. It became harder for Erin to maintain the canoe's balance and even more difficult to keep her eyes open. Particles of dust and small elements were hitting her body like little rocks, creating wounds on her face and the exposed parts of her body. The oddity of the situation was that neither the animals nor nature around her seemed to be affected by the strong wind. Colored butterflies were still flapping their iridescent wings in the air, unchallenged. Everything outside of her seemed to be unbothered, clearly untouched. It was like watching a movie on a screen while being in the midst of a virtual storm.

The experience was surreal. It didn't matter where or how Erin positioned the craft, there was no reprieve from the violent gusts. Then something even stranger began to unfold. The whole visual in front of her began to peel away, starting from the corner of her field of view moving toward the center of her vision. It was like a movie whose film had broken into frames or perhaps more fractured than that. Nothing that Erin was observing genuinely existed. It was all just a beautiful projection. The animals, the birds, the blue sky, and the golden wheat of the meadow were peeled off while still in motion. Nothing was real!

Once the whole scene was stripped away, there was nothing but stillness, the perfect absence of sound, light, and movement, the "nothing" itself. But somehow Erin knew her intuition was wrong. She was in the presence of the Shadow Kingdom. Soon the mechanics of that reality became visible to her frightened eyes, and the deception of what had been presented as reality until then became clear. It was a moment of discovery, without pain or desire. It was what it was. Erin thought she had reached the place "where light meets shadow" but she was, once again, mistaken. A soft, gentle voice whispered in her inner ear, "Trust yourself."

Erin looked around but couldn't see anyone. As her eyes became adapted to the darkness, she was able to see that there was a complex machine, almost like an intricate structure of cogwheels that was keeping everything functioning. The utopia of a few moments before had been nothing but a projection created by a shadowy mechanism. "Further," whispered the ethereal voice. At first Erin didn't know where to look, what to search for, but then a subtle feeling started to take life. The dark mechanism wasn't self-aware. It was operating with the sole purpose of maintaining the illusion.

"There must be more," Erin concluded.

Almost as confirmation, a sensation of warmth infused her being. She kept moving in the darkness without a specific direction when she finally saw a feeble light, smaller than the lumen of a candle. It was far, far away. She moved toward the light, weaving her way through the operating, oily cogwheels until she was close enough to understand that the glow was coming from a tiny window up in the corner. The window was too far up to be reached, and it was impossible for Erin to know or see what lay on the other side. Was this the end of her journey?

The voice spoke once again. "Hold the vision and trust." It was then that Erin did something she would normally not have done, something new to her. She anchored her vision to the light and allowed herself to move toward it. A higher power took over, as long as Erin allowed it to do so. In a state of no space and no time, and without reasonable explanation, Erin found herself positioned in front of a window. She took a peek to the other side and, to her surprise, saw the same scene she had experienced before the windstorm: the river, the sunny afternoon with the flock of birds, the smell of flowers, and the gentle breeze. Everything was the same but with a note of contrast. It now appeared to be more genuine, perhaps a little less perfect and more real.

In that moment she was able to see the past and the future of every single entity in the picture: the life and death, the evolution, the righteousness and the mistakes, the joy and the pain. The picture in front of her eyes was telling a story of a journey lived. Everything was in harmony because it had reached fulfillment. Something told Erin that it took a conscious effort to make it that way. It wasn't an artificial projection coming from the outside, as the machine suggested. It was a willful creation coming from the inside. The source was the conscious, dreaming mind rather than a repetitive, soulless mechanism. Something informed Erin that she was a creative part of this manifestation and not just a passive receiver or viewer. The realization was breathtaking, empowering, and frightening at the same time. In her heart she knew she had finally reached the place "where light meets shadow."

Confirmation of her thoughts came almost immediately when a mermaid softly approached her from the side. The mysterious creature was surrounded by a vibrant green and light-blue glow. The mermaid didn't say a word, but she expressed her feelings by offering a spontaneous, sincere smile. Then with a stroke of her tail, she vanished as quickly as she had appeared.

In the space between light and darkness, Erin stood: On one side she was aware of the mechanical projection of a beautiful utopia that wasn't real in her dreams; on the other side a reality that was delightful but also needed to be created, fought for, and defended, and the awareness that it wouldn't exist without effort, pain, birth, and death.

Erin now understood she was offered a choice: live in the dream world of an eternal utopia without growth or commit herself as a creator to a marvelous yet challenging reality that needed to be conquered. The second option offered no guarantee of success or happiness but rather a path to evolution. Despite there being no time in the dream, it ended before Erin could make her decision.

When she awoke from her slumber, the thick fog was gone, leaving the stage set with a cerulean, blue sky. "This might be the last one I will see for a while," was her immediate contemplation.

Everything in Inner Earth appeared to decrease in intensity and vibrancy heading toward the outside. The colors now so eccentric and blazing would eventually be replaced by pallid shades of gray and cream.

It was far from simple for Erin to fathom the implications of her strange experience "where light meets shadow." No matter, there was joy in her heart because she had persevered, and her wish to encounter a mermaid had been fulfilled.

Whatever the significance of her journey might be, Erin had finally reached the understanding that her solo exploration of Inner Earth was coming to an end.

This time she knew the path ahead would lead her back to Taras.

With a grateful heart rather than regret or nostalgia, Erin quickly resumed her return to the citadel.

If only she had met the Wasay, she thought for a moment, but knew it was time instead to go home!

CHAPTER 21: MISSING TIME

Longview Fields stretched lazily across the horizon. To Erin, they signified the end of her solitary experience but also the quickening of her arrival at Taras.

As she made her way, the air was filled with the scent of grass and the sound of wind cutting its way through the meadow. Never until that moment had Erin wondered if the Expedition crew thought she was still alive. So long had passed since the last time she saw Roger. The anticipation of what might be prompted a nervous kind of energy. She kept walking, fast, despite a lack of food the past few days. It was as if her brain were advising her to hurry up, making her feel even more tense.

Her mind was focused so deeply into her journey home that at first she didn't perceive the formless and indistinct action taking place in the field of vision in front of her. When noticed, she thought of wandering bison, even though it looked more like shadows shifting. After a while she realized the movements were too fast and too coordinated to be attributed to animals. Buffalos usually move slowly, grazing as they go and lolloping about in an ungainly way. That much she had observed.

Her alertness renewed, Erin took hold of her bow and aimed it at the dark shapes approaching. The tall grass offered a perfect camouflage, and with her patience severely tested, she remained immobile, keeping her focus on the target. Erin knew she wouldn't shoot an arrow unless it was absolutely necessary, but her solitary experience suggested that it was wiser to stand at the ready. Her breathing slowed, decreasing her heartbeat, and left her body at a standstill like an experienced sniper. Never in her previous life would Erin have guessed she would have the capacity to control her mind so well, but the training received in Inner Earth taught her skills she had not known she possessed.

Connected to the shifting shadows was a noise, a buzzing sound similar to a giant swarm of bees but more intense. The loudness increased. Erin's vigilance intensified but her calm and confident stance remained unaltered. A few minutes passed, allowing a more complete picture to take form. Her heart began to rejoice quicker than her intellect could grasp that those black dots were not animals but people, perhaps members of the Expedition.

Maybe she had not been forgotten. That simple recognition caused Erin to nearly crumble inside. It took a few more seconds to abandon her cautious attitude and comprehend that she was not in any danger. On the contrary, she had been found! Tears of joy fell abundantly as Erin moved toward what she now knew to be four-wheelers and not bison. Her whole body was shaking, and she could barely scream or even talk. She raised her arms in the air, waving them wildly trying to send a message, while staggering toward the people. But her attempts to make herself visible fell short and nobody seemed to notice her presence.

The fear of not being seen started to roar in Erin's mind. In a state of panic for survival and near desperation, Erin grabbed her gun, checked the magazine for ammunition, and with a trembling wrist fired a shot in the air. The black shapes stopped, confirming the signal had been received. Erin held her breath, waiting for guidance about her next move. She finally found her voice and while shouting ran toward what she now saw were members of her crew. It wasn't the need to be rescued that made Erin run as fast as she could but the desire to be reunited with her comrades. Words of hope thundered spontaneously. "Hey, I am here! I am alive!" she shouted, as she ran and ran with ecstatic relief.

Turning, the black shapes began moving slowly in the direction of the gunshot, but they were still too far away to be sure of what was happening. In Erin's mind, there was no doubt she had found her team, but she could not confirm the same was true for them. Erin could feel her heart pulsating inside her chest. Her throat was rasping and yet her feet kept moving forward, almost kissing the ground beneath. Tears were blinding her eyes, as she quickened her pace. All she knew was that she had to keep running and forced her body to comply.

Finally, after reaching a distance to be able to distinguish shapes and colors, confirmation of her intuition struck her like a dart. Roger was leading the small group of people! He must have recognized her because he started to run, leaving behind all his gear. The other two, still unidentified, stood in awe. In that moment the ache of missing her friends and home returned in all its force. She was a survivor, after all.

Oh, the unimaginable feeling of knowing that Roger was still a part of her life and dreams!

His hug was stronger than anything she remembered, and despite being exhausted, Erin felt lighter than air. She allowed herself to fall into his strong arms, appreciative of that simple pleasure. After a long while, Roger looked at her. "Erin," he exclaimed, almost incredulously, "Erin, you made it."

She smiled and corrected him. "Yes, we made it, Roger."

In that moment there was no need to add anything else. Erin had been found and was about to go home to Taras.

Moments later, Parker and Matt arrived, fumbling on their machines after a long run. They stared at each other, but the smiles and tears manifested on the outside weren't quite enough to convey the vortex of emotions happening on the inside. Erin's heart was still beating fast, and despite having so much to say, there were no words to be found.

Matt, as usual the strongest of the group, finally broke what seemed an eternity by offering his hand to Erin and saying, "Erin, we are so happy to have found you. We left yesterday evening with very little hope, but it looks like our prayers have been answered. Welcome back, dear Erin."

At his side, Parker was nodding, still astonished. Roger wrapped Erin's shoulders with his arm, and the four of them walked back to the vehicles. Once there, Erin was offered food and water and ate like a starving child.

"I'm sorry I caused you trouble," were her first words after the nourishment.

"No need to worry, Erin. You didn't cause any trouble. Things could have been much worse. You have been missing for only a couple of days," Roger tried to reassure his friend.

But his words had a different effect on Erin. "What do you mean only a couple of days?"

Roger smiled with fondness. "I know it's hard to count time here, but it was just the other day when Steve had that accident. Do you remember?"

Yes, Erin did remember. She remembered very well, but that was not the point. She recalled Steve being taken back to Taras by Matt, except that it was long ago. Definitely more than a couple of days! For a moment Erin felt confused but then she remembered what Agor had told her. "All your time spent here will be given back to you." Erin never paid much attention to that statement until now. Trying to hide her bewilderment, she limited herself to asking, "How is Steve doing?"

"He's feeling much better. The doctor diagnosed that he was lacking nutrients, and his genetic predisposition made him the victim of a breakdown. It looked much worse than it actually was."

Erin was relieved by the sound of those words. "I'm so happy to hear that he's fine," although she couldn't help thinking about her friend Alan. A grin appeared on her face, but it was just a noble attempt to hide her sudden melancholy and frustration.

"All's well that ends well!" Roger exclaimed, triggering a sweet grimace on her strained face.

Erin jumped on Roger's four-wheeler and leaned her chest against his back while the team made their way back to Taras. Keeping her eyes closed, she cried. Roger, on the other hand, didn't even try to hide his happiness. In his heart he couldn't wait to proudly inform Captain Miller about the success of the rescue mission. The Expedition team was once again complete, and except for Alan, there had not been any other casualties. It wasn't the perfect outcome, but considering the dangerous nature of the Exploration, it was a respectable conclusion to an avant-garde crusade.

Only two days had passed since Erin first met Agor but, in reality, it seemed more like weeks to her. Too many questions still needed to be answered, and the desire to make sense of things ignited her curiosity. But Erin knew she had more patience than the others. She had earned the capacity of forbearance. And so when the perfect opportunity presented itself later, she was prepared. The group decided to stop for a break not too far from Taras. They still had several hours of travel ahead, and Matt suggested it would be better for the team to rest before undertaking the hazardous slopes, better known as Sandy Rings.

Erin couldn't believe how much she had missed something as simple as a meal in the company of friends. After eating, Parker and Matt decided to take a short nap.

Roger laid his blanket on the grass and, with an inviting smile, asked Erin to join him while crossing his arms under his head. It was hard for Erin to resist Roger's charm, despite the fact that he was not really her kind of guy. More than anything she wanted to talk to him and so kindly accepted the invitation. The sky above them was the usual cream-gray color, so much different from the multicolored, vibrant vault of heaven that Erin had experienced only a few days before. Before she even realized it, she had become nostalgic. It wasn't the memory of her past that made her wistful but rather the imaginings of what her future held.

The longer Erin spent time with Roger, the more she was becoming convinced that he was that perfect friend, or at least he was trying to be. And so when he interrupted their silent conversation asking what she was thinking, she pondered carefully before answering. "Nothing, just looking at the colors of the sky."

Erin was surprised by the question because she knew that Roger was right. There was so much more going on in her mind.

"Everything turned out as you said it would," she said quietly.

Erin's voice was soft but loud enough to annoy Matt, who was trying to take a nap. He didn't say anything but expressed his displeasure by puffing and turning to the other side.

After a moment, Roger was the first to stand and offered his hand to Erin to help her up.

"Let's move a little bit that way so we don't bother the others," he said, while placing his hand on Erin's shoulder and guiding her a few steps away.

Even on that occasion, Roger's polite mannerism didn't fail to impress Erin. His elegant composure and charming behavior were noble and rare.

They sat on the ground not far away. The deep silence between them filled Erin's mind, but when she looked at Roger, she noticed he had been weeping. She moved closer and hugged him in a friendly fashion, as if they had never been apart and decided it was time to talk about her experience.

Erin was pleased to see how quickly Roger was able to move beyond incertitude, making up his mind that she had told him the truth. There were things she wanted to tell him, but a strange, inner feeling was advising her to be reticent. Erin honored her intuition, and Roger went patiently along with the story.

But soon enough she realized the same hesitation didn't apply to him. Roger's desire was to share his experience, and without asking for permission, he began.

He kept a pleasant outlook while narrating all the details of his adventure, from the moment he woke up to the realization of Erin's disappearance, and even included his efforts to organize the rescue mission.

Erin was delighted when she finally heard Roger say, "I knew I could have died. It was only my decision that kept me alive."

She looked at him with a questioning stare, although she already knew.

He continued. "It's hard for me to tell you this, but I have a strong feeling that my waking up was not a coincidence but the result of a conscious determination."

Before he went on speaking, Erin mentioned she had the same feeling about her experience.

Hearing her words touched Roger's heart, but he chose not to persuade her to go on. Fearing he might lose his friend again, he continued. All at once his deep, calm tone of voice ceased and was replaced by a tense enunciation.

"I looked for you everywhere, but I could not find you. I didn't know what to believe, because I couldn't imagine you had left me there to die. At the same time, I didn't want to think that something bad had happened to you. I was really worried, so I decided to go back to Taras. Somehow when I woke up, I was close by. After a short briefing with Captain Miller and some other experts, we decided to organize a rescue mission."

Following a short pause, he continued. "I could never have accepted the idea of losing you. If anything would have happened to you, I would never have forgiven myself."

Erin looked at Roger. His sincere love and concern for her was visible in his eyes. The desire to share everything with him was strong, but greater was the intuition suggesting to her that it wasn't the right moment or perhaps, sadly, he was not the right person. A few weeks prior, Erin would have paid little attention to that inner voice but now her mind was changed. She knew that her intuition was the only reason she had survived. The same insight that kept her company during her solitary journey had also kept her alive.

"I don't want to lie to you," she whispered, while keeping her head bowed.

Roger didn't seem to pay much attention to what she was saying. A smile crossed his face, barely disclosing his white teeth.

Erin quickly regretted her words, but now it was too late, so she carried on. "I have a feeling that more time has passed than just a couple of days."

Roger was silent. Resorting to what he knew to be an acceptable, scientific explanation, he replied, "That's an understandable feeling. And you are not completely wrong."

He looked at Erin out of the corner of his eye searching for interest, then continued thoughtfully. "The magnetic field appears to be different in Inner Earth. It is possible that this fact has an effect on our perception of time. But I am just speculating for now." Then he suddenly came to a standstill.

But Erin was determined to know more. "What do you mean?" she asked quietly.

"Well, as you know, time is affected by gravity. The closer you are to a source of gravity, the slower time passes. The farther we are from the point of gravity, the faster time goes. In other words, time runs slower wherever gravity is the strongest. We know this is true because we measured it with spacecraft."

"And how does this correlate to time in Inner Earth?"

Roger blushed slightly and then replied. "Every sphere has a gravitational force on the inside that pulls toward the center. This force is directly proportional to the distance from the core. The gravitational force grows as you move toward the surface of the sphere."

He waited a little to allow the information to sink in before continuing. "I can't be sure yet but my opinion is that we will find more similarity between Inner Earth and space than we are ready to admit. And this relates to the passing of time as well." He then looked at Erin pensively.

Hearing his explanation made Erin think of Agor. "He would know," she thought silently.

Roger and Erin remained for a few more minutes in a contemplative state before being interrupted by an impatient Matt reminding everybody they needed to get going. There was something exciting and mysterious in returning to Taras, and the ingenuous part of Erin couldn't wait to finally be there.

Soon enough the team resumed their journey to the citadel. The grass was slowly dwindling, exposing the white sand.

Eventually as they approached the far edge of Longview Fields, the panorama shifted completely. On the horizon, Erin could see the black waters of Origo Lake, making her content. But before she had time to fully appreciate the familiar view, a slight smell of something burning started to fill the air. The rest of the team noticed the same thing, and after a quick stop to make sure that the odor wasn't coming from the engine of one of the vehicles, Matt observed a thin but darker trail of air coming from the valley below. It didn't take long for them to realize that the gloom was actually smoke, and it appeared to be coming directly from Taras.

A sense of urgency overpowered the team. As they descended Sandy Rings toward the valley, visibility decreased, making it hard for them to follow the nearly imperceptible path.

Unaware of the gravity of the situation, Roger pointed out how hard it still was to adapt his eyes to the obscurity after so many weeks of light deprivation. "Who would have ever guessed that darkness could be so impressive?" he asked, without actually expecting a response.

Erin didn't pay much attention to what Roger was saying. She was thinking of something else more important to her. When she was a child, she used to embrace darkness without fear. It reminded her of fantastic creatures and imaginary worlds. But this was different, the kind of blackness that steals the ability to navigate the pathways of normal reality, and a thousand times more dangerous than what inspired the obscure fantasy of a young girl.

Needless to say, the unexpected situation occupied everyone's thoughts. Stretching in front of all of them lay a test of their fears, their courage, and their knowledge.

The air was becoming thick and more difficult to breathe. Stopping to put on breathing masks was the only way to endure the brittle conditions. The only thing preventing the team from rushing to base camp was the need for prudence. While analyzing the scene below, Erin could see some sporadic orange and yellow stripes emerging from the black smoke. The chilling realization that those were flames made her come to a standstill as she put on her mask. For how long she remained hostage to the horror of that moment, she did not know, but when Roger mentioned the absence of communication from base camp, a memory surfaced in her confused mind. "There are bad people in your group who do bad things," Agor had told her.

The joy of the past few hours had been replaced with anxiety and the bitter thought that what she was about to face would no longer be a lighthearted celebration of her return.

A few minutes went by, and in the absolute stillness Erin was overcome with a sense of déjà vu. She was sure she had already lived this experience, but nothing in her memory could confirm the feeling. Then she remembered her dream from a few nights prior. "Where light meets shadow" was the answer she needed. Erin knew that advancing into the obvious danger they were witnessing below was just a matter of trust.

Timidly she voiced her intuition. "I know it's hard to see and breathe, but we need to have faith and keep our vision anchored to the destination. Our minds will guide us there."

"I have been in emergency situations many times," Matt stated matter-of-factly, "and I know one must confront adversity boldly. This moment demands conviction, because we can always forgive each other but life will hold us accountable. Let confidence and rectitude give us clarity and inspire us toward the right decisions."

The silence that followed didn't last more than a few seconds, but Matt felt the urge to dissolve the fear from his companions. Extending his arms outward, he gently placed them on Parker's and Erin's shoulders, who were standing beside him. Forming a circle, they remained in what can only be described as a spiritual silence until everyone felt at peace. They all knew too well that it would have been useless to attempt to reverse Matt's decree, and so they humbly obliged.

"You will see things you have never seen before, experience situations you have never experienced before. It might scare you," was Agor's warning to Erin. More than once he had mentioned the potential danger that existed with certain people in the Expedition. Erin tried to shake such horrible thoughts from her head but they refused to be dislodged, so she made the decision to keep them tucked deep inside. Agor's warning was a heavy secret that Erin would carry alone in her heart.

Cautiously the team proceeded down to the valley. By the time they reached the boundary of Sandy Rings, the heat had become almost intolerable. There was no doubt in anyone's mind that a fire had been raging at Taras. Moving slowly along the road, Erin saw scattered debris here and there.

"Where am I?" was the question she kept asking herself while trying to recollect memories of Taras as she had known it. But the realization that nothing appeared as it was before induced a sense of utter despair in the core of her being. It was a horrific sight, and for a moment she remained transfixed observing the destruction with bated breath and eyes wide open. It didn't take long for everyone to understand that this was not just a fire but rather the result of an explosion. The sudden and chilling realization almost froze the blood in Erin's veins.

For some reason the smoke began to dissolve as they approached, allowing visibility to be partially restored. Erin searched for the tallest building in Taras, the tower, which was supposed to be visible from far away but she couldn't find it. As they moved closer to the citadel, the odor of burned things became more and more pungent, and in the midst of it, Erin could identify the smell of burned flesh. Tears started rolling down her face, leaving white streaks of pain on her soot-covered cheeks.

What kind of tomorrow could there possibly be? she questioned, staring bewildered at the devastation.

After so many days of journeying through unknown territory, with all the many wonders experienced and messages of hope, this wasn't exactly what Erin was expecting on her return. And yet in the midst of such desperation, she couldn't help but think about how her life had been saved. So sorrowful and exhausting was that moment, so deep the agitation, that it was only with great difficulty that was she was able to restore her composure.

Then all of a sudden a faint spark ignited a ray of hope inside her. Maybe it wasn't too late. Maybe there was still someone who could be saved. Erin and her team were determined to advance, but cautiously. However, they soon realized that the only things left of Taras were the basement walls of some buildings and a large amount of wreckage.

The darkest night of their adventure had arrived, and it was insolently demanding everyone's attention. Erin looked at her teammates and saw fear, desperation, and misery reflected in their eyes.

Without saying a word, Matt rushed to the end of the settlement toward the shores of Origo Lake hoping to find Admiral Q-Oho still anchored in all its majesty. To his immense desolation he found the only thing left of the noble vessel was a rubble of smoking metal. After a few minutes of solitude to collect himself, he calmly decided to reengage the world and slowly walked toward his team.

"Admiral Q-Oho has been destroyed and we have no way out of here. We are in trouble." He looked at his companions and saw the terror in their faces. With little emotion in his voice, he added, "I have reminded myself why I am here and I think you all should do the same. I have been in war and lonely before, and I know strength comes from conviction. In situations like this, ruthless determination is necessary to avoid desperation and to take charge of responsibility. The choice belongs to each of us. How do we want to live the last days of our lives? Because this is it, folks. We have reached the end of our mortal existence."

The team was stunned by Matt's words, everyone except Erin. She knew that her time to make a difference had arrived.

"Not everything is lost. I know someone who can help us."

Everyone's eyes widened at the sound of Erin's words.

"We have a long journey ahead," she replied, smiling quietly at the idea of seeing Agor again. It wasn't easy to admit. He had been right since the beginning.

CHAPTER 22: THE END OF WAR

"Every man must do two things alone; he must do his own believing and his own dying."

— Martin Luther

Earlier that afternoon, the SOTIS team had received the long-awaited phone call. General Curtis had been found dead in his office with a single bullet to his head. His body was discovered early in the morning lying prostrate on the floor with the weapon still in his right hand. Blood was smeared on the walls and on the floor. After a quick investigation, the case was ruled a suicide and subsequently closed to avoid bringing unnecessary attention to the situation. Despite the request of the family, no autopsy was performed.

The President of the United States had already released a statement from the White House addressing his sorrow for the loss of a valued staff member and friend, together with his condolences to the family, whom he knew very well. Many who had lived and worked with General Curtis were aware of his generosity as well as his honesty. Those who were asked were able to confirm that General Curtis appeared to be his usual self and hadn't shown any sign of distress in the days preceding the "accident."

"Another one bites the dust," was the distant comment of agent Kelly. There was no compassion in his words. To his mind it was just cold and impersonal business as usual. But more than that, there was something about the whole situation that brought him a surge of passion like nothing he had experienced before.

TJ wished he had the same internal flame when he loosely commented, "I guess this is the signal we were all waiting for."

He looked at his leader with inquisitive eyes, seeking a note of confirmation.

"You are correct. We shall proceed with the plan." Agent Kelly retorted, with a glint of evil in his eyes. "But for now, I will enjoy another glass of this superb whiskey," and with the most polished manners served himself a generous glass of bourbon without ice.

Kelly's answer didn't carry much weight with TJ and Jordan. They moved away with the intention of taking a good nap, but a muttering from their leader warned them to be on the alert.

In the meantime, Captain Miller had already been informed of the tragic news. The thought of his fond friend being dead concerned him deeply. What was even more troubling was the awareness that he had committed suicide. General Curtis just wasn't the type of person who would consider such a senseless action! Everyone who had the pleasure to know him could have confirmed that.

Sitting in the silence of his office, Miller grabbed the phone and dialed a number to the outside world.

"Hello, Susan, this is Jeff." His tone was deep and calm.

A long silence on the other end, then a faint voice responded. "Jeff ... I guess you have already been informed."

"Yes, they have just briefed me. I am sorry, Susan. I wish it weren't true. You have no idea how much I would prefer to be there with you right now."

General Curtis' widow, Susan, burst into tears. It was hard to even talk for Captain Miller, and it took him tremendous effort to keep his composure without crying. Years of service in the military taught him to control his emotions well. He allowed the widow to vent all her pain over the phone. Then he continued. "Susan, our Expedition is coming to an end very soon. I will be able to see you after my return. I just wanted to tell you that I'm sorry for your loss. Your husband was a very talented man and a good friend of mine. I will miss him a lot." A note of emotion transpired through his voice.

"Thank you, Jeff. He was so proud of his friendship with you. He kept talking about you. He really loved you very much."

"Thank you, Susan. I appreciate that. The sentiments were mutual. I will always carry with me a fine memory of David." Captain Miller's voice was full of affection. "I will call you when I get back, Susan. Stay strong, my friend."

"I'll do my best, but it's hard." Susan paused for a second, sniffling. Then she added, "Promise me that you will call me when you come back. I would love to see you, Jeff. I need to know why all of this is happening."

"I don't have an answer, Susan. I don't think there is one. But I would be honored to share my memories of your husband with you."

"Thank you, Jeff. I would really appreciate that. I shall see you upon your return to this part of the world," she said, forcing a weak chuckle.

"Bye now, Susan," Captain Miller responded, with a strong inclination to cry.

"Good-bye, Jeff," were her parting words as she hung up the phone.

A mysterious voice whispered in his inner ear that someday, somehow, everything would be made known. But there was also a less noticeable feeling, a sort of call to action, a pressure to do something, that was making him extremely anxious. His thoughts were lodged in the memory of his friend and his absurd action. The last phone call with General Curtis was just a few days ago, and Captain Miller hadn't noticed anything terribly unusual in his friend's attitude. But obviously there must have been something troubling his mind, and it never occurred to Captain Miller to understand what. That thought made him feel indignant. Why did Curtis kill himself? Why didn't he seek help or even a small word of advice?

Captain Miller had a lot on his plate, and it wasn't just the Expedition. Thoughts about his career and a potential resignation were occupying his mind more often lately. Never in his life had the desire for freedom been so intense. Maybe it was the result of being restricted in an unfamiliar place and having no liberty to leave, or perhaps the stress and depletion from being in charge of other people's lives, but a sense of unfamiliar rebellion was starting to spread in his mind like a contagious disease that had no cure. He knew the task he had chosen to undertake was not an easy one, but he had always hoped for the best. Would he refuse to comply with his obligations? No, that would have been senseless. But what was once a privilege and an honor was rapidly becoming nothing more than a primitive emotion: the fear of being stuck in a reality that he had very little power to change.

Then as if an internal clock reminded him of his duties, he switched off all of his sorrow and brought his mind back to the present moment. He needed to inform the crew. Still with his mind conflicted and half unconsciously, he began to write his speech for the occasion. The perfect draft came after a couple of different versions. Almost in a mechanical manner, he convened a council. As he prepared to leave his office, he was already caught up in the feeling that he was about to give the last speech of his mission.

As he walked through Taras toward the conference room, it occurred to him that love and sorrow often appear together. The pain of his loss was real and it seemed to be coming and going like waves on the shore, leaving his mind dry at one moment and flooded with memories the next. He needed more time to think, so he resolved to make another round of the peaceful settlement before entering the building.

The conference room was already filling up. Some people were happily chatting, unconcerned about the upcoming message. Others, more seasoned and experienced, were already showing signs of puzzlement and curiosity on their faces. A few young employees nodded at Captain Miller in a sign of respect, but nobody approached him with questions or comments as they were accustomed to doing.

At first Captain Miller didn't pay much attention to that minor change, but then he began to wonder if the expression on his face betrayed his usual professional and authoritative presence. To him, it was like a bittersweet epiphany. Ever since he had arrived in Inner Earth, an unusual impression had started to take form in his mind. It was the perception of something invisible and yet very noticeable. Somehow he knew that the essence of his message had already been delivered from mind to mind. Any action in the physical world was secondary to a reality that had already been preceded by his decisions. If only people could be more aware of the invisible, he caught himself pondering. There was an unsettling energy in those types of thoughts, he soon noted. He was able, however, to recover from his baseless fear and return to his normal mood.

From the rear of the room, Captain Miller studied the people gathered. The quiet and older individuals were mainly located at the edges of the hall and mostly seated by themselves. The majority, however, were chatting and laughing excitedly, sharing food and jokes with friends and coworkers.

Captain Miller looked for Clyde and found him, as expected, in the very back of the room by himself. As soon as their eyes met, Clyde gasped and started to wave his hand in the air, holding what appeared to be a folded piece of paper. Captain Miller had always retained a good eye for reading people, and he could immediately identify the scared look on the face of the young man. It was evident that Clyde had something important to say. He chose, however, to put that understanding away with willful determination and focus on something more important to him in that moment — his friend David.

In the meantime, the crowd inside the hall had become aware of Captain Miller's presence and a spontaneous chant filled the room. "We stand united! We stand united! We stand united!"

With all the inner strength he could command, Captain Miller took steps toward the stage and smiled. A few tears drifted onto his cheeks.

"We stand united! We stand united! We stand united!" The unified voice was followed by another addition, sounding like,

"Where we go one, we go all! Where we go one, we go all! Where we go one, we go all!" It was now clear to him that the Expedition crew was not ready to return home unless everyone had been accounted for. That included Erin and the rescue team. His smile broadened. He was proud of his squad. With a trembling hand, he pulled the microphone closer to his mouth and pronounced, "Yes. Where we go one, we go all."

Instantaneously, the room became energized in an explosion of joy. When the excitement calmed down a little, Captain Miller continued. He decided he wouldn't need his notes after all and tucked the intended discourse in his pocket. It was almost as if he could hear the guttural laughter of General Curtis behind him.

He was finally ready to deliver his speech.

"This adventure we all share began with a very simple, common story. It was the story of love and discovery. This little story, called 'the exploration story,' was nothing more than the fantasy of a small boy. But this young fellow also had a dream that one day, one fine morning, he would wake up to see his story become reality. Most of his life was dedicated to this devotion, the exploration story as he knew it could be. He committed himself to his passion even when he didn't know how to accomplish it. He committed himself to his passion even when there were no means available to do it. You know, the boy never felt the need to prove that he was right or capable of achieving something. He never had any intention to have an impact on the world. There was only his genuine desire to live his story, fully and sincerely.

"Time passed and the little boy became a man. People in his life came and left. Some changed and some did not. But his ability to pursue his dream never changed. His determination to hold onto his story never changed. I had the privilege to meet this man, and I can assure you he didn't always have an easy life. One time I asked him how he was able to endure in times of incertitude. He replied with only two words. Those two words changed my life forever. He said, "Trust God." Just these two words, trust God. You know, I wasn't a person of faith before. I have never believed in any God. But with his words, he made me wonder. He made me look for something more meaningful in my life. He said to me one day, 'Jeff, you keep making the same mistake. You insist on wanting to understand the future. It is foolish for any person to do that because the future cannot be known. The future can only be trusted. You need to look at tomorrow with trust. Only the past can be understood. You can attempt to connect the dots of your past but not of your future. You don't know enough to do that.' He was right.

"Going back to his story, it so happens that one day, one fine morning, the boy's dream became a reality. This Expedition is his story. This adventure is his dream. I want to repeat this again: We are here today because of a little boy's story and his ability to hold onto his dream. Our journey began just as he envisioned. I guess many of you are curious to know who this person is. Unfortunately, he is not here with us today. His doctors advised him not to take part in this Expedition because of some medical problems. They said it was too risky. Some of you may ask why? Why would he refuse to live out his dream now that he was finally able to accomplish it? I asked him the same question. He replied by saying, 'Why do you think I am not participating? I have been taking part in this adventure ever since I was a child. Now it is your turn to enjoy it.' He never stopped living his dream, I can assure you that much, until one day, the day that he died. Till that day, which happens to be today."

Captain Miller paused briefly, took a few deep breaths and then continued. "Plato once said that only those who die have seen the end of war. But I can tell you, nobody wants to die. Even those who want to see God don't want to die to meet him. I have asked myself the meaning of many things, and there is no difference this time. I still don't have all the answers, but one thing I do know: Sometime, somehow, we will be able to connect all the dots. I want to trust that there is a bigger plan for us than dying. I want to trust that there is a higher purpose for us than our mortal existence. In this moment of incertitude and confusion, I would like to remind each and every one of us of those two simple words that my friend once said to me, 'Trust God.'

"Let all of us trust our ability to dream and to live our story. If not for someone else, let's do it for ourselves. Let us give our story permission to take us to places that we have never seen, to meet people that we have never met, and to live experiences that we have never lived, even if we don't know how to do it, even if we don't have the tools to do it. Let us trust God and move toward our future with joy and determination. But, most of all, let us all give a happy ending to the story of our friend, whose name was General Curtis. He was found dead today in his office in D.C. Please join me in honoring his name because we now know that only the forgotten ones are truly dead. May his memory live in our hearts and his inspiration guide us for the remaining days of our mission. We owe it to him. We owe it to us. We owe it to God. Thank you all for coming and God bless."

Captain Miller stepped away from the microphone. For several minutes nobody said a word. Then someone from the back of the hall shouted, "I have a dream!" The rest of the crowd almost mechanically started to chant in unison, "I have a dream! I have a dream! I have a dream!" Captain Miller was weeping profusely. He gave the crowd one last look, raising his right hand in a salute, then walked out of the room. Clyde was standing there waiting for his opportunity to speak. Captain Miller approached him, as he promised. "What's in there, Clyde?" he asked, gathering his emotions when he saw the young technician holding the piece of paper so carefully.

"Sir, I have been working on the communication that was sent on my terminal and I was able to decode the message. It doesn't look pretty, sir."

"Excellent, Clyde! What exactly doesn't look pretty?"

"It appears we are in danger, sir."

Captain Miller opened his eyes wide and remained in silence for a few moments giving Clyde the opportunity to continue. "The people … uh … the message seems to be coming from space, sir. And there is something else. There are entities who live in Inner Earth. They are warning us of a potential danger."

Captain Miller was baffled. "Okay. Hold on, Clyde. You are saying that the message is coming from space and it is alerting us to a potential danger in Inner Earth? In addition to the fact that there are other entities living here? How am I supposed to make sense of everything you are saying?"

"I know, sir. It seems very confusing, but this is exactly what the communication says. As you said before, one day we will be able to connect all the dots. But for now, please take a look for yourself, sir. I have printed the message for you to see, sir."

Clyde handed the folded piece of paper to his boss. Captain Miller grabbed the note and read, "Humans not alone here. Humans not aware of dangerous situation. High alert. Please withdraw efforts to expand. X21CQT-OK+"

"What does X21CQT-OK+ mean? Have you been able to decode it?" Captain Miller's voice was showing signs of anxiety.

Clyde didn't reply, so Captain Miller continued, "Are you sure this is a valid communication and not a hacking attempt?"

"Yes, sir. The message didn't follow the proper channels used for this type of communication and I was able to secure the source. Given the information I have, there is no doubt in my mind that this message comes from space."

Captain Miller didn't wait too long before commanding, "Let's go to my office! If what you say is true, this is a matter of security and it must be addressed immediately!"

Captain Miller grabbed Clyde by the elbow and hurried outside of the arena and down the main street of Taras. He purposefully ignored the many people trying to approach him with questions or condolences. As they were drawing closer to Admiral Q-Oho, Clyde spotted the SOTIS team leaving the vessel. The three agents were wearing the usual black uniforms but curiously carrying some heavy-looking backpacks. They were headed toward the center of the citadel, oblivious to the presence of the Captain and Clyde. Something about the picture perturbed Clyde, but he quickly acknowledged it was probably his nerves due to the last inconvenient meeting he had with them in his office.

As they climbed the stairs to the second level where the Captain's office was located, time seemed to slow down dramatically. Clyde saw the unfolding of every single action as if he were in a slow-motion movie, and despite his efforts, there was no way to accelerate what was happening. Then all of a sudden he perceived what seemed to be a loud noise followed by darkness. When he finally reopened his eyes, he found himself floating in the air. From this privileged position, Clyde was able to observe everything and everyone down below. Captain Miller was laughing from the chair at his desk, cuddled by his wife Molly and their son Jake. They were waving at Clyde, so he returned the courtesy. Joy and lightness were in his heart. A sweet energy pulled him toward another direction where he saw Megan smiling and dancing in a field of flowers. She had a picnic ready and was calling him with her gentle hand. In a moment Clyde was there in front of an altar with the woman he loved. Images from the future revealed a lovely family of four kids and plenty of animals. Clyde looked closely and was able to spot a wonderful farm in the mountains. He knew everything he was observing belonged to him. That was a happy life he had created for himself!

A pat on his shoulder demanded he look in the opposite direction, and there he saw all of his friends from the Expedition gathered together to be celebrated. Each and every one of them were called out and rewarded with a medal of honor. A deep sense of pride and belonging infused Clyde's soul as he allowed himself to be coddled in that sweet vision. Somehow he knew that he had been a part of something majestic and that the efforts of every single member were going to be rewarded, not forgotten. Somehow he knew the Expedition would make history.

Desiring to go back in time returned him to Taras. What he saw was unexpected and painful. The citadel was completely destroyed, every single building was razed to the ground, and countless, lifeless bodies were lying on what was left of base camp. A veil of sadness coated the scene below. Clyde stopped there for a few moments. There was a feeling of anguish that caused him to cry. As he became aware of it, a tear fell onto the dark ruins of Taras. From that little drop of salty water, a flower of light emerged, emanating rays of energy all around. The whole scene transformed into something completely different. Taras had risen again — stronger, bigger, and more populated. Inner Earth was a reality for the multitudes and not a dream only for a few, select people. Races of beings from different dimensions were living harmoniously together in mutual respect. The ultimate sacrifice had been paid by a small group of brave men and women for the benefit of humanity. The names of those who sacrificed their lives were embedded in every tree, plant, and flower that existed. They would be remembered forever. Clyde knew he was one of them and his sense of despair was quickly replaced with peace and joy. He knew that it had all been worth it.

In the blink of an eye, Clyde found himself walking with Captain Miller upstairs toward his office when a tremor shook the boat. Captain Miller looked at the young man at his side with a glance of terror in his eyes, but this time Clyde was the one who knew. With the deepest sense of love in his heart, he whispered, "We are not alone, sir. I can assure you, sir, everything will be fine."

The noise that followed echoed across the grieving town of Taras issuing, amid a terrible realization, the horrifying sound of an explosion.

CHAPTER 23: EXPEDITION ADMIRAL Q-OHO

"Whatever else history may say about me when I'm gone, I hope it will record that I appealed to your best hopes, not your worst fears; to your confidence rather than your doubts. My dream is that you will travel the road ahead with liberty's lamp guiding your steps and opportunity's arm steadying your way."

— Ronald Reagan

Jeff M. – captain
Clyde T. – cyber security technician/devices specialist
Megan S. – nurse
Scott A. – surgeon
Erica K. – medical assistant
Dennis B. – nurse assistant
Rachel V. – biologist
Steve G. – photographer
Jennifer B. – psychologist
Alexa P. – cook
Eva W. – archery coach and ballistic expert
Jeffrey B. – cook assistant
Greg S. – barista
Linda C. – waitress
Morgan N. – janitor
Beth B. – janitor
Chuck M. – physical therapist
Frank L. – storage manager
Luke T. – tailor

Kelly P. – librarian
Jessy T. – law enforcement officer
Jackie E. – law enforcement officer
Mike V. – security guard
Brenda T. – scientist
Logan H. – researcher
Devin P. – researcher
Amanda G. – robot technician
Robert C. – filming and video editing
Alison R. – audio recording
Paul T. – scientist
Ricardo P. – scientist
Cody R. – communication specialist
Matthew C. – computer technician
John N. – computer technician
Johnathan B. – anesthetist
Larry R. – fitness trainer
Nick D. – hair stylist
Michelle W. – massage therapist
Rob C. – delivery manager
Charlie F. – civilian
Jake M. – civilian
Susan G. – exploration guide
Jim J. – survival expert
Henry M. – pilot
George M. – pilot
Karl R. – construction worker
Kevin P. – electrician
Paul P. – plumber

Admiral Q-Oho Inner Earth Expedition Members – Deceased

CHAPTER 24: WHAT ONCE WAS

By the time the blast occurred, the SOTIS team was already in a secure location far from the epicenter of the explosion. The small but powerful devices installed in critical areas of Admiral Q-Oho didn't fail their expectations, and a few other explosives located in strategic positions around Taras added to the macabre achievement. There were no known survivors except for the rescue team and possibly Erin, but that was no reason for concern for the three agents.

Kelly, who was never less than arrogant, looked at TJ and Jordan with a smirk of satisfaction. It didn't matter that the majority of their work was done, because nothing could crack his heart with joy. The level of self-importance he attributed to himself by virtue of his position was hard to please. Kelly knew that the most crucial and dangerous part of their mission was yet to come. In order for them to be successful, the few remaining survivors had to be found. "Dead or alive" was the mantra repeated in his twisted mind. At this point, nothing else mattered to him.

TJ pulled a radio device from his backpack and informed their leader in the outer world of the current situation. "Boss, it's done."

A rough voice from the other end of the line responded, "Excellent! Can you confirm that there are no survivors?"

"Not at this time, boss. A few explorers are currently on a rescue mission to extract the civilian lady, but even if they return, their chances of survival are slim. No human being can make it in this environment without food and water. It will be a breeze for us to get rid of them." There was a tone of pride in his voice.

"Oh, I forgot about the civilian lady! The underdog never gives up. Remember this old saying! I recommend you proceed cautiously. Timing is very important. Don't take anything for granted, and do not underestimate anyone. Now that we have entered the most delicate phase of our mission, I will be in touch with you on a regular basis. In order to do that, I need you to confirm that this line is safe and secure."

"Yes, the line is 100% insulated, as per instructions. We can speak freely, boss."

"That's what I needed to hear." A coughing attack interrupted the communication. "Sorry, I need to grab some water."

"Boss, are you okay?"

"Yes!" the individual shouted while slurping the water.

The line fell dead shortly after. Impatiently TJ made a second attempt to call his boss but without success. The line was busy.

"You know that he has a temper. Leave him alone," was Jordan's brief comment after the call. He had been listening to the entire conversation.

TJ nodded and placed the device back inside the backpack.

Kelly's face was engraved with a harsh expression blended with fatigue. Opening the map that he held in his hands, he pointed his finger at an unnamed location.

"Exactly here! This is our next target!" His tone of voice made him sound like a tyrant.

TJ and Jordan looked at the map. Although Kelly's behavior was annoying at times, they decided it best to go along.

Kelly's eyes wandered to his companions, and with a weary tone of voice he added, "This is our next infiltration point. In order to access this location, we need the civilian. She is the only one who can take us there." He pondered a moment before adding, "I've been scanning her movements through the device since Steve's accident. I was able to detect that she met someone but shortly after, her direction became impossible to tell. I believe her device has been removed by someone who lives in Inner Earth."

"We don't even know if she is alive or not," TJ replied.

Kelly's voice rose above the others. "She is alive. I have just spotted the rescue crew outside of Taras, or what is left of it, I should say. Anyway, she was with them and apparently in good condition. There is nothing to worry about. Everybody understand?"

"Roger that."

"Yup!"

Kelly folded the map and put it back in his pocket. Using a pair of binoculars, he tried to locate the survivors. It was hard to see through the smoke, but eventually he spotted the remaining members not too far from what was once the tower.

"I can see them: Roger, Parker, the civilian, and Matt. Just what I was hoping. We are left with the best ones. Let's give them some time to despair. They'll come around for help once they realize we are the only survivors. I suggest we spend the night here and get ready for action tomorrow."

But this time TJ and Jordan seemed confused by their leader's words.

"What now?" Kelly asked with a tone of sarcasm in his voice.

TJ replied, "Tell me again. How are we going to explain that we survived the explosion? It would only draw attention to our mission. Forget about the others, but that Matt is no idiot. He'll figure it out pretty quickly."

Kelly paused for a moment, with his face lowered looking at the ground. Of course he had thought about that.

"I am not concerned about Matt as much as I am worried about the civilian. She has made contact with the alien race and I am afraid of what she knows. However, let's stick to the plan. We left late for the rescue mission and when the explosion occurred, we came back to see what happened. Why is this so hard to conceive?"

"That's not the original plan, and I don't think it's going to fly."

"We will make it fly!" Kelly's reply was cold and domineering just like the expression on his face. There was no point arguing with him. So much damage had already been done.

"It will work like we said it would." Jordan grabbed TJ by the elbow warning him not to continue.

Kelly didn't say a word but spat on the ground and left shortly after.

TJ and Jordan stayed behind, mulling over their unverified future. "Do you want to be killed? You know that we have a plan, and you know what happens when someone doesn't follow the orders. We need to finish this. There is no way out at this point!" Jordan's unease filtered through his words.

TJ replied, without any fire in his eyes, "I know, but I don't trust Matt! He's too smart to believe we were on a rescue mission."

"No, he isn't. Everyone in this Expedition was selected with a specific purpose. And, by the way, even if he didn't trust us, he knows that he needs to survive, just like the rest of us. We will have to rely on each other in order to make it. This is when we'll make our move. The civilian will have no other choice but to spill the beans about what she has found out during her disappearance. With that information handy, we'll be able to attack our final target."

"I hope you're right," he muttered, with sorrow in his voice before turning his gaze away from his friend.

"TJ, you seem to be reminiscing about your past. This is not the time. We can't afford to have a weak link right now. It's about the success of the operation. Moreover, it's about our lives! Where do you stand?"

TJ, who was already ignoring his friend Jordan, turned around and replied, "Don't worry. I'm still into this and I will prove it. You can count on me."

And with those words he walked away, becoming shrouded by the thin layer of smoke still in the air.

Despite the immutable gray color of the sky, TJ knew it was night. It was cold. He wrapped his arms around himself and stood in silence watching what was left of Taras. The fire had almost burned itself out and the smell of scorch was slowly declining. A sense of "what once was" pervaded him for a brief moment, as he contemplated the results of his actions. For some reason the view of a burning city didn't flatter him as much as he thought it would. What was that strange feeling of discomfort that was stirring in his soul? All that he could feel was a hollowness — no longer desire or interest. Something hard to describe was bothering him. TJ looked back at his friend Jordan. He was peacefully enjoying his cigar, almost as if the pleasure of smoking could protect him from his pain. The bond with his friend TJ was undeniable and, at the same time, barely tolerable. TJ walked back and sat not too far from his ally.

Jordan opened his eyes and looked at TJ. "You are having second thoughts, aren't you?"

TJ felt embarrassed in the presence of his buddy. It was the first time. "Not exactly second thoughts. I can't explain," he said, timidly.

Jordan glanced at his friend and his expression changed to amusement. "We are not supposed to have emotions."

TJ decided to laugh it off and asked for a cigar. "I almost forgot the power of intoxicating your mind."

Jordan didn't reply but smiled at his friend, while keeping his eyes closed. Strangely enough, that little endorsement was all that TJ needed.

CHAPTER 25: NEW PLANS

By the following morning, the SOTIS agents were ready for action. They spotted the Delta team — Erin, Roger, Parker, and Matt — just outside of Taras at the base of Sandy Rings. The air in that location was still fairly unpolluted, making it a good location to camp overnight. It appeared that the four survivors had just woken up, as they observed them sipping coffee around a campfire. Their dismay from the dramatic events of the previous day was clearly visible. Knowing there wasn't much time at their disposal, the SOTIS agents decided to make their move quickly.

At first when Roger saw the three men walking toward his team, he felt a spark of joy burst into his heart. Then when he realized it was the three SOTIS team agents, his elation rapidly diminished. He wasn't exactly thrilled to see them, and he had no intention of lying about his feelings.

"Hi, guys," he shouted, more with the intent to alert the rest of his team than a desire to be friendly.

Matt, who was absorbed in sipping his coffee, almost fell off his perch with astonishment that someone else was alive. The rest of the team looked mystified and sincerely touched at the sight of other survivors. They hugged one another as they never thought they would, considering the impassive and guarded attitudes of the SOTIS agents.

Parker, expressing concern for their well-being, offered the agents a cup of coffee and a spot around the fire. In an attempt to behave appropriately to the stressful situation, the three operatives gladly accepted the invitation. After a few informal exchanges, the SOTIS agents began to explain why they weren't able to be on time for the rescue mission: a phone call with the Department of Homeland Security had caused their delay. The story appeared justified and credible, and the rescue team was easily convinced of the veracity of the information provided — all of them, except Erin, who cautiously avoided coming to any conclusion.

Agor's warning regarding some bad people in the Expedition resonated inside of her louder than ever. This unexpected development was exercising a particular caution in Erin's mind to where her first doubts didn't take long to manifest.

To everyone's amazement, Kelly made an unexpected statement. "The explosion was not an accident."

As anticipated, the team's curiosity was thoroughly aroused by his words, although the insolence in his voice was just a little more than what some would tolerate.

Impatiently Matt asked, "How do you know?"

Kelly looked at him before resuming. "Our communication system had been hacked a few days prior to the explosion. The reason why we voted against the rescue mission was because it wasn't considered safe."

He paused for a moment, carefully measuring his words. Then he continued. "Some things cannot be revealed yet, but we have reasons to believe that this place is inhabited with entities who don't want us here."

Erin was shocked. That was exactly what Agor had told her. "Humans are not welcomed here; they must go back," he kept reiterating. How was it possible for the agent to be aware of that information?

Kelly continued. "We believe what happened was a premeditated attack perpetuated by these entities with the intent of informing us that humans are not welcomed in this place."

"More than informing us that humans are not welcomed here, they actually got rid of most of us," was Matt's broken comment. Frustration was clearly noticeable in his voice.

The silence that followed was filled with tension and confusion. The information Kelly had provided was hard to digest and needed time to be absorbed. The three agents waited patiently for the knowledge to soak in.

After several moments of reticence, Erin was the first to speak. "If there were even the slightest doubt that the Exploration crew was in danger, why wasn't anyone informed?"

"As I said, some information needed to be kept secret. Those were the orders. Captain Miller's plan was to return as soon as possible. There were only a few people who had the full picture of the situation and he was one of them. His decision was to allow the rescue mission before leaving Inner Earth. We tried to warn him about the risk of such an undertaking but in the end, he had the final word."

Kelly looked at Matt and, almost touched by the sorrow in his eyes, added, "To be honest, I'm not sure this situation could have been avoided."

"But how did it happen? Which type of weapons did these 'people' use?"

"Regular explosives, very similar to TNT," was the quick response of Jordan. Kelly nodded, admonishing the other two agents with a glare to let him be in charge.

Roger, who had been silent until that moment, took his turn to say something. "The question we must ask ourselves is not how did they do it but who are these people? Where are they now? Are they watching us? Listening to us? Planning to kill us? Where do they live? Unless we can confirm this is true, I'm sorry, but for me it will remain just another conspiracy."

"I can confirm there are other entities living in Inner Earth." Erin's statement was as shocking and unexpected as lightning out of a blue sky. Parker, Roger, Matt, and even the SOTIS agents turned their heads and stared at Erin, their mouths open incredulously, all of them waiting for her to go on.

Erin took a deep breath. Then she continued. "During my disappearance I had the opportunity to meet some of these beings. They have been living here for thousands of years, and I can confirm what Kelly said. They don't want humans here. But

I have to say that my experience with them was very positive, and the only reason I survived was because they saved me."

"You ... you have actually seen them?" Parker's astonished response to Erin's comment sounded shrill.

"I have actually met them. I can't even begin to describe what lies behind Longview Fields. There is a whole new world, and it is beautiful."

Matt, feeling the responsibility of his seniority, made an attempt to neutralize the situation. "Erin, we don't know what happened to you after you got lost, but it is feasible you suffered some trauma and that could have caused some confusion. It is possible that you are perturbed right now ..."

Feeling insulted and angered, Erin stopped Matt before he had a chance to finish his sentence. She always held a good dose of respect for the old veteran but not this time.

Trying to keep her tone of voice to a minimum, she exclaimed, "No, Matt, I am not confused! I know what I have seen and done."

With some madness in her action, Erin grabbed her quiver and pulled out the golden arrow given to her by Agor. "This is proof that what I am saying is true."

She handed the treasure to Matt, who remained mystified and astonished by Erin's quick reaction.

He eventually took the arrow and examined it thoroughly. "How did you get this?" He looked at Erin perplexed, raising his eyebrows.

"One of the people who live here gave it to me. His name is Agor. He said I will need it one day." Erin stretched her arm forward, demanding the arrow back. There was a great display of dignity in her action.

The interest among the group was becoming intense. All eyes were pointed at Erin, who felt it necessary to provide more information. However, prudence told her to filter out a large part of the message received, including her own personal realizations. For Erin, it wasn't clear yet who to trust and who was unreliable.

Kelly decided to take advantage of the situation and made an attempt to gain some clues. "Do you know where these people live and how to get there?"

Erin wasn't sure. She had never been allowed beyond a certain point, not even under Agor's supervision.

"I was told they live in a city deep inside Inner Earth, but I have never been there." Kelly stared at her, signaling that he wasn't satisfied with her response, so she continued. "I was never invited. The place where they live seems to be strongly protected and I don't think one can simply decide to go there."

Kelly had the confirmation he needed and gave his mates TJ and Jordan a quick look of connivance. So far, all the information received by Erin confirmed what the SOTIS agents already knew.

Roger intervened. "We need to find a way to meet these people. They are the only hope we have to survive in this place and the only ones who can potentially help us to contact our government and ask for some backup."

"I agree," was the joint response of Matt and Kelly.

"As unfortunate as it seems, this is the only option we have left," Matt added.

Roger looked at Erin and asked, "When you said yesterday you knew someone who can help us, were you referring to these people?"

Erin nodded pensively but didn't say a word.

Parker, who was probably by this time the most fearful among the group, finally voiced his concerns. "If they are the ones responsible for the destruction of our base camp and the killing of everyone else, what makes you guys think they won't do the same to us? I would assume they would want to finish what they started. Am I wrong?"

"There is no way for us to know that. It is a gamble. But if we stay here, we will die for sure and in a matter of days. Our supplies of food and water are limited and there is no way we can navigate Devil's Passage without a proper vessel. Even if our government could send an investigative team, it would take too many days for them to get here. We have no choice." Ironically, Kelly's voice was reassuring.

Matt had to concur that Kelly was right. It was a risk, but also the only option left at that point.

"I agree with agent Kelly. We must take our chances. Maybe our lives were saved for a reason. Maybe they want us to go home and inform our government to avoid any future exploration attempts in Inner Earth."

"We need a plan and we need Erin's help to find them."

This last statement from Kelly slightly bothered Erin. A strange feeling of annoyance was aroused in her heart, accompanied by a prompting to be careful. But she felt betrayed by her own words when she heard herself pronounce, "I will help you. I think I know how to get there."

A gratified smirk appeared on Kelly's face just in time for Erin to notice it. Feeling she had put herself in an uncomfortable position, Erin decided to leave the group and scouted for a place to be alone not too far from her companions. Roger didn't take long to join her, leaving the rest of the team still boldly discussing their next step.

Erin was sitting on the ground hugging her knees with her arms, a position she would usually adopt when she needed to think or when she was feeling nostalgic. Roger approached her with kindness. "How are you feeling? I can sense there is something wrong. What's up, Erin?"

For a brief moment Erin was tempted to vent everything she hadn't yet revealed to the only person she could really trust. But the warning for prudence was still burning inside and prevented her from sharing her thoughts. "I think I'm just tired. Confused, maybe."

Roger didn't reply and kept his glance lowered. A few moments of complete silence went by before he added, "I want you to know that whatever happens here, I have always respected you. I am on your side, Erin, even if I understand only a little of how hard it must be for you to trust anyone, especially now. Just remember that if you need anyone to talk to, you can always count on me."

Having said that, Roger looked at Erin dearly for a few seconds, then left to rejoin the others.

The remainder of the morning passed quietly without Erin's involvement in what the rest of the team was planning. "Seek the path of least resistance and go with the flow," she reminded herself. It was in that moment of self-reflection that she recognized there was indeed the spark of a "true sailor" inside of her, and that simple concept made her feel appreciative and encouraged.

The sky at the horizon was still dark from the smoke, but considering how the visibility had improved, Erin thought it a good time to walk around what was left of Taras. Despite her idea having been unanimously rejected by her teammates, she made her way alone toward the citadel.

"It won't take me long," she assured them before jumping on the motorized vehicle and driving away.

Parting admonishments from her companions were useless because she was already gone, leaving behind a small cloud of dust. Matt was expecting a different reaction from Roger and didn't hesitate to inquire, "Are you letting her go by herself? I thought the two of you were friends."

But Roger gave a harsh look to Matt and walked a few steps away. When he turned around, his face was pale. "There is nothing between us." His voice betrayed all of his weariness. "I need to let her go."

"If she is not back within a couple of hours, I will go and bring her back," replied Matt. "There is nothing left alive in that place. She will find out quickly enough."

Despite sympathizing with Matt's words, Roger didn't say anything further. He hovered there dejected, his hands inside his pants' pockets and his head bowed.

After a few minutes, Erin reached the beginning of what was once the settlement of Taras. A scrap of metal with the words "Inner Grounds" still legible caught her attention.

Memories of her time spent at the cafeteria surfaced and her attempt to hold back tears was useless. The base of the tower was still partially standing, but instead of the big metal door there was now a gigantic, shapeless opening. Erin walked through the aperture slowly and then carefully clambered over the ruins searching for anything that reminded her of Alan, maybe some residue of the steal coffin, maybe something that could awake any memory of him, maybe … maybe … Erin was sure she was at the same location where the refrigerated room once stood. There was no doubt about it, because she had been there many times, always with a different excuse.

The upsetting moment of realizing that nothing was left was hard to reconcile. All that she could do was linger in contemplation, wishing she could have the opportunity to bring justice to her dear friend. But how? She was good in surviving events that had been fated for others: Jessica, Alan, and everyone else. Even the last of her friends, Roger, she knew had to be sacrificed. Surviving Inner Earth cost her everybody. What was it all worth?

All of a sudden a gentle touch on her left shoulder made her jump. It took Erin what seemed an eternity before she had the courage to turn around. In her youthful heart she was hoping to see Alan. A smile of anticipation illuminated her face, but when she turned around, there was nothing … nobody. It was all just an illusion. Her dejected heart sank even deeper, until she finally decided it was time to go back and face the harshness of the situation. "Good-bye, Alan. In the end, fate has decided for you. Maybe you belong here. Maybe we all belong here. I will never forget you."

Erin took a deep breath and, despite the absence of walls, walked outside through what was once the main door. It was then that something white and small caught her attention. It was a piece of paper, carefully folded to make an origami in the shape of a hummingbird.

"How beautiful!" Erin exclaimed, loudly. At a closer look, she could see some blue ink transpiring through the paper. Carefully she opened it, trying not to damage the origami.

Milady, my friend,
know at the end
those who remain
have something to gain,
and those who leave
don't want you to grieve.
It is called life,
no need for strife.
Destiny is a choice,
let your heart rejoice.
You have come a long way.
Believe me, there will be a day
when all of this will make sense,
but for now, don't be tense.
You have more than you know,
now it is time for you to grow.
Always keep the long vision
and make the right decision.
A bright future lies ahead
if you conquer your dread.
Fight the good fight
and be a light in the night.
You will always find me in your heart,
I was there from the very start.
I will tell you how to lead your team,
all you must do is look for the gleam.
When it is time to make your choice,
never fear, listen to this voice.
The battle you have fought
will be done when the arrow is sought.
When the moment is right,
let it take flight.

And remember what seems tragic
always hides some magic.
The meaning is for you to find,
never forget to trust your mind.
Milady, one last tip:
Don't ever forget to enjoy your trip.

By the time she was done reading the poetry, Erin was sobbing uncontrollably. Tearfully, still shaking, she folded the paper trying to reproduce the shape of the hummingbird as best she could and carefully put it in her pocket. Gratitude could not encompass what she was feeling inside. There were no words or images that came to mind, only the certitude that the dream of Inner Earth was not over. To Erin, it had become immortal. She climbed back onto the vehicle and before leaving gave one last look at Taras. "One day you will rise again," she pronounced, and then drove away.

Images of a flourishing Taras, rising from the ashes like the mystical Phoenix, occupied Erin's mind as she returned to the camp. She parked the four-wheeler and ran toward Roger, who was preoccupied and not yet alerted to her presence. "Alan!" she exclaimed, almost without thinking.

Roger turned around. "Alan?"

"I mean, Roger …" Erin tried to hide the sudden blush on her cheeks. A smile appeared spontaneously on her face when she looked up at the horizon and saw an image of Alan smirking back at her. It was another note of confirmation that everything was going to be all right.

CHAPTER 26: AN ODD ENCOUNTER

The next day the extended team began their adventure in search of the people of Inner Earth.

All in all, it was the type of journey never to be undertaken without foreknowledge of the geography. Therefore Erin was put in charge of leading the group, despite being considered the least experienced member of the Expedition. The crossing of Longview Fields this time was rather easy, considering the motorized vehicles at their disposal.

After a safe beginning, Erin led Roger and the team to the hazardous and less hospitable Forest of the Giant Trees. The woods were darker than what Erin remembered and the path she had previously opened was already nonexistent. For the most part, the group advanced in silence. Occasionally a shaky voice would ask if they were going in the right direction, to which Erin would respond with a dismissive and annoyed "Yes."

Beyond timber and creeks, they eventually arrived at Lake Tumira, the first of the five lakes listed on the west section of the map. The lake had little grass, just some shrubs and a few other broken and blackened stumps.

Erin tried to explain to her companions that the basin was inhabited by a sleepy mastodon named Tugar, but all she received in return were skeptical looks of mistrust.

"This is just one of the many strange things we will encounter," she concluded.

The landscape that had previously captured Erin's imagination was quite wild, but none of her fellow adventurers realized just how dangerous it could be. Occasionally Erin would recount some of her experiences in Inner Earth, including the description of the five lakes, each one inhabited by some kind of prehistoric creature, including, she had been told, one that resembled a dragon. The fact that she had never seen one allowed her greater, figurative freedom.

The SOTIS agents weren't the least bit interested in Erin's adventures, which they considered trivial and a distraction to their real purpose. Roger and Parker, on the other hand, were becoming ever fonder of the young female explorer and, after their initial skepticism, were becoming captivated with the idea of walking into a fantastic world. Their interest only grew stronger.

Perhaps that change in attitude allowed them their first encounter with a strange creature. The experience wasn't meant for everyone, and that made it even more precious for those who participated. It was during a recess that the SOTIS agents, accompanied by Erin, decided to venture inside the forest in search of some sweet berries. The rest of the team — Roger, Matt, and Parker — waited lazily in the neighboring meadows not too far from the river.

While lounging comfortably in the makeshift camp, a crunching sound, almost inaudible at first, began to intensify, followed by the approach of a large, ominous shadow. Initially their instinct was to flee, but a more strategic decision to stay hidden took hold instead. The gloomy, shapeless form advanced toward them, apparently oblivious of their presence. As it came closer, the outline began to assume a more definite form. Whatever it was had the appearance of a huge bear walking upright on two feet. It was obvious the creature was looking for food because it was shaking the bushes and shrubs along the way. Except for the noise of broken branches and sticks, the creature was making no sound of its own.

When the frightening thing was less than a few feet away, it suddenly changed direction, turning toward the river, as if something or someone had called it. At the touch of the water, the creature began to transform into a giant fish, dark in color and luminescent. The limbs turned into fins and the fur into scales. It was amazing to watch. But it didn't last long because in a matter of moments, the mysterious critter was gone, having plunged into the murky waters. All that was left were some ripples on the surface.

Matt, Parker, and Roger looked at each other, utterly stunned.

"What was that?" was the only thing Roger could say after a long pause, but none of the others could come up with a reasonable explanation.

"A mutant Big Foot, that's what it looked like to me," Matt offered, and the look on his face confirmed that he wasn't joking.

"Let's ask Erin when she comes back." Parker failed at holding back a smirk on his face. "Maybe that was one of her spooky friends."

Despite Parker's comment not being received humorously by the others, the prevailing understanding following the unusual encounter was that Inner Earth was filled with more than what met the eye. Maybe it was prompted by the ambition to live the novelty of the experience to its fullest or perhaps a simple curious impulse, but a new sentiment began to arise in each of them — the desire to enjoy their journey more than the need to be saved. Matt voiced what everyone else was thinking with a few simple words. "If we are to leave this place, it's better that we experience it first. Maybe we should learn how to walk before we run."

Not long had passed before the SOTIS agents and Erin made their reappearance with a large load of berries and some other edible fruits they had found in the forest. It was clear that they had enjoyed a good time together. Roger had not seen Erin that happy for a while, possibly since they first met in Tromso. But he was also aware that the woman standing in front of him was not the same young lady he had encountered months before. Something in her had changed and now Roger was beginning to understand a small part of it. It was hard to explain, even for his analytical mind, but in that brief moment of clarity he realized his assumptions of her trying to hide something had been too hasty.

While biting a soft plum-like fruit, Erin queried, "Is everything okay? You look different ..."

Roger smiled without answering. However, it didn't matter because Erin wouldn't have paid attention to his words anyway. He knew she was too busy relishing the sweet delicacy Inner Earth had provided from her foraging.

"Maybe we should learn how to walk before we run," Roger said to himself, while grabbing one of the large, orange berries and sinking his teeth into it.

It was the end of a bountiful day and the explorers decided to stay where they were and camp for the night. The amicable atmosphere was noticeable and remained undisturbed.

Erin, Roger, and Parker were playfully following some giant fireflies in an attempt to film and document their behavior, while the SOTIS agents were positioned away from the rest of the group, silently studying the map and some undisclosed documents. Matt sat alone, starting to become curious about the agents' confidential behavior and lack of participation. Without letting anyone know, he decided to take a short patrol around the camp.

The first thing that caught his attention were the bulky backpacks of the three agents. They were strangely ponderous, and something was telling Matt there was more than just simple survival gear in those sacks. The idea of knowing the content of those bags had been battling in his mind ever since the agents' arrival, but he had never had the audacity to ask. Somehow he had the impression it was better not to know. That night, however, the impulse to find out who he was dealing with was more gnawing than ever. Carefully and very discretely he had moved away from the group, making sure that no one was following him, and slowly wandered by the area where all the gear was placed.

His strategy was soon interrupted by the severity of Kelly's voice coming from behind his shoulders. "Is everything okay?"

The unexpected question hit Matt like a cold shower and gave him chills down his back. Agitated, he made an effort to recompose himself before turning around, and then responded. "Oh, yes, yes … I heard some noises coming from behind those bushes … but probably it was just my imagination."

Agent Kelly didn't appear to rely on those words because there was a relentless, indiscernible expression on his face. Matt smiled nervously, attempting to defuse the situation, then striding in front of the agent went back to sit with the others. The campfire was lit, and the rest of the team seemed relaxed and unconcerned. Kelly rejoined his team shortly after but not before opening his backpack and making sure that everything was in order. That simple gesture gave Matt the confirmation he needed that something was odd.

Considering the questionable situation, Matt decided to wait till the next morning before talking to Roger and spent the rest of the evening reposing by the fire, burdened by his thoughts.

The beginning of another day was assured. A freshening dew covered the green landscape like a veil of silk. It was the first gift of the silent morning. In this new Inner Earth environment, the shift from night- to daytime had become more pronounced.

Despite the sparkling light, agent Kelly didn't look like himself. There was a lackluster in his eyes and the color of his face seemed as though it had faded during the night. His appetite was poor and so was his attitude. His protestations to ensure that everything was under tight control gave the adventurers no other choice than to resume their quest without further worry.

When the moment was ripe, Matt, still contending with his ambiguity, took Roger aside and shared his concerns. Despite having mentioned the episode from the night before, Roger didn't seem overly alarmed. In his opinion, the SOTIS team was dealing with highly classified information and a certain level of secrecy was to be expected from them. "He's so fascinated with the environment, his guard is down," Matt thought to himself.

"The strategy of a true enemy is to alter the perception of its adversaries," was Matt's best argument, but it still fell short on Roger's ears

"You need to relax." With those words Roger ended the conversation, leaving Matt alone to dispute his own doubts.

A few more days went by and the team finally faced the Rusty Mountains, land of the giant eagles. Erin could hardly believe they had come so far. The valley was ringed by the majestic mountains that rose from the ground and stretched to the sky. As the name suggested, the peaks were covered in bauxite, setting them ablaze with a blanket of red and brown light.

Parker looked at Erin somewhat in shock and said, "Please don't tell us that we're supposed to climb those mountains!?"

Erin replied with a slow and measured tone of voice, "If you think the mountains are challenging, you might not be ready for what we could find on the other side."

Hearing that sent Parker to a new level of discomfort as he retraced his steps. His reaction placed a burden on Erin's spirit because she knew she had not been fair. Keeping her head bowed, she looked at Parker out of the corner of her eye while attempting a timid smile. The next few minutes were filled with an ominous, brittle kind of silence that penetrated the blood more than the chilling cold coming from the mountains.

"There will be conflict, mostly internal," said Matt. "Sometimes life gives us the ability to choose, but for us ... we have been forced to take an unusual path. With commitment there will be resolution." He gave Erin a brief glance of caution and slowly resumed the hike.

As they trekked toward the ascent, the mountains began to exhibit their temperament. The pass was becoming narrower and, occasionally, protruding rocks almost completely blocked the light. As they crossed an area of exceptional wilderness, the landscape became as fascinating as it was treacherous. Hiking from gorge to gorge, a few in the team began to show signs of fatigue. When they finally halted for the night after the challenging day, almost all immediately drifted off to an exhausted slumber, except Matt, who volunteered to be the sentinel and spent the night sitting close to the campfire. He was feeling more anxious than tired.

On the opposite side of the camp, another explorer was nervous. Fearful of exposure, agent Kelly never completely closed both eyes at the same time — quite a feat but obtainable in a job as demanding as his. Although he knew that sleeplessness was a good part of his current occupation, he always envied those who could drift off with the serenity of innocent children.

Eventually the quiet of the early morning brought the calm anticipation of another day.

Waking refreshed from a dreamless night, Roger, with his usual, conscientious outlook proclaimed, "If things go according to plan, we should be able to reach the summit before the end of the day. Once at the top, we'll have a better idea of what lies on the other side."

"So be it, my friend," said Kelly, with an exaggerated bow.

The rest of the team submitted to the upcoming challenge without saying much.

After a quick meal and feeling somewhat refreshed in body and mind, everyone was already on their feet in less than an hour.

For the rest of the climb, Erin became very quiet. She was fighting her conscience.

CHAPTER 27: ALDORA

The hypothesis advanced by Mr. Windsor of a sun and an ocean inside the planet was about to find its first validation. A small sun, the maker of time, finally made its early and rightful appearance.

As the team reached the summit, the Inner Earth sun had already begun its decline on the horizon. It was their first sunset since the beginning of the Expedition, and they were in awe of its splendor. Night was about to fall once again after weeks of continuous daylight.

From the top of the mountain under the orange-pink sky, the view was marvelous to behold. The rocky peaks gradually descended to welcome a deep and calm blue sea. In its midst, a white city emerged pompously from the glistening water. It was like a pearl surrounded by a carpet of blue sapphires. Somehow it reminded Erin of the "Birth of Venus," the famous painting by Sandro Botticelli.

A sensation of wonder and peace overcame the explorers as they stood silently, captivated by the view that lay before them.

Aldora, the beautiful empyrean of Inner Earth, had been discovered at last.

The city wasn't exactly large, as one would expect, but it was breathtaking. The island that gave Aldora the appearance of floating was oval-shaped, almost round. They could see four alabaster towers, on top of which perched four giant thunderbirds ready to fly. The rest of the buildings were quite small, with the exception of a circular edifice located in the center of the city. The aforesaid building was disproportionally large compared to the rest of the structures, and unlike the other buildings it appeared to be made of opal. There were no visible trees or flowers, which seemed curious considering the abundant and colorful vegetation of Inner Earth.

Erin felt immediately smitten with Aldora, and in a surge of longing she wished she could stay there forever.

In that moment of fulfillment, the only thing that would have made her jubilation complete was someone to intimately share it with. Roger had an idea of Erin's thoughts and, experiencing his own euphoria from the fantastic sight that lay before them, placed his arm over her shoulder. He pulled nearer, and his comment sounded like a soft whisper. "I feel like my individuality is looking for balance. What I have in front of my eyes has never been seen before. I have the impression I could be a part of it if I asked, but at the same time I am scared to lose myself if I do."

"Strange," commented Erin. "The more I look at Aldora, the more I feel like a river that has no other choice than to become the ocean. It's something inevitable. I sense the same urge as your mind, but unlike you I feel that I have no choice."

The look that Roger gave Erin was one of friendship and compassion. He was able to perceive much more than he could express in words. He knew she was right. Aldora was for Erin more than what it was for everyone else.

"Do you feel there is something you have to do?" he quietly asked.

"I do. I just don't know what." Erin's voice was almost trembling.

Roger hugged her even tighter. "Not so fast, my friend. The river will become the ocean, as it always does, just not today." Then turning his attention to the rest of the group, he exclaimed, "We made it, people! We have come as far as we could have imagined we might come!"

Happiness, tied with relief, was visible in all of their faces. The smiles and laughter came out with ease, except for Kelly. Kelly was one of those individuals that no one could read easily. Enjoyment was something almost elusive to him, and the closest sign of contentment was an occasional smirk on his face. While the rest of the team was exultant, he remained distant, staring silently at the horizon. From the expression on his face, Roger knew that Kelly was enjoying his own train of thought, whatever that was.

Erin was also attempting to escape the excited energy and chatter coming from the rest the group, although her reasons were quite different, or so she assumed. Under the blanket of the starry night that soon descended, she asked for guidance. More than that, she asked for a miracle.

Just as Erin was about to drift into a deep slumber, a vivid voice penetrated her semiconscious state.

"Do you think a miracle is the only way to win your inner battle?"

The hush that followed instead of being comforting was worse than an enemy. She looked around. The group was resting peacefully. It was as if nature conspired to keep everyone asleep except her. In that moment of suspense, all she craved was reassurance and normality. Any primitive desire she might have held to be different and important didn't seem that attractive anymore.

The voice spoke again. "Be careful what you wish for," but this time it carried no surprise. Agitated, Erin left the small cavern where they had sheltered and moved toward the ledge of the cliff.

The white city of Aldora, so bright during the day, was now covered with a myriad of pastel lights gently moving in harmony, almost like a dance. After her initial reaction, Erin allowed herself to be captivated. As if by magic, the lights she could see emerging from Aldora looked just like the northern lights. Was this the place then where the aurora borealis originated? Could the northern lights be a reminder that human civilization is not alone on Earth? Or maybe, more metaphorically, they represent an invitation to explore inward?

"This must be just one of those weird, lucid dreams," she thought to herself, skeptical, wondering how to get out of whatever that was. But the vision in front of her persisted. It was not a dream.

"Fighting a reality costs more energy than to allow it. Be careful how you apply your spiritual force." The voice was coming from somewhere behind her and seemed to have intensified her sense of gravity.

Erin suddenly felt heavy in her body, unable to move. Trying to wrestle with the meaning of what was happening was to completely miss the point. She knew that much. So she waited, still — utterly still. There was no sound other than her own breathing.

In that eerie peace, nature's voice was once again silent.

Gradually the tranquillity outside became reflected inward. Before she knew, everything had returned to normal. A calmness settled within Erin, the sort of calm that brings assurance and washes away the past, a state of mind she would grow to love more each day.

The colored lights radiating from Aldora had ceased. Everything was again concealed in darkness, not the darkness of fear but a gentle, hopeful darkness. It was that frame of mind that Erin would ultimately need to carry her forward in her journey. In reverie she sank to the ground and lost all awareness.

CHAPTER 28: QUEEN MELANY

"Welcome, human."

At the sound of those words, Erin opened her eyes.

That was an uncommon voice, she thought. As she arose from the ground, she couldn't help but catch her breath. She found herself inside a large, stately building. Most of the walls were decorated with silver and gold mosaics. In the middle of the room on top of a round, golden table she saw a regal vase of translucent roses. As she turned her attention toward the back of the room, her eyes fell on something more familiar — the figure of what appeared to be a man. The entity was very tall in stature and wearing a sort of loose robe, ivory in color. His head was bare except for a short beard, perfectly trimmed and entirely black.

"Come nearer," he commanded.

Erin felt more than perplexed by the situation but said nothing as she approached. The entity was scanning her with his black eyes and smiled vaguely as she moved closer.

"The Queen has expressed the desire to see you. I will guide you to the garden where she is waiting. You will speak only when you are asked to do so," he said, formally.

There was a short pause. Then he continued in the most charming manner. "Would you please follow me?" And without waiting for an answer he began walking toward a long, glass tunnel.

Erin halted, despite the fact that the entity's pleasant invitation had given her some reassurance. Then as if being pushed by an invisible force, she started to follow the commanding figure. She had barely walked fifty meters when the scene began to change. A soft, pink light now infused the walls of the glass corridor, and a delicate fragrance of flowers

279

began to fill the air. Erin could see an arched door blocking the view at the end of the tunnel. As soon as she walked through, she found herself entering the most delightful garden.

The central patio resembled a small arena and was profusely decorated with pink, white, and yellow flowers. In the middle, she was amazed to find a sizeable, golden hummingbird feeder and a countless number of the mystical creatures nourishing themselves from its nectar. What had Agor said to her? *"You cannot put new wine in an old bottle. Change your way of perceiving things and you will see them."* Erin was greatly cheered by the view and allowed herself to be immersed in the loveliness of it all when, before she could murmur any appreciation, a soft voice from behind interrupted her reverie.

"Welcome, SunAlaka."

Erin slowly turned toward the origin of that regal voice. The figure in front of her appeared more ethereal than human, surrounded as she was by a sunny, pinkish glow. The lady was clearly blending in with the background but without the intent of camouflage. She had the deepest green eyes and a smile that melted Erin's heart. She was wearing a delicate rose-colored robe that touched the ground, hiding her feet. The velvet garment was soft and lightly decorated. A golden belt was wrapped around her waist, accentuating the tall and flawless figure. With a simple gesture of her hand, the lovely woman moved her dark hair behind her shoulders and took a few steps closer to Erin.

"Welcome to my garden," she repeated softly, and before Erin could say anything, the young lady continued. "I have been told you have encountered some of my people. I asked to see you, and I hope you don't mind."

Erin waited until she was sure the lady had finished. Then she spoke in a gentle tone. "It is my honor to meet you, Your Highness."

It was not long before the lady responded in a voice that was filled with music. "I suppose you have been told I am the Queen." She stood severely dignified, much as she looked pleased.

"Indeed, Your Highness." Erin bowed slightly.

"I like the simplicity of the human mind, although sometimes the human tongue reflects a lack of subservience to a higher understanding." The Queen spoke with ease.

"Lack of subservience to a … a higher understanding?" Erin stumbled over the words.

"Assuming to know and not knowing is very deceitful to the human spirit and yet an elixir hard to decline. It keeps entities from evolving."

Erin halted and an anxious whine began inwardly. Fearful of her lack of comprehension, she refrained from commenting.

The Queen looked pleased. Then softening her voice, she added, "Be cautious in your presumptions, SunAlaka. If you learn how to listen patiently, you will save yourself from inevitable troubles."

Erin bowed assent but was still confused.

It was then with a great display of dignity that the Queen proclaimed, "I am Lady Melany, descendent of Floridus, and Queen of Aldora. This title was given to me not by royal bloodline but because I am the oldest person in Inner Earth. I demand no obedience to myself but subordination to a moral covenant of virtue. I am, indeed, a servant to my people, and I shall perish if I allow myself to be deceived by greed and power."

Somehow things were starting to become less complicated for Erin, and as they did, she humbly responded with a little embarrassment. "Queen Melany, I have been quick all my life in action as well as in judgment. But it's not too late to make a change, and I do solemnly promise not to come to conclusions so promptly."

The Queen continued. "Words are easy to understand and yet very hard to practice. If your command is weak and without authority, it will be easily dismissed."

Not only did Erin not know what to say, she was starting to feel weak on her feet. "I should just say nothing," she thought to herself, but her pitiful attitude was swiftly interrupted.

"Come and see," said the Queen, while holding a colorful hummingbird in the palm of her hand. "This noble, little creature is very close to excellence because of its courage, strength, intelligence, and humility. For many reasons it reminds me of the hidden potentials of the human race so easily overcome by fear. As you become aware of this being, you should ask yourself what is stronger, the big or the small?" The Queen paused for a moment and a smile played around her mouth. "You look at it but don't see it. May I hear from you the essence of your thoughts?"

"I feel very small right now. I have been told that small can be big and big can be small. But I am not sure I fully comprehend the meaning of it. Maybe Your Highness could help me with that?"

"There is so much to admire in you, SunAlaka, but your raw honesty is the most endearing." The Queen turned her back to Erin as she walked toward a white bench where she sat. "Please join me," she invited.

Erin was quickly losing her stiffness and, trusting the invitation, sat down beside her. All she wanted was for the Queen to understand how grateful she was.

"What is necessary for you, my child, is to stop being concerned about what you don't know but rather seek to be worthy of knowing."

"How would I do that?" Erin asked, humbly.

The Queen gave Erin a long, compassionate stare, then proclaimed, "Set your mind to truth, and what is right will follow."

After stalling for a moment, Erin soon recovered her spirit. "It seems easy to do, now that I am in your presence, Your Highness. However, I am not sure I will be able hold the same confidence once I return to my reality. The people in my world think much differently."

The Queen bent slightly forward, gently touching Erin's shoulder. "I dare to ask you, what do you know? If I stay with you, will your insecurity go away? Are you sure that your strength will arise because of me? Focus your mind on righteousness instead of favors, gain, and comfort. When you live by this rule, more virtuous people will appear in your life. You will know you are not alone. You never were. The truth cannot be hidden. No one is left to stand alone. My people and I are fully aware of the human situation. There is a spiritual battle in your world that only those with knowledge can see is occurring. It's a battle between light and dark, truth and lies, freedom and slavery, and ultimately between life and death.

"Remember, truth is not always kind and kindness is not always truth. You have been conditioned to be weak and kind instead of strong and honest. You have been conditioned to seek value and dependency in others while your spirit longs for meaning and sovereignty in yourself. There was a time in your world when truth was openly celebrated. But when humans realized that truth wasn't something friendly or gentle, they decided to hide it for the sake of social gain and personal power. By doing that, humans disclaimed their own divinity. Now truth is being despised, and those who speak it are shunned, ridiculed, or, worse, killed. Humans need to restore honesty in their words, actions, intentions, and thoughts. They need to reclaim their independence as divine beings. There is no other way forward for the human race."

Without a doubt, Erin started to experience some anxiety. She felt the need to move but tried to stay calm. Eventually words came to her. "There is a part of me that knows that something is wrong, but I can't understand the origin of my trouble. Why is it so hard for me to understand?" Erin could barely look at the Queen.

"I can only bring before your eyes what you are capable of seeing. If your mind was tenebrous, I would not have revealed these lofty subjects to you."

"Tenebrous?" There was commotion in Erin's eyes, so the Queen continued. "You have already been warned. There are some entities in your company that foster no benevolence and neither are they straightforward. Those entities need to be managed without weakness. The first test in virtue is to recognize the legitimacy of my words. Let there be truth!"

"Lofty ideals ... How can this be so when you ask me to betray members of my own team? We have survived together. We have come here together. I don't think I would be able to go against anybody in my group." There was sadness in Erin's voice.

"You don't have to be in favor or against anyone. Know what is right and your actions will follow. Righteousness is a higher virtue than devotion."

Erin clutched her arms and stayed silent, oppressed by her own thoughts. When the Queen began to speak again, she listened with utmost interest.

"The day for my people to meet your friends has not yet come. We understand those who approach us with simplicity and those who have concealment. Those who cannot value the law of our kingdom have none of our respect. It is my duty, as Queen of Aldora, to protect my people and safeguard the motherland where they live."

At the sound of those words, Erin sat motionless. She was completely in the dark as to what they meant, and that made her sad. There was something Erin wanted to ask, one thought that oppressed her.

It wasn't long before she finally found the courage to put the question to the Queen. "Who are these people you are warning me about?"

The Queen's reply was short. "My answer might not satisfy you but I will respond according to truthfulness. There are those who lead the blind and there are those who help the blind see. Which one am I?"

Those words lifted a heavy pressure off Erin's mind and, even more, carried a sudden realization. At the beginning of her journey, Erin's only concern was that people did not know her. But now she wasn't worried about that anymore. She was concerned about not knowing herself. "Which one am I?" she repeated in her mind.

The Queen smiled, pleased. As she rose to her feet, a hummingbird landed on her shoulder. "You can be as excellent as this little creature, SunAlaka. If righteous and virtuous leaders will govern your land, humanity will arise to a higher level of knowledge and experience. The contribution of one entity is never too small because we all stand as a minority of one that makes up the many. Know that you can change the rules of the game. What if instead of languishing, you could prosper? What if instead of being a survivor, you could thrive?"

The Queen gently placed a kiss on Erin's forehead and whispered softly, "You will do well, my child."

Without further engagement, she departed. Her duty was complete.

Chapter 29: From Dark to Light

Erin stood alone but not for long. Just as she was about to leave, a friendly voice made her gasp.

"I hope you enjoyed your visit here. It was short, but at least now you know a little more about us." Agor watched her with a stare so steady and considerate that Erin almost cringed at the sight of it.

She hurried to straighten herself up, beamed at him, and replied, "It has been so long since the last time we spoke."

"Is it really so? Time might be used for self-orientation, but it doesn't really exist. We have already talked about this."

Agor's statement put a damper on Erin's excitement, but it was only for a few moments because she saw nothing short of gentleness and empathy in his face.

"Treasure your knowledge and remember that it comes with responsibility. Keep your mind unoccupied with worries about time. As I promised you earlier, all the time you spent here with us will be given back to you." Agor looked up toward the ceiling and a wide grin of satisfaction appeared on his face. "I will bring you back to your people. Pepecus is already waiting for us."

Erin's feet refused to move. "What will happen to me? To us? My friends and I came here asking for help, not just spiritual help. Our city has been pulverized, our vessel destroyed. Every other member of the Expedition is dead. How are we supposed to leave this place and go home?" Erin's eyes were suddenly tearing up. Mastering her confusion, after a few moments she continued. "I was hoping you could help us."

Agor didn't say anything right away but watched Erin with kindness. He then spoke to her on a level her mind could grasp. "Life undergoes continuous changes. Your actions will either lead you to safety or to more deception. It is important that you understand which road needs to be pursued."

In absorbing those words, it became clear to Erin that Agor wasn't simply giving general advice. He was bringing her to an understanding that some sort of peril was hanging over her head, a danger that was more certain than any suspected.

"Some of my companions think that your people are responsible for the destruction of Taras." Erin spoke openly but kept a composed appearance.

Agor's answer was measured. "I don't perceive any condemnation in your words."

"There isn't, only the desire to know what happened. I stand between two fires, and I am afraid I might lose my mind." There was no appeasement in her words, no suggestion of a smile.

"Inner Earth has given you a lot. Now it is time for you to put everything to the test. Only in that way will your knowledge be complete."

Agor's challenge left Erin in doubt, and her hope sank faster than a rock. But the feeling was only temporary because she began to realize that there was a sort of heavy pressure against her back. Erin turned, perhaps too slowly, to be considered brave. At first she saw a bright light, something similar to an apparition. She rubbed her eyes nervously. Gradually a familiar figure materialized in front of her. Before she could understand that Alan was there, his usual encouragement already filled her ears.

Hello again, my dear Milady,
I'm here to tell you, don't be shady,
it's time for you to show
what you have come here to know.
My words were not vain,
and here we meet again.
Access your inner power
and bloom like a flower.
If you remember to shine,

all will be fine.
As dark days are ended,
your future life will be splendid.
Don't be flawed,
be awed ...
and just trust God.

When Erin tried to speak, she could not articulate. She struggled to lower her heartbeat, but before she could do that, Alan had disappeared.

Streaming tears glided down her pale cheeks. It was almost too much to bear. Agor, who had remained patiently out of the way, moved closer in an attempt to bail her out from that bittersweet rumination. She looked at him and a melancholy smile graced her lips. In that split second it occurred to Erin that she had never truly mastered standing alone.

"When contemplation becomes anguish, it should be interrupted," he said, in a fatherly manner.

Sure enough, in the next moment Pepecus magically made his appearance. It was clear to Erin that the time to return to her friends and her destiny had come.

One last time she walked close to the giant eagle and fondly stroked his head. The eagle responded with a growling sound. It was the first time she had found that courage.

Flying with Pepecus was as delightful as Erin remembered. Giant, outspread wings graciously defied gravity, as the eagle tacked through the sky.

"I want you to always remember," shouted Agor, while steering Pepecus away from Aldora. The view below was a tapestry of charming buildings, lakes and fields, woods and rivers. Everything seemed so modest from the sky, even the giant, prehistoric animals so long gone from the exterior of the planet. The magnificent sight stole Erin's breath away. She was enchanted. Inner Earth was no longer foreign to her. Everything that ever mattered to Erin was there — a world within a world.

As her joy increased, so did her awareness. She could trust *herself.*

In a flash of insight, Erin knew. She knew it all — the deception, the pain. Who would have known that all it took was a journey within from above? "A change of perspective ..." she thought to herself.

"... Goes a long way!" exclaimed Agor, who once again was mentally following her train of thought.

The wisdom of Aldora locked in her heart forever, Erin was ready to go home. Her choice had been made. Ironically, long conversations with Agor about alien races and universes, galaxies and time travel, taught her the meaning of simplicity. Everything wasn't perfect, but it all made sense. She didn't feel small after all, not even in a world inhabited by giants. Erin's future was not undefined anymore. She knew there was a role to play in the big picture that had been arranged just for her, and it was something she was willing to do.

"Humanity will not be destroyed and neither will the benevolent entities of Inner Earth. This place will have its heroes," said Erin, grabbing the golden arrow from the quiver.

That was the signal that Agor had been waiting for.

Drifting over the calm sea, the eagle flew back toward the mountains. Everything was still silent, almost deceptively so. It was the time of day when the darkness of the night unites with the light of day. It was a meaning that only the awakened soul could comprehend; the eyes could not.

When Pepecus was close enough, Erin aimed and waited. Her arm was strong and her mind clear, perhaps as never before. Enough destruction had already been done. Now the time had arrived to end it all.

Inside the cavern the team was still sleeping, oblivious to the imminent turn of events.

Kelly was the first to wake up but without contentment, as if something had ended the night before. His vigilance was heightened to the point that sleep had become a dangerous choice. He looked at his fellows who were still in deep slumber, and with a lonely feeling of urgency rose to his feet to greet the sunlight. The rays hadn't even touched his skin when he became aware of a shadow hovering on the horizon. The ominous gloom advanced as Kelly stood nervously, almost hypnotized by the menacing apparition. Soon enough a bright, golden light started to emerge from the center of the shadow. It was coming toward him fast. Before the realization dawned on him, Kelly was struck by a golden arrow.

Time had ceased to be his friendly companion.

Then everything went dark. But this time it happened only to him.

Chapter 30: New Beginnings

FIVE MONTHS LATER

The news was all over the papers. "Erin Palmer, two-time survivor, is launching a new reality show called *Thrive*. The show takes its inspiration from *The Last Templar* but it will require a different type of behavior. Hard work, clarity, and honest thinking will be the qualities needed for success. Has the time of dominance via deception come to an end?"

Erin put the newspaper on the table and looked out the window. "Those curtains should have been cleaned long ago," she thought, while sipping her coffee. She was now able to appreciate the joy of little things, something that she could never have known before. After all, Erin was happy. Something in her had changed, perhaps forever.

In some ways, her life's journey separated her from everyone else. Her priorities had evolved. She knew something that most people had forgotten: She felt loved. It was in that state of mind that she thought of Jessica. They say that being honest sometimes costs more than it pays, but it was a risk worth taking because it represented the awakened embodiment of Erin's soul. Among all her memories, the ones that carried the most lasting significance were the ones when she did the right thing.

Without hesitation, Erin started her computer and began to write.

Dear Jessica,

I never expected that I'd be known to the world, but I never wanted to be lost to the people that I love. I suppose I'm writing this hoping that perhaps you might still cherish a memory of me.

Some people see me as a survivor, a 'lucky' person that somehow made it home. Some others hate me for the same reason. In their mind, the privilege of my existence should have been appropriated to someone else.

During my time in Inner Earth, I spent many days in isolation. There was a part of me that never wanted to escape childhood, but I was forced to find safety in an unknown world. Something in that experience showed me how to manage my troubles and gave me the opportunity to develop a stronger character. I had to become humble, because I learned the hard way that survival could never be achieved from the sanctuary of self-importance, nor could greatness. My unfulfilled expectations taught me to become more sensitive to others in sorrow. So if you tell me about your afflictions, trust me when I say that I can now understand you.

I wish you could assume that there is no duplicity in my words if I say that everything I did and said was motivated by a pure and honest intent, challenged by the moment. I also know that my actions had a profound effect on you and left untold pain in your heart. I prefer not to indulge in what could have been, because the mistakes I made sailed me to the greatest adventure.

The person that I once was seems so grown-up now that I have embraced a new state of joy within. It's no longer about being a survivor. I am thankful for every day I have been given. I have no regrets. I want to thrive.

I guess we all need to choose how we want to live our life. If I could share something with you, it would be what I have discovered about my existence. Don't be afraid to fail but approach life as an equal.

If we cross paths again, please don't ignore me.

Sincerely,
Your friend,
Erin

SOURCES

For those interested in knowing more about the topics discussed in this novel, below are some useful links.

CHAPTER 2: TROMSO
https://www.scientificamerican.com/article/how-fast-is-the-earth-mov/
https://www.space.com/33527-how-fast-is-earth-moving.html

CHAPTER 4: ANTARCTICA
https://www.theblackvault.com/documentarchive/operation-highjump/
https://www.britannica.com/topic/Operation-High-Jump
https://www.britannica.com/biography/James-V-Forrestal
https://mysteriousuniverse.org/2019/06/james-forrestal-suicide-or-something-way-more-sinister/
https://www.history.com/news/hitler-nazi-secret-expedition-antarctica-whale-oil
https://www.nature.com/news/2011/110328/full/news.2011.188.html
https://www.nationalgeographic.com/science/2019/11/deadly-virus-spreading-marine-mammals-as-arctic-ice-disappears/#close

CHAPTER 7: LIFE
https://www.ancient-origins.net/ancient-places-europe/cairn-de-barnenez-one-oldest-structures-world-005771
https://www.britannica.com/science/law-of-superposition
https://www2.lbl.gov/abc/wallchart/chapters/13/4.html

CHAPTER 9: THE ART OF SEEING

http://www.bbc.com/future/story/20170512-what-causes-that-feeling-of-being-watched
https://www.thecut.com/article/the-psychology-of-feeling-like-youre-being-watched.html
https://brainrules.blogspot.com/2010/02/we-do-not-see-with-our-eyes-we-see-with.html
http://www.cycleback.com/eyephysiology.html
https://www.akc.org/

CHAPTER 21: MISSING TIME

http://thescienceexplorer.com/universe/how-gravity-changes-time-effect-known-gravitational-time-dilation
https://www.quora.com/Where-is-gravity-greatest-on-the-surface-or-within-a-sphMattal-mass
https://www.math.ksu.edu/~dbski/writings/shell.pdf
https://news.berkeley.edu/2010/12/16/earth-magnetic-field/
http://hyperphysics.phy-astr.gsu.edu/hbase/Mechanics/sphshell.html

About the Author

During the winter of 2008, everything changed. After completing the Camino of Santiago pilgrimage — known in English as "the Way of St. James" — Cinzia realized that her career as a psychologist wasn't as exciting as she had hoped. It became clear to her that being surrounded by nature was more stimulating than working in a clinic, so she decided to follow her deeper intuition. However, a few more years of working in the Big Tech industry went by before she finally understood that life was worth the risk of leaving a safe but unfulfilling place for the unknown. After quitting her job in the greater Seattle area, she moved with her husband to Montana, where she now lives an adventurous life exploring nature and the outdoors. To this day, Cinzia maintains her passion for hiking, outdoor sports, traveling, and nature exploration.

SUNALAKA, LLC.

P.O Box 800
Somers, MT 59932, U.S.A.
https://sunalaka.com/
info@sunalaka.com